Cholesterol

CHOLESTEROL

by
Tony Drury

Cholesterol
Copyright ©2013 Tony Drury
Published in 2013 by City Fiction

Edited by Laura Keeling

City Fiction
c/o
Sue Richardson Associates Ltd
Minerva Mill Innovation Centre
Station Road
Alcester
Warwickshire B49 5ET
T: 01789 761345
www.cityfiction.com

A CIP record for this book is available from the British Library.

ISBN 978-0-9572017-5-0

Printed and bound in Great Britain by TJ International, Padstow, Cornwall

The word 'cholesterol' comes from the Greek *chole* (bile) and *stereos* (solid) and *ol*, the chemical suffix for an alcohol. It is a waxy steroid of fat that is produced in the liver or intestines. High levels of cholesterol in the human blood are associated with arthrosclerosis and heart disease; but the body also needs cholesterol to build and maintain membranes.

There is 'good' cholesterol which is a function of high-density lipoprotein (HDL) and 'bad' cholesterol which is a function of low-density lipoprotein (LDL).

This is more than most patients will be told after seeing their doctor for a blood test to ascertain their cholesterol reading. They will just be told that their result is 5.8 and they must keep taking the statins.

But there is good and bad cholesterol inside us all, just as there is good and bad inside most human beings.

Also by Tony Drury

Megan's Game (2012)
The Deal (2012)

Prologue

May 2008

His chest was exposed and there were electrodes attached to his skin. The steel canopy moved slowly over him.

"Breathe in and hold. Hold. Hold. Release. Breathe in slightly deeper please. Hold. Hold. Five more seconds please. Hold. Release. Rest."

The process from start to finish lasted about twelve minutes.

Adrian Dexter remained still, awaiting further instructions. He thought back to the start of the medical journey to Harley Street and the scanning centre. He had visited his optician who'd photographed the back of his eyes and then pronounced that he suspected Adrian might have high cholesterol. A visit to his doctor followed; a blood test; a second appointment a week later; a diagnosis of a high cholesterol reading and a mandatory prescription of statins, the wonder drug.

The problem was that he flatly refused to accept the doctor's instructions. He attempted to discuss his concerns about taking drugs with his GP. Was the evidence water-tight? How could he be certain that his arteries were clogged with fatty tissue? The doctor brought the consultation to an end. He told Adrian to return to the surgery in four weeks' time for a further blood test.

Adrian had torn up the prescription and booked an appointment with his private doctor, whose surgery was near to Monument tube station in the City of London. The same process followed, with a blood test, a high cholesterol reading, and a proposal that he take statins. But this time it paid to pay. The doctor attempted to address Adrian's concerns but was unable to confirm, without equivocation, that the blood test provided definitive evidence of the need for the prescription.

"Mr Dexter. You have the option of going to the scanning centre in Harley Street and letting them check your heart. That should answer your questions."

So, he'd duly trotted off to Harley Street, discussed the process with the receptionist, paid the fee of over five hundred pounds and made an appointment for three days later.

A voice brought him back to the present time.

"Thank you, Mr Dexter," said the voice attached to a white gown. "That's fine. Please return to the waiting room and the consultant will see you in about forty minutes."

He spent his time drinking coffee and reading the *Financial Times*. He laughed out loud at the attempts of the Prime Minister, Gordon Brown, to calm frayed City nerves as a result of the growing subprime mortgage crisis in the US.

He was called through and sat down in front of a pleasant-looking man who handed him a folder containing four separate papers.

"Let me take you through the results of your scan, Mr Dexter. I suggest we take it page by page. The top one is, as you can see, your Coronary Calcium Scores in Asymptomatic."

"I thought you were testing for cholesterol?"

"We're looking for calcium deposits and the test shows that you are free of them. If you lower your eyes to the bottom of the page, beneath the graphs, you will see that you have a score of zero. The diagnosis shows as 'No identifiable atherosclerotic plaque. Very low cardio-vascular disease risk.' You're fifty-five years old, Mr Dexter. Not bad, I would suggest, but let's read on."

Adrian's eyes scanned the column headed 'Clinical Interpretation':

A 'negative' examination. Greater than 97 percent chance of absence of coronary artery disease.

Adrian turned the first page over. He looked at the heading, 'Recommendations'. The consultant spoke for about five minutes. He emphasised that, despite the findings, if there were any chest or cardio-respiratory symptoms, Adrian must immediately consult with his own doctor.

He turned to page three which showed a series of twelve sections of his heart.

"We're looking for white spots of calcium in the arteries, Mr Dexter. As you can see, there are none evident here."

The final page showed two pictures of his heart. It looked like a small, red chicken.

"I'm delighted to be able to give you such encouraging news, Mr Dexter, but please continue to be careful. You're in good shape. Let's keep it that way."

"So I don't need to take statins?"

"Absolutely not, Mr Dexter."

"So why did my doctor prescribe them?"

"I suggest you discuss that with him."

Adrian left the centre and walked thoughtfully up Harley Street towards the Euston Road. He was not to know that nearly four years later he would return to the centre and undergo the same process.

However, at that time the events following the test would have far reaching consequences and would end with Adrian suffering the most violent chest pains that it is possible for a person to experience.

PART ONE

The Fatty Tissue Starts to Build

Chapter One

February/March 2012

The clinical consultant sighed. He looked down on yet another woman who was depending on his skills to realise her dreams. He knew that he was battling to help nature take its course but still, he would complete his well-paid part without a hitch. Yet the physiology of the female body never ceased to challenge him. He knew the drugs and their properties perfectly; he would administer the prescriptive regime without a moment's uncertainty. She would lie there, her eyes pleading with him to ensure a success.

This was his last surgical appointment of the day and he was hoping that he would have time to see Leila before going home to his wife and their three children. They had not been together for three days and he was feeling horny.

His patient lay on the treatment table, hating this moment despite the fact that she was there of her own free will and she wanted it to happen. She knew that he would treat her with his usual sensitivity. He had a nice, avuncular face and warm hands. She had complete faith in him, his training and his skills.

It was the intrusion that really upset her, the sensation of a foreign object over which she had no control. She had spent the last hour preparing herself for the coming procedure.

After discussion they had selected the natural cycle IVF process. The actual term *in vitro fertilisation* was misleading because the first two words mean *in glass*, more usually known as a test tube baby. Their choice involved the monitoring of the woman's natural cycle in order to collect an ovum for fertilisation.

The preparation of his sperm was not a problem – it went through sperm washing, where inactive cells and seminal fluid were removed. The sperm and the egg are then incubated together in a culture medium for eighteen hours. If a fertilised egg appears it is treated and left for forty-eight hours. It was now time for the transfer of the ovum to her uterus.

She tensed as she listened to his soft and reassuring voice. She closed her eyes tight and thought of him. "It's so bloody unfair," she said to herself, before gasping with the discomfort.

Adrian had finally made his decision. It would completely change his way of life, but unfortunately not in the way he intended.

This, in itself, was surprising. As the chief executive of MXD Capital, a corporate finance house based in the City of London, he was used to planning detailed and successful fund-raising campaigns for his clients. He had achieved results by concentrating his resources into teams of eight individuals. Their rewards for completing assignments were decent salaries and staggering extra payments. Even though the financial press continued its attack on bankers' bonuses, the City still knew how to reward success.

Yet, to most people, his was a secretive and esoteric world which used a language nobody on the outside could understand. They worked strange hours in expensive offices and earned astronomical amounts of money. Many of them lived in the South Downs, drank expensive champagne and had holiday homes in France.

'Corporate Finance For DUMMIES', if ever written, would tell a rather different story. Most of the senior management and directors of London's corporate finance houses are public school-educated and in office due as much to birth as to ability. They pay huge salaries to their staff because they earn vast fees. Essentially, they find companies wanting to borrow money, put together a share promotion document, raise the funds and make paper millionaires out of the directors. The new shareholders then hope that the company achieves its anticipated results over the next few years so that the shares rise in price and they can sell at a profit. The better companies may also pay a dividend, which is an important source of income to many retired people.

But, as Adrian knew all too well, it was not that easy.

When he'd become chief executive seven years earlier, he'd analysed the company's recent failures carefully. He knew that the incentive of money alone was insufficient to guarantee success. He realised that an important element was the group ethos. He had therefore concentrated on identifying natural leaders amongst his senior staff. Their essential qualities included empathy and stamina.

He was willing to try controversial moves. This was put to the test when he had initiated the creation of a team which went on to complete the twelve million pound fund-raising for a Manchester-based retail business. It was led by a twenty-nine year old corporate lawyer.

Michelle Rochford was quietly spoken and inwardly determined. Adrian had watched her for two years and then caused outrage within the firm by promoting her. The senior member of her team quickly regretted his verbal objections and drink-fuelled tweets when Michelle made him redundant. Within two weeks she had moved out another two married individuals, who were having an affair, and recruited their replacements. She ignored the howls of protests from their former leaders who were furious at losing what they considered their best staff.

She knew that she had the support of the chief executive provided she succeeded with her first assignment. After she was given the retail business deal, she gave her team twenty-four hours to read the documentation and then promptly transported them in a twelve-seater coach to Manchester, where they spent two days with the client company and its executives. Michelle then took her colleagues to Eskdale, situated in the glacial valley area of South West Cumbria, where they underwent a three-day Outward Bound course. This included sleeping alone on the banks of the river Esk and climbing Scarfell Pike. As the group stood on top of the three thousand, two hundred and nine foot mountain, looking out over the Lake District National Park, she breathed a sigh of relief that all eight of them were present.

They returned to London and on Monday morning at seven o'clock they began the assignment. She introduced hugging. This took place when a member booked a commitment of over two hundred and fifty thousand pounds. If any person recorded a sum of this amount or more, and it did not materialise, that individual was banned from hugging for the duration of the assignment. The first outburst came late on Friday afternoon when a South London fund manager faxed over a signed application form for shares to the value of four hundred thousand pounds. The bodily contact was wild and resulted in a row between Adrian and his protégé.

"I did not promote you, against the advice of all my other colleagues, to turn this place into an orgy centre!" he'd yelled.

"Oh, grow up, Adrian," she'd replied.

"I beg your pardon?"

"They were hugging. That's all."

"They?"

"OK, Adrian. We. I was in the middle of it."

"What's hugging – or whatever you call it – got to do with raising twelve million pounds?"

"You're too old to understand."

The total amount needed was raised with just three hours to go to the deadline. The last two days were increasingly tense. A pension fund pulled out of a three million pound commitment. Two members of Michelle's team worked through the night analysing the earlier rejections by fund managers into their possible potential for reconsidering the proposition. They then revisited every investment executive who would see them. It was a huge effort on their part. It paid off in that three investments were secured to complete the fund-raising.

Adrian shook the hands of all the team members and then took Michelle to the Royal Exchange bar, opposite the Bank of England, where they shared a bottle of champagne. It took him nearly fifty minutes to ask the question uppermost in his mind.

"Michelle," he slurred slightly. "When you said I was too old, what did you mean?"

"Whoops," she laughed. "Well, you know, you're not George Clooney… but you've still got it."

"Got what?"

"That something," she said, giving him a beaming, corporate lawyer's smile.

"I'm not suggesting we should… er… connect." He stopped and refilled their glasses. "Actually, that's not true. I am. But to get back to the point. Why did you say I was too old?"

"Well, are we or aren't we?" She sipped her champagne and laughed.

"Connecting you mean? Do you understand what I'm saying?"

"Yes. Though I'll admit to the fact I've never been asked to 'connect' before. Sounds like fun."

Adrian called over the waiter and ordered a second bottle of champagne.

"Is that a good idea?" she asked.

"You said I was too old."

"I said that you were too old to understand. I was referring to hugging."

It was now six-thirty in the evening and the subdued lighting, together with the champagne, was slowly bringing the two work colleagues closer together. Michelle put her glass down on the table and took his right hand in both of hers.

"Adrian. You're a lovely man. You're a terrific boss. Your great talent is that you let people show initiative. I know that you took a chance with me and we all heard the shouting that went on in your office. But it was my success. Don't try to understand it. I'll deal with the team. Trust me, it's never dull." She squeezed his hand and kissed him on his cheek. "That's my world. Your world is being the boss." She kissed him again. "And you're bloody good at it."

"But why was I too old?"

"Age, Adrian, is an attitude of mind. My team is the youngest in the company. When they reached the top of Scarfell they became adults. There wasn't a single personal issue during the assignment. That's why we succeeded. And one more point, boss."

"What?"

"Don't ever again give me a transaction that has been rejected by every other group. I now get first option on any deal. Do we understand each other?"

He nodded resignedly and slumped forward.

"You tried first with Bill's team and they refused it on grounds of valuation and sector. You then tried the venture capital unit, who rejected it because you had offered it to Bill's group first. Finally you imposed it on the private client funds section run by Mrs 'Wonderful' and Harriett swore at you."

He was now reduced to shaking his head and avoiding her eyes.

"Michelle Rochford comes first. Right. Got it?"

He had got it. The future rules were firmly established.

As he sagged in the back of a taxi, which was taking him home to St. John's Wood in North London, he now understood why he'd always felt a little nervous when dealing with Michelle.

Another woman also occupied his thoughts. Four thousand four hundred miles away, a middle-aged woman waited patiently for him. He checked his text messages and was disappointed that the screen was blank.

When he reached his home he found a note from his wife telling him how to heat up his supper, and that there was a chilled bottle of wine which she'd opened earlier in the evening in the fridge. She said that she'd see him in the morning.

As he'd lost his appetite, he put the meal in a black sack and deposited it in the appropriate bin outside the rear entrance. He found the wine, poured himself a large glass, retired to his study and put on a CD of Rachmaninov's piano concerto number one, perhaps number two. He couldn't remember which and he didn't care. He then slumped into his favourite chair and started to think about Michelle.

He remembered all the details available to him. She had soft black hair and a high forehead. Her eyes were green. Her skin was clear. She had generous lips which were made more appealing by the pale-coloured gloss which she'd applied. Her smile lit up her already attractive face. She'd been wearing a business suit. Beneath the jacket she'd chosen a white blouse which she had left open down to the third button. Beneath that he could see the outline of a white silk bra. Her breasts pushed against the material and he had been able to sense her nipples. The skirt was quite short and when seated revealed her stunning thighs.

She'd worn low-heeled black shoes. At one point in the evening, her skirt had risen and Adrian had glimpsed a flash of her white panties.

His growing lusting for younger women was beginning to concern him.

He had become aware of the current trend for couples in their fifties and sixties to divorce. The post-second world war baby boomers were now reaching retirement age. They were, as a group, healthier, wealthier and more libidinous. The trend was raising its head at dinner parties – recently a banker friend in Fulham had announced that he and his wife were calling it a day. There was, so they said, no other party involved. There were three children.

He'd read in a newspaper article that pensioners were the only age group where the divorce rate was rising. He could recall the statistics given for 2009 which revealed that more than eleven thousand, five hundred over sixties divorced in that year: a rise of 4 percent. Other age groups had seen a fall of 11 percent in the separation rate.

There was the usual avalanche of opinion polls, blogs and tweets. Men in their sixties, it was said, were viewing life anew.

Adrian considered his wife his best friend. He liked his three daughters, especially one of them, had a good social life and relished his professional work. When he'd told his wife that he was thinking of leaving his company and devoting his life to helping enterprising businesses she'd immediately committed one million pounds of her inheritance to his cause.

But he'd spent the previous three months thinking about his life. He'd turned fifty-nine just a few weeks ago. Annie and their three children had given him a memorable weekend. Honeysuckle, his eldest daughter, had flown in from South America with her Spanish husband to announce that they were returning home for good. Victoria, the youngest, had given a speech at the private birthday dinner party telling the eleven couples present that her father was the most special person she had ever known. She did not fail to mention the grandchildren upstairs in bed.

Adrian knew that he was going through the male menopause. He was aware that his body was reducing its production of the testosterone hormone. Whilst his reproductive system was still functioning, he knew from his reading up on the subject that he might lose some of his libido and, possibly, his potency. He'd noticed that his powers of concentration were wavering and recently he'd experienced a hot flush in the middle of the night. But he was rarely nervous and never depressed: life was too good.

He was with Annie. They had been married for thirty-four years. With the exception of his South African dalliance and a few other adventures, especially during the early eighties, he had been loyal and committed. She remained faithful and totally in love with him. He would now complete the re-evaluation of his work/life balance and prepare for the next stage of his life. He would leave full-time work and dedicate himself to financing small businesses. He would play his part in getting Britain moving again.

He attributed some of the impetus to his change of regime in the last twelve months, following the death of a colleague from prostate cancer. Adrian had joined a gym, cut down his alcohol intake, researched diets and lost nearly thirty pounds in weight. After a number of months, he'd begun to feel younger and he sensed that people were more at ease with him. Now and again he'd indulge in the occasional escapism that drink offered – though he usually regretted it the next day.

Recently he'd started to notice that women on trains were beginning to excite him more. At seven in the morning, on the tube to Bank Station, he'd look at the more attractive ones and silently lust after them. Several looked stunning in their business suits and their figures tantalised him. He eyed them cautiously. One day a girl knew exactly what he was doing and he'd got off the train as a measure of self-protection.

He knew that he could not seriously consider divorcing Annie. Even if he did ponder that option, any thinking in this direction had been partly eradicated during an evening drink with a public relations executive he knew quite well.

"Adrian," he'd slurred. "Fucking Kenneth Clarke. It's all his bloody fault."

"What is?"

"Mediation. It's part of the review of the family justice system. It's because Beth and I have two kids."

He'd paused and gone to the bar to fetch two more drinks.

"I really do object to buying you fizzy water, Adrian," he'd said, as he banged the glasses down on their table.

"Ok. You were saying about mediation?"

"We've had three meetings now. Bloody awful they were." He'd pulled a piece of paper from his inside pocket. "Listen to this crap." He'd begun reading.

"Don't sweat the small stuff and get hung up on detail or broken promises. Try to remove criticism and blame from the way you communicate and instead explain why something is important to you."

"Ronnie," Adrian had said. "I think I get the…"

"No, no. Let me finish." He'd read on:

"Think about what you can do to improve things rather than focusing on what your ex doesn't do."

"And do you know what Beth said? 'I concur'," he'd mimicked. "'Perhaps if Ronald hadn't spent his time fucking all the women in his office and losing all our savings in stupid investments…' – and those were the more repeatable things she said!"

"Interesting idea this mediation," Adrian had suggested, as they'd left the bar together.

The flashing red light told him he had a text message. He knew already who had sent it and he was fairly sure of the sentiment. He read it to be sure.

Still love you. Still miss you. Still pray that you'll return. Always yours. S x

Sonja had been his only serious affair in the last fifteen years, and it had been sudden and unexpected. He had flown to Johannesburg to secure a major investment into MXD Capital from a South African bank that wanted to gain a presence in the London markets. He'd spent two days with Nigel de Groot, the director assigned by the board to complete the transaction, and at the outset met their personnel director, Sonja Redmaine, during a reception held in his honour.

It was electric from the start and he'd taken her out for dinner. She'd gone back to his hotel room and they'd ended up in bed together. He'd sent a message to London saying that he'd caught a stomach bug and would be staying for an extra two days. They'd made love nine times and he was within twenty minutes of missing his return flight.

During their last twenty-four hours together they'd talked exhaustively about their individual situations. Sonja was financially secure due to the payment received from her ex-husband.

"Usual story, Adrian," she'd said. "He ran off with a younger version... it cost him big time."

He'd made it clear that he had no intention of breaking up his own family. She'd cupped his face in her hands and spoken quietly to him.

"I understand completely," she'd said. "You're a lovely man. I'm willing to live in hope. I'll contact you regularly to let you know that I'm here waiting for you to return."

"That can never happen," he'd replied.

""Never" is not in my lexicon Adrian. Ok, you're leaving in four hours' time. I'm going to make sure you never forget our last meeting."

Well, he hadn't forgotten it yet. Now he waited eagerly for her weekly texts – and the intensity of feeling that had passed between them stayed with him on a daily basis.

He sent a loving message back to South Africa, and then thought again about the text he had received from Sonja the week before. It had been very different in tone and contained some worrying information.

An hour later he went to bed but couldn't sleep. He had yet to advise the board of directors of his impending departure from the company, and his intention to use Annie's money to set up his small business fund.

Many people struggle to understand how businesses operate. How can a chief executive be dismissed because the trading results are poor and then receive a two million pound pay-off?

Where is the logic in an American-trained management consultant going into a British utilities company, making thousands of workers redundant, sacking the board of directors and then sailing off into the sunset with a mouth-watering bonus which is paid in dollars and finds its way into an off-shore bank account? Who are the so-called 'funds' that raid the stock market 'short-selling' shares? How can you sell a share that you don't own only to buy it back at a lower price a few weeks later? There must be a set of rules somewhere.

Two of the most misused words in financial circles are 'corporate governance'.

These are the principles that are supposed to mean that businesses are correctly operated and the directors are focused on generating shareholder value. This is the capitalist system at work. Businesses acquire money (capital) from others (shareholders) and use it to generate profits (which are paid out as dividends).

There are Companies Acts, stock market codes of conduct, regulatory requirements and an ever-growing willingness to use litigation if there's a claim that can be substantiated. However, government is forever messing around with the rules. There are some Members of Parliament who think there should be a mandatory number of female board members. The European Union (Brussels) has proposed that 40 percent of directors of a company should be women.

A company is controlled by a board of directors. There are executives who run the business and non-executives who attend meetings and protect shareholders' interests. Most boards are dominated by either the chairman and/or the chief executive. If the two are working together then the chances of proper corporate governance are slim. In recent times the former Knight of the Realm, Fred Goodwin, demonstrated at the Royal Bank of Scotland that even the biggest companies could descend into chaos and wrong decision making when it comes to proper corporate governance.

Lord Singleton, the chairman of MXD Capital, was a good leader and had a healthy respect for Adrian. He tried to ensure that board meetings were quick, positive and accountable.

He sat back in his chair and thanked Chrissie Williamson, the finance director of MXD Capital, for her report. He had listened attentively to the chief executive's fifteen minute presentation of the overall position a little earlier, but was now struggling to maintain his concentration as Chrissie took her colleagues through columns of figures. He forgot to ask if there were any questions from other directors.

He was keen to return to the House of Lords so that he could register for his three hundred pound daily allowance. He was due to meet with his lawyers later in the day to discuss access to the family trust funds so that he could pay off his debts. The recession had hit him particularly badly: he had lost two directorships as companies cut their overheads. His youngest daughter had required a rather expensive abortion and his son, having walked out of his Oxford college, was starting an internet business which required some risk capital. He'd also bought shares, on the advice of his stockbroker, in the semi-nationalised Lloyds Bank. His losses now stood at over two hundred thousand pounds.

As he looked down at the agenda to remind himself of the next matter, he was unprepared for the sudden outburst from Nigel de Groot.

"Mr Chairman," he said. "This is unacceptable. The losses for the last three months are over three hundred thousand pounds. The cash balances are now below two million pounds. The loss for the year is projected to be over one and a half million pounds. The chief executive talks about his competitor analysis and how MXD is not the worst-performing finance house in London. Yet did I hear that we have completed only two trans-actions since the last board meeting? Did I also hear that on the twelve million pound fund-raising, nearly 50 percent of the earnings were paid out as commissions to the sales team? Man, are you all crazy?"

"Thank you Mr…"

Lord Singleton was abruptly prevented from continuing his statement.

"When my bank invested eight million pounds for a 22 per-cent stake in this business only two years ago, we were assured that a London listing was being planned at twice the valuation. We were expecting to double the value of our money. But what do I hear? Losses, bonuses to sales teams, poor market conditions!"

"Do you have a solution, Mr De Groot?" asked the chairman.

"This is a leaderless company. My colleagues in Johannesburg no longer have any confidence in Mr Dexter. We ask that he resigns. We are prepared to buy the 78 percent of the business we do not own for ten million pounds."

"That values us at around twelve million!" yelled Russell Warren, the marketing director. "This is plain opportunism, Mr Chairman."

"This is not the way we do things in London, Mr De Groot. I am amazed you did not notify…"

"Have you heard of Bailey Mayhew?" interrupted the South African.

The board of directors was aware of the reputation of the identified City lawyers.

"They are awaiting my instructions to issue proceedings against every member of this board."

"For what?" asked Chrissie.

"Oh, my dear woman. Let's start with the financial forecasts you gave us in your 2009 presentation."

"Adrian. Do you have anything to say?" asked the chairman.

The chief executive reached under the table and brought out bound folders for each of the other six board members. He asked that they be passed around the table. He spoke in a strong tone.

"Mr Chairman. I am grateful to Nigel de Groot for focusing our attention on the difficulties MXD Capital is having. The market conditions are dire. Chrissie and her unit simply cannot cut overheads any further. We've streamlined into four fundraising teams and I have already listed three new mandates we have won. The success Michelle Rochford had in raising the twelve million pounds has started the jungle drums beating in our favour. Mr De Groot might also like to know that to my knowledge she has received three, perhaps four, offers to join other finance houses."

"But she's staying?" said Mark Webster, the compliance director.

"She's staying and she's just started on her next assignment."

"After her team climbed Ben Nevis!" laughed Chrissie.

"You are laughing. You are all crazy!" barked Nigel de Groot.

"Yes, I agree that English humour is sometimes puzzling to foreigners," said Adrian, "but it's good to ease the tensions. Now, let me provide you with something that will show you how serious we are. The folder I have distributed concerns a takeover of Silicon Capital. This is a corporate finance house with great potential that specialises in technology companies. It is based in Cambridge, although it has a small London office. We've already received a draft letter of engagement from a leading adviser stating that we can float our shares on the market at a combined valuation of seventeen million pounds. We will also raise around five million pounds from the institutions. I will stay on for six months before handing over to their Mark Appleton who will become the new chief executive. This is all subject to board approval of course, Mr Chairman. I would ask that you look at appendix three on page fifty-three. I am proposing that on the completion of the deal each member of this board receives a performance bonus of seventy-five thousand pounds each, with the exception of you Mr Chairman. My proposal is that you receive one hundred thousand pounds."

Lord Singleton wondered whether he might not need the scheduled meeting with his lawyers later in the day.

Nigel de Groot stood up and slammed down his folder.

"I'm off to see Bailey Mayhew!"

"Ok. You might want to mention Zambian Goldfields to them," said Adrian.

The South African director stopped in his tracks, turned and advanced towards him. Adrian stood up and faced his aggressor.

"There are two security officers outside the door, Mr De Groot. I suggest you sit down."

As he did so, glancing behind him, Adrian brought out from under the table six copies of a thinner report. He asked that they be circulated around to the board members.

"Nigel de Groot," said Adrian, in a quiet voice, "is being

investigated by the South African authorities and the banking regulators for his bank's investment in a speculative investment called Zambian Goldfields. They are estimated to have lost almost six hundred million rand, which will wipe out 50 percent of their equity capital. Mr De Groot is being pursued separately by the authorities for a suspected personal bribe from Zambia."

"Mr De Groot. Do you wish to comment on these remarks made by our chief executive?" asked the chairman.

"No. You will hear from my solicitors."

"Earlier this morning, I spoke to the bank's chairman and offered him personally one million pounds for the 22 percent stake that they hold in MXD Capital. That offer was immediately accepted," Adrian continued.

Nigel de Groot rose to his feet.

"You have made a very big mistake, Mr Dexter. Nobody crosses Nigel de Groot and gets away with it."

"Mark, please ask the security guards to escort Mr De Groot off the premises. But can I suggest that you sign this letter of resignation first please, Mr De Groot?"

Nigel de Groot snatched the form out of Adrian's outstretched hand and put his signature at the bottom, before storming from the room.

For the next hour the remaining directors went through the proposed merger with Silicon Capital in great detail. Adrian explained that the stake that he'd purchased from the South African bank would be sold as part of the market flotation. He told his colleagues about his wish to leave the industry, but reassured them that he would ensure Mark Appleton was well installed before he departed.

"And the timing of these proposed payments?" asked the chairman.

"Subject to the board's approval, we start the process in the morning. As finance director, Chrissie will lead our team."

"I don't think we need a formal vote," concluded the chairman. "I am sure the minutes will confirm total support for our chief executive's brilliant work."

A little later Chrissie entered Adrian's office and shut the door.

"How did you know?" she asked.

"Know what?"

"Don't play games with me," she replied.

He laughed. "Chrissie, it's good to have friends."

Later that evening Adrian was relaxing in his study at home, listening to the music of Bach, when a red flashing light on his mobile interrupted his reverie.

Still love u. Have u heard? NdeG to be arrested when he arrives back in SA. Fancy. S x

He thought for several, long moments before sending his reply.

I'm aching with desire. I want to thank you. A x

He listened to the cadence as the organist played the Toccata and Fugue in D Minor. The red light flashed again.

There's a plane leaving Heathrow in five hours' time. S x

He knew that he was fantasising. He was committed to his decision to stay with Annie, to complete the merger with Silicon Capital and then to pursue his dream of developing his trust fund.

But Sonja simply would not go away. He was recalling the seventh time they had made love... he had never felt so physically and emotionally compatible with a woman. She had a body which oozed sensuality.

This time he had penetrated her and whispered into her ear, urging her to hold on. He'd felt her legs grip him even more firmly and her arms wrapped around his neck. He'd pleaded more urgently: "Hold on, Sonja, hold on." She'd groaned. "Please, please, now!" "Hold... now, Sonja, now."

They'd climaxed together in a perfect moment of passion. She'd felt him explode and her juices cascade down inside her. They'd held on and on and on before, finally, they'd slumped back into the mattress.

As he flew back to London he'd decided not to let that happen again. He would resume his married life with Annie and their occasional love-making.

But he had the memory of that occasion. It could never be taken away from him.

Chapter Two

April 2012

She gently lifted herself off the bed and moved across the surgery to join the consultant in a further discussion.

"I know that you want answers. I'll do my best. You're healthy, your weight is right, normal blood pressure – but," he paused, "but you are rather tense."

He took a piece of paper from the top of the file and started to read out its contents:

"The latest statistics show that for a woman of your age there's a 38.9 percent pregnancy rate of success and a 31.7 percent live birth rate."

She gasped and her hand flew to her mouth.

"Statistics. That's all they are. In my judgement you have a more than 50 percent chance of giving birth to a healthy baby. In fact I'd say perhaps 60 percent."

He sat back in his chair and sighed.

"I wish it were better still, but nature has its own ways of doing things. So far the treatment has progressed perfectly. I just wish that you weren't so nervous."

Londoners had been enjoying two weeks of milder weather and in many areas the authorities were beginning to discuss possible water conservation measures. The mayoral candidates Boris Johnson and Ken Livingstone were hurling increasingly personal insults at each other; interest rates were being held at record-low levels and the budget was neutral as the Chancellor had little room for fiscal expansion in the stubbornly tight economic conditions; and his proposed fall in the rate of corporate tax had pleased the City.

MXD Capital was experiencing slightly improved trading results and two of the fund-raising groups had achieved success. The chief executive however, who was focusing on the planned merger with Silicon Capital, found himself in an intense discussion. The sun was pouring through the windows of his Cornhill offices. Michelle Rochford was wearing a pink outfit and an angry expression.

"No, Adrian, it doesn't. It's short by three thousand pounds."

"Michelle. It's correct. That's your commission payment. Stop bloody arguing."

"It's wrong. You must be trying to short-change me."

The chief executive of MXD Capital sighed.

"I've got a board of directors saying I'm too generous and a team leader who's just plain greedy."

Michelle exploded.

"GREEDY! Do you have any idea how hard we worked on the deal? You gave me thirty-six hours and we still brought in the half a million pounds your fucking client needed!"

"Don't swear please, Michelle."

"You used the word 'bloody'."

"Because you keep arguing. That's the correct figure. That's what I'm signing. I wrote the authorisation slip out myself."

Michelle stopped and looked around the office. On the left-hand wall was a calendar – the page for April showed a picture of Big Ben. She went over, lifted it off its hook and placed it on the table.

"Adrian. Please look at this. What time is it showing on the face of the clock?"

"Michelle, I have a company to run. Please. Take your payment slip."

"What time is it showing, Adrian?"

"If I must. The clock is showing... er... it's plain to see... er... two-thirty. Right. Take your slip to Chrissie and leave me alone."

"It's showing twenty to eleven, Adrian." She placed the payment slip in front of him.

"What figure is that?" she asked.

"Eight. Eight thousand, two hundred and three pounds."

"It's a five, Adrian. Five thousand."

He sat back and took off his glasses.

"I'm sorry, Michelle. I need to get my eyes tested. This isn't the first error I've made recently. I thought it was just because

I was tired."

He altered the authorisation slip, initialled the change of 'five' to 'eight', and handed it to his now-smiling colleague.

"Will you go today?" asked Michelle.

"Go where?"

"To get your eyes tested. When you pay me one of your regular compliments I want the satisfaction of knowing that you can actually see me." She turned and flounced from the room.

"As if I could miss you," sighed Adrian under his breath.

He was due to have lunch with Mark Appleton, the chief executive of Silicon Capital, at Gow's Restaurant in Old Broad Street near to Liverpool Street Station. He realised that he would pass the opticians in London Wall.

Two hours later he called in and, much to his surprise, was told they had a slot at three p.m. due to a cancellation.

"Well congratulations, Mark. When's the date?"

"Cate and I haven't quite got there yet," said the head of the finance house. "To be honest, Adrian, I'm still pinching myself that she's mine."

"And it was my introduction!" laughed Adrian.

"Indeed. I met her a year ago at one of your receptions. Incidentally, MXD Capital does those events very well, Adrian. It's something I'll want to continue."

"Cate's in public relations, isn't she?"

"She's a specialist in brand management change. She's currently working for an Australian bank which wants to change its name. It feels it's been tarnished by recent events. Cate's been in Brisbane for ten days."

After that, they spent most of the lunch discussing the proposed merger of their two firms. Both men were convinced that, contrary to the current economic evidence, there were signs of improved conditions. In City speak, a 'bull market' was emerging.

"Adrian," said Mark, "you've had far more experience than me, I know, but I'm wedded to the idea of market cycles."

He sipped his sparkling water and smiled at his lunch companion. Gow's, a popular City fish restaurant, was busy, reflecting the increased activity of the local firms.

"We had the years of excess during the Blair years and, in particular, Labour's second term following his 2001 election victory."

"Fuelled by the Americans," interrupted Adrian. "It was propelled initially by Bill Clinton and his enthusiastic funding of house-buyers in the southern states."

"Agreed, but it was going to happen anyway. There was a natural credit exuberance and so, while everybody blames the Fed's decision to let Lehman Brothers go into receivership in 2008, really, the cycle has simply been adjusting to re-establish the value of money. We've been in a period of austerity for nearly four years. The pound is probably valued correctly now against the dollar and the euro."

They were not to know, at that point in time, that their assessment was wrong and the country's recession had much longer to run. The value of the pound was to move further downwards against most major currencies and, in particular, the American dollar and the euro.

He picked up his wine glass and toasted the situation.

"This is a great time to merge our firms. Together we can really attract the better business. I was impressed by your retail deal in Manchester."

"Hmm, yes, and you've yet to meet Michelle," Adrian chuckled.

"The head of the fund-raising team? My people already know about her."

"And you managed to raise the ten million pounds for that mobile phone company."

"We did." Mark hesitated. "But it was very tough – in the end we found half the money from sources in Hong Kong."

Their plates were cleared away. Both men chose to avoid the desert menu and finish with coffee.

"So you'll stay on for up to six months while we merge the businesses?" confirmed Mark.

"Yes. I'll commit to three full days a week and come in on Thursdays if I'm needed."

He drank from the white cup in front of him and opened the Gow's chocolate.

"I gather our two chairmen are dining together in the coming week," said Mark.

"Yes, and I suggest we let them battle it out. I think, when push comes to shove, Lord Singleton will agree to stand down."

With that, Adrian settled the bill and the two men rose to leave the restaurant.

"I'm looking forward to meeting Cate," said Adrian.

"Me too," laughed Mark. "She arrived back from Australia this morning. Perhaps you and your wife will join us for dinner in the next week."

"Possibly. Annie is a rather home-loving person, but I'll ask her."

Thirty minutes later, he found himself peering through several different machines, wearing various pieces of equipment and staring at spots on various coloured backgrounds.

"Hold still, please," said Rick, the ophthalmologist, "I'm photographing the back of your eyes, Mr Dexter."

"Well," he continued, a few moments later, "how old are you?" He looked down at his folder. "Right. Fifty-nine. Your eyes are fine, but you need much stronger reading glasses. No problem. I'll write out the prescription and they'll sort you out downstairs. Your long sight is unchanged. There is nothing to worry about." He paused. "But there is something I should mention. When we look at the back of your eyes we can tell various things. It's the only part of your body that can provide health guides without intrusion."

"What are you talking about?" asked Adrian.

"By looking at the capillaries on the back of the eye, we can check for high blood pressure and diabetes. The good news is that you're clear of both of those."

"No high blood pressure?"

"If you have doubts go and see your doctor, but there's nothing here to suggest any concerns." He turned his head away and coughed. "But there is strong evidence of cholesterol."

"What makes you say that?"

"Well, I can see a yellow seepage from the blood vessels. You need to see your doctor, Mr Dexter."

It was déjà vu. In 2008 he had been told by the optician that his back of the eye examination had suggested evidence of cholesterol. He had seen his doctor, who had ordered a blood test. This had confirmed a level of cholesterol that required treatment and he had prescribed statins. Adrian had read quite extensively about this drug and had refused to take it without better evidence. So he'd consulted a private doctor in the City, who'd suggested that Adrian visit the scanning centre in Harley Street. He'd taken the doctor's advice, and two weeks later had been given a clear prognosis and told there was no need for him to take the statins.

He returned to his office, shut the door and telephoned the scanning centre. He made an appointment for the following day. As he replaced the receiver on its holder, Michelle burst through the door.

"Adrian. Bob's fund-raising team. They can't generate interest in the five million pounds for the private health care company. It's ridiculous. With the NHS reforms, private medicine is going to have a bonanza! Give it to us. We'll raise it."

"You know I can't do that, Michelle. I have to wait until Bob tells me officially."

"Wimp."

Adrian stared at his colleague. The pink outfit had remained immaculate. He realised with an inward groan that he could see through the material of the skirt. Her thighs were already tanned.

"Come and see me at eight o'clock tomorrow morning and I'll authorise you to start."

"No, now, Adrian. My team's ready to start now. I'm meeting a medical fund investment manager tonight."

"Eight o'clock tomorrow morning, Michelle. If you make any move before then I'll suspend you."

She looked at him and smiled.

"I withdraw the 'wimp' comment with apologies," she said. "See you in the morning, boss."

As she swirled round her skirt followed the contours of her buttocks.

Once again Adrian sighed. His thoughts returned to Johannesburg and another pair of sun-drenched legs.

That evening, the team leader, Bob Archer, who had been with Adrian for a number of years, resigned and stormed out of the building, caught the tube train at Bank Station and then took the main line route home to Reading. His parting comments were rather pointed.

"What's it going to be, Adrian, you bastard, her body or my years of dedication to MXD Capital?"

Early the following afternoon, Adrian visited the scanning centre in Harley Street. He commented to the receptionist that he was surprised he was able to make an appointment so quickly. She explained that the recession had resulted in a fall in business account bookings.

The process was similar to the one he had experienced four years earlier and after an hour he found himself sitting in front of a consultant. The results were similar to his first set of test results, although there was evidence of minute deposits of calcium in the artery on the left anterior of the heart. However, the overall results gave a reading of 1 – 10 and a diagnosis of 'minimal plaque burden' plus a clinical interpretation of 'significant coronary artery disease very unlikely'. In other words he was free of any immediate heart problems.

The consultant smiled at his patient.

"Frankly, Mr Dexter, with these results you do not need us to test you again for another five years."

On his way back to the City, he exited Bank tube station and walked up Cornhill towards his office. He decided to call in at Green's Runner Bar and have a glass of champagne to celebrate his medical clearance. He entered the converted banking hall, made a beeline for the circular bar, and ordered his drink.

As he turned round, he spotted Michelle at a table with a companion. He approached and asked if he might join them. She seemed genuinely pleased with the suggestion, so he sat down.

"Adrian, this is Pollett," said Michelle.

Adrian put out his right hand which was promptly ignored by the dark-haired individual sporting three days' growth. He was wearing a grey suit and an open-neck red shirt.

"Sorry about the situation at the office," whispered Michelle to her boss, "But we're certain to raise the money."

"Which is why I agreed," said Adrian. He turned back to the man.

"Pollett. Is that your first name?"

"It's Pollett."

"We call him Pollett, Adrian," confirmed Michelle.

"Ok, no problem. What do you do, Pollett?"

"I move from car crash to car crash."

Michelle took Adrian's hand and squeezed it.

"Pollett's a rather private person," she said.

"I'm raising two young children, that's what I'm doing – ever since the bitch walked out on me."

Adrian glanced at Michelle.

"He's very dedicated to them," she said.

"Shall I buy a bottle of champagne, Pollett?" asked Adrian.

"I thought you might say something useful if we gave you enough time," he responded.

Adrian called a waiter and ordered champagne and canapés.

"Are you aware that I'm Michelle's boss?" he asked, looking at Pollett.

"Bollocks. You can't do without her. She tells me that she's the best fund-raiser you'll ever have and now you've lost your senior team leader, you've no choice. If Michelle doesn't perform, your credibility will be shot to pieces."

Michelle leaned forward and touched Adrian's hand again.

"Pollett takes a keen interest in what I do," she said.

"You're one of the greedy bastards, aren't you." It was not a question. "Screwing ordinary people for your massive bonuses." Pollett downed the remains of his lager.

"The financial services sector is a big earner for the economy, Pollett."

"Spare me the crap, if you will. Going to sing 'Land of Hope and Glory', are we?"

"We spend too much time running ourselves down," said Adrian.

"If there was a fucking apocalypse this evening, England wouldn't even get started."

"Apocalypse. What does that mean?"

"The fucking end of the world."

Adrian shook his head as he tried to understand the man's social observations.

"So, how long have you been carrying your chip?" he asked.

"No chip, sir. I just don't take crap from your type."

"My type?"

"Wealthy fucking snobs. I've told Michelle. She's not going to let you patronise her."

"You're obviously well-experienced in these matters, Pollett."

"I get my relationships with women right. Michelle and I are compatible because we're honest with each other."

"Just as you did with the mother of your two children?"

Pollett glared at Adrian and then turned to Michelle. He stood up. "Give me a ring, babe," he said and stormed out of the bar.

The bottle of champagne was now served up by the waiter, along with the canapés. He filled two fresh glasses and handed one each to Adrian and Michelle. A few minutes passed before they spoke.

"Pollett?" asked Adrian.

"He's my stepbrother. His father was a colonel in the army and a keen historian. He named his son Montgomery Patton Pollett. My brother so hated his names that he decided to become Pollett. We're all used to it now."

"Does he work?"

"He's a musician. He plays saxophone in a jazz band. He's very good."

"And the marriage?" Adrian paused. "Do you mind me asking?"

"No. I'm really not certain what happened. It was fine until the second child arrived. That was three years ago. She walked out a year ago and we don't have any real idea where she's gone – although I think he might know more than he's saying."

They decided to walk back to the office together after drinking a second glass of champagne, and then finishing the bottle. They remained silent, each lost in their own thoughts.

Chrissie Williamson was consumed in her thoughts and did not realise that she was the last member of senior management left in the offices of MXD Capital. Her desk was littered with pages of accounting information, though she didn't need more than her summary sheet, which never left her side, to know that the losses were continuing. Now she needed to factor in a settlement with Bob Archer which she had provisionally calculated to be around three hundred and fifty thousand pounds. MXD Capital had already received, within hours, the opening salvo from his solicitors and she knew that it would be settled on the steps of the court. That was the way the financial services sector seemed to operate these days. Loyalty, both ways, had gone. The more you earned, the more expensive your solicitor and the more ready he'd be to resort to litigation on behalf of the client.

He had run a good and effective operation and staff turnover under his watch was low. He completed, on average, a transaction every two to three months. His last involved raising ten million pounds for a distribution company in the Midlands who were building a 'state of the art' warehousing centre near to the M40 motorway. The deal earned the company a two hundred thousand pound transaction fee and fund-raising commissions of 4.5 percent, netting a further four hundred and fifty thousand pounds in revenues. There were further charges of twenty five thousand pounds for finding a non-executive chairman for the client and an introductory commission of fifteen thousand pounds for introducing the business to a London-based public relations consultancy. On top of that MXD Capital received shares worth two hundred thousand pounds and an annual retainer of fifty thousand pounds.

Chrissie smiled and raised her glass of wine to toast the health of the former prime minister.

"Cheers, Gordon," she laughed.

The recession gripping the country's economy had resulted in fund-raising becoming more difficult, and thus more expensive, as sources of external finance dried up. The price for success had risen dramatically and Bob Archer's last deal was particularly lucrative. The problem was, however, that there were simply not enough transactions to go around.

She liked Bob and would miss him, but she was cautiously supportive of Michelle and liked her innovative approach to team building. She sipped some more wine.

"I wouldn't mind a bit of hugging myself," she chuckled.

Many people, especially those who have reached sixty and beyond, can remember where they were when they heard the news on two specific dates. Adrian could most certainly recall the circumstances when he learned of the events of 22 November 1963 and 31 August 1997.

He was now to add a further occasion to his memory: 11 April 2012. He had arranged to visit the opticians to collect his glasses. Little did he know that it was the start of a series of events that would change his life; the day he met Helen and she pressed her hands into his groin.

When he was later to look back at that day and his first contact with her, he knew that he had been given instinctive warnings but had failed to heed them.

To that extent he was in the same category as the thirty-fifth president of the United States of America. In 1963 John F Kennedy ignored the concerns of his security advisers and with his wife Jacqueline, drove in an open-top vehicle, through the streets of Dallas in Texas, only to be assassinated by Lee Harvey Oswald. He had been president for less than three years.

Diana, Princess of Wales, had also been warned of the risk to her personal safety if she continued associating with Dodi Fayed. As the car crashed in the Pont de l'Alma in Paris, her injuries were such that she died several hours later in the Pitie-Salpetriere Hospital.

Adrian had received a call to say that his replacement glasses were ready for collection, so he left the office during the afternoon and called into the opticians. He immediately ran into Rick, the ophthalmologist, and proceeded to tell him about his experience at the scanning centre and the limited risk of cholesterol.

"I know what I saw," Rick said, in a loud voice, "but I'm pleased for you."

A few moments later he found himself sitting at a work station. A woman was undoing the packages and removing the glasses contained within. She looked at the designer frames and nodded.

"We have two pairs here, Mr Dexter. I'll fit them both to make sure they're comfortable."

She began by placing the first pair on his nose and wrapping the sides around his ears.

"How does that feel?"

Adrian signalled his complete satisfaction and so she removed the glasses and replaced them with the next set.

"So, what was my colleague pleased about?" she asked, as she adjusted the strength of the fitting.

Adrian pulled back and looked at her. "Pleased about? Who?"

"I heard Rick say that he was pleased for you."

Adrian told her briefly about the back of the eye diagnosis which Rick had given, his trip to the scanning centre and the results."

"I was simply telling Rick that I don't have to worry about cholesterol."

"This is your second pair, Mr Dexter. I want to be sure that we've got the prescription right. Can you read this chart?" This he did without difficulty.

The new pair was such an improvement that Adrian was able to read the optician's name badge. It said 'Helen Greenwood. Manager'.

"Well, you're lucky, aren't you? Not having a problem with cholesterol. You'd be surprised the number of clients we have to advise to see their doctors."

"I'd not thought of it as lucky," said Adrian. "There are still plenty of other conditions that can affect me!"

Helen Greenwood looked at him.

"My Matt had high cholesterol. He ran the last four London marathons and we knew nothing about his condition."

She went to put the glasses in their case but decided to check the fitting one last time.

"I want to be absolutely sure they're right for you," she said. She placed them on his face but then loosened her grip and they fell into his lap. She immediately grabbed at them and fumbled, pressing her hands into his groin in the attempt. She pulled away immediately and apologised.

"It's Helen, isn't it?" said Adrian.

She nodded and busied herself by putting the glasses into a case.

"I don't think you've finished fitting them."

She placed the glasses on Adrian's face once more. She tightened the left-hand screw and Adrian confirmed that they were perfect.

"I wouldn't have mentioned about cholesterol if I'd known…"

She looked up and smiled.

"Don't worry about it, Mr Dexter. What matters is that we're providing you with the right glasses."

"You've looked after me very well. Thank you."

He collected his package and asked Helen whether the amount he had paid on his previous visit was correct.

"I don't think I can justify taking any more money off you, Mr Dexter," she laughed.

He turned to leave the shop. He couldn't think of any further reason he could contrive to stay longer. As he left he noticed in the reflection of the window that Helen was watching him.

He arrived home several hours later, finding that Annie had gone to bed as usual.

He settled into his study and read a text message that had arrived earlier.

DeG arrested. Missing you as ever. S x

He texted a reply and then deleted it. He couldn't stop thinking about Helen. He put a Beatles CD on to play and, as 'Love Me Do' echoed around him, he tried to recall every single moment of his time in the opticians. He stopped the CD player and replaced the disc with his favourite group (whom he considered the best group of all time). He put on track seven, his favourite song on the album. The lyrics did not actually fit his mood:

'If you should ever leave me...'

He had met her a few hours ago.

He realised he was beginning to make a fool of himself. She was perhaps in her late thirties. He had never met her before, and he had forgotten to check whether she was wearing any rings. And there was this Matt, whoever he was. That's assuming he was alive after that cryptic comment about his high cholesterol... But she'd pressed her hands into his groin... She was merely retrieving a pair of glasses. She was wearing an alluring perfume. She had such wonderful hands!

He poured himself a large scotch and sat back in his chair. He was married to Annie and he knew that he'd always remain committed to her. He had no choice in the matter.

So why was he sitting in his study thinking about an optician he had met just a few hours ago?

Perhaps The Beach Boys were right: 'God Only Knows.'

He slept badly and went to work early the next morning. His colleagues sensed he was ill at ease and even Michelle decided to avoid him. Late in the afternoon, he left Cornhill and visited the opticians. He looked around but could not see Helen. He was asked if he needed any assistance and he occupied the time of a young girl who, hard as she tried, could not find any way to make the one pair of glasses fit any better. She mentioned that she had seen Helen attend to him the day before and she was the best of the best. He gave up and left the shop. In the doorway he ran into Helen, who was returning with three large cardboard cups of steaming coffee.

"Mr Dexter!" she exclaimed. "Nothing wrong, I trust?"

Adrian hesitated and mumbled about the glasses not fitting properly.

"That's dreadful. Come back in and let me check them for you."

"Don't worry – your colleague has done that already."

"No. I must be sure. Please come on in."

The coffees disappeared and Helen invited Adrian to sit at a workstation. After fiddling around with the glasses for a few minutes, she looked puzzled.

"Mr Dexter. The glasses fit perfectly. There's nothing wrong with them."

"I know."

Helen gave him a rather quizzical stare.

"I wanted to see you again."

She straightened the buttons on her suit jacket and pulled her skirt down to her knees. She then ran a hand through her fair hair and gave him a wonderful smile.

"Well, in that case, I think you've achieved your objective, Mr Dexter. You've seen me again."

"Yes, but I won't see you again for probably two years unless I manage to break these things."

"That would be a pity."

"Not really – I'd pay, of course, for any repairs."

"That's not what I meant," she said quietly.

"What did you mean?"

"It would be a pity not to see each other again."

"Would you join me for a glass of wine this evening?"

"Oh," she sighed, "I have a staff training session tonight."

"No, of course, it was silly of me to ask. I realise…"

"But I haven't said 'no' to tomorrow night, have I?"

She put her hand in her pocket and pulled out a card.

"My mobile number is on that. Text me."

Chapter Three

April 2012

Helen read the text message with a certain amount of surprise.

Davy's Bar & Grill: 57 High Holborn: 6.00pm: please confirm. Adrian.

"Well, that sounds romantic," she said to herself, a little disappointed. Her hopes of a lush cocktail bar in a lavish London hotel were dashed.

She sent her reply.

Thanks. Looking forward to it. Helen.

She decided that she shouldn't get him too excited. Where the hell was 'Davy's Bar & Grill'?

But the moment she walked in to the wine bar she felt comfortable, and she instantly loved the oak caskets and old-fashioned decor. She saw him immediately, sitting in the corner. He helped her remove her light raincoat, and hung it on the hooks by the wooden hat stand.

She sat down and immediately picked up the menu.

"I'll just have a glass of house white, please."

He looked at her and smiled.

A waitress had already arrived and was busily putting two glasses on the table. She showed the bottle to her client who nodded, before unscrewing the top and pouring a small amount into his glass. He looked at it, swirled the wine around, lifted it up to his nose, smelt deeply and nodded to the waitress.

She then poured a generous amount of wine for both of them.

Adrian raised his glass and smiled at Helen.

"Thank you for coming," he said.

She tasted the wine. The aromatic German grape hit the back of her throat and she sighed with pleasure.

"Good choice," she said.

"Not difficult," he replied, "a Riesling is rarely disappointing. This one is a 2009 from Warapara in New Zealand. But you can still smell the river Rhine can't you?"

Before she could answer, the waitress had reappeared with two white dishes and laced serviettes. She returned a few moments later and served them each with a plate of canapés.

"I couldn't decide on just one item so I picked all the things that I like the most." He laughed. "I'm happy to swap if you wish."

She looked at the food in front of her.

"You've been served tiger prawns wrapped in smoked salmon with lemon and dill mayonnaise," he said.

She laughed. "I don't rate your chances of me exchanging any of mine. What have you got?"

"Mine's chopped Cumberland sausage with Mediterranean tapenade and crostini."

"How could you do this to me? I want all the prawns and some of your Cumberland sausage," she smiled. "Are you open to negotiation?"

"I could order some more?" he proposed.

"Just a minute," she said. "Is there anything else coming?"

"You'll have to wait to find out."

The waitress returned once more with a large bottle of sparkling water and two iced glasses.

Helen settled back into her chair and sighed. She liked his dark suit and open shirt. She'd checked his records and knew his age, but decided he was wearing remarkably well. There was grey in his hair but this only added to his appeal – he looked fit and he sparkled, somehow.

"How are the glasses?" she asked.

"Finance department have not returned a single request slip since you sorted me out."

"I looked at your notes. You've got good vision."

"Which is why I asked you to have a drink with me. On that note, you're looking incredibly attractive tonight."

"Do you say that to all the opticians you meet?"

"I've lived a rather sheltered life. You're actually the first optician I've ever invited for a drink."

She leaned across and put her hand on his arm.

"Well, on that basis, I must be the best."

"That's why I didn't bother with the others." He smiled at her with a twinkle in his eye.

The waitress reappeared and topped up their glasses. She took Adrian's plate away but saw that Helen had left two tiger prawns.

"I'm feeling generous tonight," Helen said. "Would you like one of my prawns?"

"With dill mayonnaise?"

"Of course. No short changing here!"

She picked up one of the crustaceans, rubbed it in the remaining sauce, leaned across and put it in his mouth.

"I'm willing to forgive you for eating all the sausage," she said.

He wiped his mouth with his serviette before nodding to the bar staff. Within minutes a second bottle of the Riesling was served. Helen lifted her replenished glass and smiled.

"It's certainly very good service here."

"Well, I came early and gave the manager ten pounds. I told him there would be another ten pounds later if the service was up to standard."

She laughed. "We seem on our way to having an open and honest relationship!"

"Would you want it any other way?"

There was a long pause while she considered his words.

"So who broke Adele's heart, Helen? Who inspired the songs on her album '21'?"

Helen looked at Adrian with some amazement.

"Who do you think it was, Adrian?"

"The DJ Ned Biggs, some have suggested James Corden, but I can't believe that... the rock singer Jamie Reynolds is a possibility."

"You know your pop scene, don't you?"

"One tries."

Helen looked thoughtful. "Tell me Adrian, which song did you prefer: 'Love Forever Love' or 'My Dream Is Coming True'?"

He reflected on her question for some time.

"I liked both," he replied, "but, for me, 'Love Forever Love' was the best track on the whole album.'

"Interesting answer. Just one small problem. I made those titles up. You've no idea who Adele is, have you?"

Adrian drank some wine.

"Where did you get the question from, Adrian?"

"My daughter. I texted her. She suggested Adele because of the controversy about who she was thinking about when she recorded her songs. I meant to go out this afternoon and buy the CD, but somehow the finance director wanted time with me…"

"So you told your daughter that you wanted to impress a younger woman so that she might sleep with you?"

"I told my daughter I was taking some of the younger staff for a drink and I wanted to appear 'cool'. That's her word by the way. She thought it was funny."

"Our open and honest relationship hasn't lasted too long, has it?"

Their conversation was interrupted by the arrival of the mini chocolate pots. There were six pots, three for each of them, all topped with fresh cream.

"Oh, wow. This is delicious," Helen sighed.

"Sorry about Adele," said Adrian. "That was a stupid idea."

"I'm flattered that you're making such an effort! But I'd prefer you to be yourself. You're proposing to cheat on your wife."

"That's a bit forward, isn't it? I invited you out for a drink, that's all."

She put her spoon down and looked across the table.

"I'm going to the cloakroom. When I come back, we're going to start again."

"I want to tell you about MXD Capital, Cate. No, don't do that, darling. Please, Cate, stop it." He groaned. "On second thoughts, carry on." Ten days away from his fiancée were ten days too many.

She sat up and threw off the bed covers.

"You like this Adrian, don't you?"

"Yes. He has a good reputation and he's a deal maker. The merger is a great development for us."

"And you'll be the boss, Mark. Wow. My Mark, the head honcho. I think this deserves something special…"

She disappeared under the sheets.

"I'll take over in six… oh God… in six… Cate, please."

She reappeared and leant over to the side table. She then opened a drawer and took out a parcel covered in 'congratulations' wrapping paper.

"Happy anniversary, darling."

He opened it and took out a copy of Robert Harris's *The Fear Index*.

"Fantastic. They were talking about this book at work today. It's all about…"

Cate had returned to her beneath-the-sheets activities.

"It's about a computer… oh… based… oh hell…"

He pulled her from under the coverings.

"Cate. What anniversary? What are we celebrating?"

"Guess."

"Hmm. We're celebrating something special?"

"Very special."

"The first time you cooked a Sunday roast without burning it?"

"Quite close. Anyway I haven't managed that yet. Try something more dramatic."

"Got it. The gym. A year ago you beat your target for running a mile on the treadmill."

"Not bad. Certainly physical prowess was involved."

"Life's too short. Tell me. What's so marvellous about today?"

She kissed him and let her tongue linger in his mouth while she did something with her right hand.

"A year ago today, at twelve minutes past midday, you fucked me for the first time."

"And I suppose you've been adding up ever since?"

"I had a week off with the flu if you remember – and I'm sure you do – but otherwise I stopped counting after two hundred and thirty times."

49

The telephone rang but almost immediately went to answer-phone.

She had now lifted herself up higher on the bed and was straddled across him with her thighs across the top of his legs. She was massaging his testicles. He could not take his eyes off her body. From the very beginning he had been transfixed by the silky sheen of her skin. She had little body hair and he would never forget the night she had decided to shave everything off...

"You can't take your eyes off me, can you? There, you're looking at my..."

"It's the sex act, Cate."

"I thought it was my alluring body!" she laughed.

"Same thing."

"What is?"

"Why is my penis erect?"

"Probably because I'm playing with it!"

"Ok, go and stand over there."

"Right. This gives a new meaning to the term 'foreplay' – but you're the chief executive!"

"How far away are you?" he asked.

"Seven and a half feet, or do you want it in centimetres?"

"What's my penis doing?"

"From here it looks very large indeed."

"See. That's my point! So much of sex is visual. How do animals mate? Two chimpanzees don't say they love each other. The female simply displays her genital area and that drives the male mad with desire. That's why most sex is from behind. The female bends over..."

"I get the idea, Mark. You want me to spend the next twenty years of our forthcoming marriage bending over like an orang-utan."

"Well, it's in your best interests to do so."

"Excuse me? Why is it in my best interests?"

"A woman experiences the deepest penetration when a man enters her from behind. In fact, the human being is the only creature that practises sex from a front to front position. If you watch pornography, the film makers know what their customers

50

want. That's why so much porn shows women having sex from behind."

"I didn't know you watched porn."

"I don't. But did you know that nearly all our hotels show explicit sex movies and make a fortune from it?"

"That's just for dirty old men."

"There was a survey recently which said that, on average, a male visitor to a hotel will turn on the porn channel within four minutes twenty seconds of entering the room."

"Ok. Have you done with your voyeurism now, Mark? Can I come back to bed?"

Within seconds, they were locked together in a passionate embrace. Cate broke away from his lips and whispered a command in his ear. Mark did as he was told and went and stood by the side of the bed. His fiancée lay face down on the bed and allowed her buttocks to settle. Mark had thought from the beginning that they were near to perfection. She then slowly opened her legs and imperceptibly raised herself. She remained motionless and said nothing.

Mark checked with his fingers that she was moist before entering her, moving his hands under her upper body and fondling her breasts at the same time. His lips rested on her neck as he began to rock in and out.

A few minutes later, Cate experienced an orgasm more intense than anything she had ever known before.

The theatregoers had moved off in their taxis to the West End to ensure they arrived before the stage curtains rose. The vacated tables were quickly filled with young people enjoying wine and nibbles. Adrian noticed that the couple to his right, towards the bar, were clearly not getting on.

Helen strode back across the floor with an athletic poise. She was wearing a black pencil skirt, white shirt and low-heeled stilettos. He saw that the only items of jewellery she was showing were stud earrings and a gold pendant.

She sat down, lifted her glass to her lips, sipped some wine and asked Adrian if they could have some coffee.

"It's on its way," he said quietly.

"No more food, please," she smiled. "It was marvellous. You've been very thoughtful."

"I've been a fool."

She looked at him and frowned.

"Adrian, do you want to go? Shall we call it a day?"

"Is that what you want?"

"No. I'd like to stay here and get to know you better."

The waitress arrived with a tray carrying a cafetiere, cups, saucers, serviettes and a white bowl filled with Davy chocolates.

"Sorry about Adele," Adrian said.

Before she could answer, they were interrupted by the couple at the adjacent table who were now volubly disagreeing. Adrian looked across and then back at Helen, trying to ignore the commotion.

"Adrian, forget..."

But the man had now stood up and, before anyone knew what was happening, smashed a pint glass against the edge of the table. He suddenly had his left arm around the girl's throat and held the jagged edge of the container against her neck. Blood was already trickling down her skin and staining the top of her yellow blouse.

"Bitch, fucking bitch!" he screamed. "Let's see if he fancies you with your face altered!"

The girl screamed. Tables cleared. Chairs were knocked over. Adrian had run round and put himself in between Helen and the fight, but he suddenly leapt up and threw himself at the couple. He managed to grip the man's right arm but struggled to ease the pressure on the girl's throat.

"Helen," he hissed, "take your shirt off."

She looked at him with her mouth open.

"Now, Helen, please – take it off."

She unbuttoned her garment before removing it and pressing it into his left hand.

"No. Wrap it around my wrist, Helen, as tightly as you can."

She completed her instructions and stood back. She was wearing a low-cut white bra.

"Move back further, Helen. Get back."

The pulsating blue lights and the piercing sirens announced the arrival of the police.

"Let go of my fucking arm or I slash her!"

Adrian held on and whispered something to the girl. She nodded. Her eyes were wide open and filled with terror.

"I'm Adrian. What's your name?"

"What do you fucking mean 'what's my name?' Fuck off. Let go!"

"Pete. I heard her call you Pete."

"Bollocks. You've been chatting up that bird with the bra. Nice tits. I've been watching you. Gagging for it, aren't you?"

"Pete. That is your name?"

"My fucking name is Zac, not fucking Pete!"

"Ok. Great name, Zac. I hate my name. Adrian. It makes me sound like a poof."

As he spoke, he managed to move his grip about an inch up Zac's arm, towards the wrist and the glass.

"She doesn't think you're queer. I watched her put something in your mouth. Hey. Don't do that, bitch."

He had seen that Helen had lifted her coat off the hook and wrapped it around herself.

"Bitch! Yes, you! Fucking take it off. I was enjoying your tits."

Adrian once more whispered into the ear of the hostage. The police inspector was holding his arm across his two colleagues. Outside the wine bar the police had halted all traffic in High Holborn, and there were two ambulances and a medical team waiting to go into action. The armed response unit had also arrived. The inspector had his attention fixed solely on Adrian's face.

"You like tits do you, Zac?"

"This bitch fucked my mate. Last night. Told me she was working late."

Adrian felt him imperceptibly ease his hold of the glass against her throat.

Helen was standing alone, immobile. She had tightened her garment around her.

"Pissed you off did it, Zac?" asked Adrian.

"I'll sort him out later. I've got her to fix first."

"You're going to fix nobody, Zac. You're a sensible guy. Let her go."

"She fucked him."

"Zac. I've been down the same road, mate. There's this woman in my office. I was going to fuck her. But what happens, Zac? She arrives with a bloke called Pollett."

"Pollett. Fucking stupid name. What's her name?"

"Michelle."

"Nice name. Good body?"

"She climbs mountains. Fantastic legs."

"Your woman's got nice legs. I watched her cross the…"

"Now!!" shouted Adrian.

He wrenched Zac's arm away from the girl's throat; the broken glass slashed across his left arm. He was saved by Helen's shirt, which was ripped to shreds.

The inspector had now reached the girl and pulled her away. The police had Zac flat on the floor and were handcuffing him.

Adrian staggered away and into Helen's arms. Her raincoat was open and he thrust his face into her chest. She hugged him to her. He was shaking.

Forty-five minutes later, Adrian had completed his statement and agreed to visit the police station the next day. He refused all offers of help from the police and the staff of the wine bar, who had managed to find Helen a Davy's t-shirt to wear.

The inspector shook his hand.

"Where did you learn that trick, Mr Dexter?"

"What trick?"

"Wrapping the shirt around your left arm. Smart move."

"I just watch a lot of old James Cagney films!" he replied.

The inspector laughed. "You dirty rat," he mimicked.

"Cagney claimed he never actually said that!" laughed Adrian.

They all moved off. He was told that the girl had needed three stitches in her neck. Her parents were with her at the hospital and had sent him a personal message of thanks.

Adrian stood with Helen on the pavement.

"I'm going home. I'll phone you."

She looked at him with a mixture of admiration and frustration. She didn't want him to leave her.

Before he stepped into the taxi she had hailed, she kissed him.

"Adrian," she said, as he closed the door, "please take care. And who's Michelle?"

He didn't answer. She called herself a cab and felt very alone.

She was feeling better; and she needed to feel well. A Swedish study involving a hundred and sixty-six women had drawn one worrying conclusion – the psychological stress experienced by a female during the process, due to changes in her body, could lead to clinical depression. The report also suggested that some couples were financially stretched by the costs involved.

She thought about the receipt of their latest bank statement and the meeting with the personal finance officer. A thirty-three minute meeting could be summed up in one word: 'No'.

She decided to go for a walk in her local park.

She knew she needed to find a solution, but regretted the transgression it would mean from her Catholic faith. What had the church leaflet said?

It separates the procreative purpose of the union act from its unitive purpose.

'Holy Mary,' she thought to herself. 'Father forgive me: I will have sinned twice. IVF and now sex with a married man.'

Sonja Redmaine felt uncomfortable for two reasons: one, the evening breeze blowing onto the balcony of the fifteenth floor hotel room and two, the look in Nigel de Groot's eyes. She knew she should not have accepted his invitation to join him for evening drinks, but had had little choice in the matter.

"Nouja? Hoe gaan dit met jou?" He did not wait for an answer as he did not care how she was. "Thank you for the envelope from Bailey Mayhew. You're certain nobody else saw this package?"

"No. It arrived by courier this morning and I took delivery myself." She sipped her vodka and tonic. "It was a surprise to receive your call."

"A storm in a tea cup, Sonja. The authorities received a tip-off about Zambian Goldfields. I know who it was. That's being dealt with."

"So will we be seeing you back at the bank, Nigel?"

"No. I'm moving on." He took a swig of his scotch and water. "But I'm puzzled by one thing. It's clear that Adrian Dexter knew about my proposal to the board. He was well prepared. Now, how do you think that happened, Sonja?"

"We were all aware of the agreed strategy, Nigel. It was discussed by the board."

"But how did Dexter know about it?"

"Ekskuus? Are you sure he did?"

He moved around slowly and stood in front of her. Suddenly he raised his open hand and slapped her across the face, knocking her from the chair to the floor. He kicked her in the stomach, making her scream out in pain. He then grabbed the top of her dress and dragged her into the lounge of the hotel suite. He ripped off her clothes in one violent movement, so she was left with only her underwear. He took a knife from his pocket and sliced the bra strap in one movement. He pulled the garment away. Sonja's hands flew up to try and hide her modesty. With one hand, he ripped off her panties. He then went over to the table and removed several photographs from a folder.

"Sit up," he ordered.

"Fok jou! I'm naked, Nigel. Please."

He went to the bathroom and brought out a white towelling robe which he threw at her. She wrapped it tightly around herself and went and sat on a chair. She was terrified.

He handed her the first of the photographs. She gasped in amazement. They showed her naked with Adrian in a bed in a Johannesburg hotel.

"Would you like to see some more?" he asked. "My favourite is where you seem to have something in your mouth." He laughed. "Thought you'd fooled everybody. You should know by now that Nigel de Groot is always one step ahead."

He returned to the table and removed the top from a wooden box. When Sonja saw its contents, she cried out in dread. He was holding a sjambok, a whip made out of the hide of a hippopotamus. A strip of between three to five feet is rolled into a cylindrical shape and fixed to a handle. This whip is usually used to ward off dangerous dogs, or by the police for crowd control. Occasionally it is used for corrective purposes.

"Stand up," he ordered.

Sonja stood up.

"Take off the robe."

She let it fall to the floor.

"Go over to the bed."

She walked slowly across the room.

"Kneel."

She slumped to her knees and looked up at him.

"Vlieg in jou moer!" she swore. He pushed her forcibly, so that she was leaning over the edge of the bed.

"Lean over the side of the bed."

Her buttocks showed her white bikini lines. The pale flesh glowed. He sat beside her and put his hands on her skin.

"Very nice," he said. "I bet Adrian Dexter enjoyed these... So, did you tell him?" he snarled. She was silent for a minute and he shouted the question again.

She eventually nodded her head, knowing that it was useless to deny it.

He stood up and raised the whip. As it lacerated her flesh, she cried out, "Eina! Jou doos!"

Downstairs at the hotel bribes had been paid, and the in-human noises went unheeded.

"I was surprised to get your call, Mr Appleton."

"Mark."

They were together in a coffee shop in Moorgate. Both had ordered skinny lattes.

"Our firms are merging, so I thought I'd better meet with some of the key staff. Adrian's aware of this."

"But I'm a team leader. I'm not senior management."

"Michelle, you are building a great reputation. You've pulled off three fund-raisings in the last six weeks. The private hos-pitals transaction was very impressive. I'm hoping we'll work well together."

"I'm not comfortable about this. You're going to ask me about my colleagues, aren't you?"

"This is about you and me. It's important that we get to know one another. I've heard you've had approaches from other finance houses."

"Yes, and I'll be accepting one of them if this is the way you manage your business."

"I have a close-knit team at Silicon Capital, Michelle. The merger makes sense. We want to work well together."

"Well, this is not the way to go about it, Mr Appleton. We haven't even officially been told what's going on."

"That's just because we need regulatory permission. It's taking time."

"No. I don't like this."

Michelle stood up and walked out of the coffee house.

The text message arrived mid-morning the following day.

Please can we meet? H.

Adrian answered, suggesting a lunchtime coffee.

Two hours later, they were together in a London Wall restaurant, drinking black coffee and eating sandwiches.

"I just don't know what to think," said Helen. "One minute we're having our first drink together and a little later you're holding me with your arms around my bare stomach."

"Well, what do you want to think, Helen?"

"I didn't sleep. It's as though we've known each other forever. But I know nothing about you really. Are we going to see each other again?"

Adrian laughed. "I think that's what we're doing at the moment."

"No. I mean something else. You know what I'm trying to say. You asked me out hoping that I'd sleep with you."

"And will you, Helen?"

"It doesn't happen like this. We meet. We have a drink. We have dinner a few times. We begin to touch. Eventually…"

"Do you not think that Zac short-circuited the process for us?"

"Who's Zac?"

"The man with the broken glass last night."

"Oh, I see. Him. You were fantastically brave. He could have smashed that glass in your face."

"Saved by your shirt!"

"But I know nothing about you!" she exclaimed, suddenly.

"You know I have good eyesight. Long distance, anyway."

"And you have great reading vision now, due to Rick."

"Rick?"

"The ophthalmologist."

"Yes. Right. Rick. So what else do you know? I'm fifty-nine. I'm married. I have three daughters. My work is in corporate finance, and I run an advisory business."

"Don't forget that you're handsome, fit – and you fancy Michelle."

"I just said that to divert Zac's attention," Adrian said with a smile.

"It worked. Who is Michelle anyway, and who's Pollett?"

"Pollett is her step-brother. Michelle is one of my group leaders. She has eight colleagues and they raise funds for our clients."

"She's attractive?"

"Very."

"So have you tried it on with her?"

"She's a work colleague. I'm the chief executive."

"So you have and she rejected you."

"No. I have never tried – but that's only because she made it clear there was no point!"

"We're back to our honest and open relationship. That's good," Helen smiled.

"So, your turn to answer my question. Are you interested in a relationship with me?"

She looked across at him. "It just doesn't seem right. Surely you should court me first."

"That's a lovely word. I'm definitely up for courting you."

"You did a bit of that last night. Though not quite as planned, I admit!" she laughed. "Shall we go and have a proper drink?"

Within minutes they had found seats in the crowded bar next door and Adrian had bought two glasses of red wine.

They talked and talked for the next thirty minutes, and Helen didn't remove her hand from Adrian's knee the entire time. They then both realised with disappointment that they needed to return to their offices.

"I'm free tonight," said Adrian.

"So am I."

"Would you like to go and see 'Jersey Boys'? It's on at the Prince Edward theatre."

"I'd love to. The story of the Four Seasons."

"We took clients to see it. Marvellous. The music's great."

"You're happy to see it again?"

"I'll be with you."

As Helen walked back to work, she became lost in her thoughts. She passed the bank and the coffee house and then stopped. She looked at her reflection in a shop window and brushed her hand through her hair.

"He's just about perfect," she said quietly to herself.

Chapter Four

April (third week) 2012

Cate felt as though she was fifty shades of pink. Mark loved early morning sex and he'd woken up in a particularly playful mood that morning. After he'd kissed her and left for work, she lay back and basked in her post-coital glow. She had a few hours to kill before lunch with her ex – she felt slightly guilty about the plan, but she wanted to know why she had lost him.

She sighed, picked up her Kindle and re-read one of the final sentences:

The pain is indescribable… physical, mental… metaphysical… it is everywhere, seeping into the marrow of my bones. Grief. This is grief – and I've brought it on myself.

'You deserve all you got, stupid cow,' Cate said to herself. While in Australia, she'd come across a book which was being hyped up on social media. She'd never heard of EL James, but she'd trawled her way through the ludicrous story of a high-flying entrepreneur establishing a sexual relationship, based on a written contract, with a pathetic literature student.

Cate had decided that Anastasia was too unreal to be true. How she continued with him when she couldn't touch him made no sense at all. She'd hated Christian from the beginning and had dismissed his so-called 'inner demons' as irrelevant. He was just in love with himself: a typical man. And the sex scenes? Really? Did she need all that… detail? She did not. She pressed the button and deleted *Fifty Shades of Grey* from her reader.

"Utter nonsense. That'll never catch on," she thought.

Pollett couldn't get the cadence quite as he wanted. He knew he had a great ability to play jazz in his mind, accompanying it on his saxophone. He'd lain in the same position on Hampstead Heath for over an hour going through the variations that Louis Armstrong had introduced into the genre. He stopped, wiped

61

his mouth, and waited for Louis to tell him that he was ready to sing 'It's a Wonderful World'.

He finished the performance and waited for the applause. As he moved a little to his left he knocked over the can of strong lager. He was late. Who the fuck cared? The bitch could take care of the kids – and anyway, they'd told him they wanted to live with her, not him. Bitch. She'd brainwashed them. He'd put in three extra sessions so he could buy them presents. She was such a mean, selfish whore.

He had a great life ahead of him. Well, that's what Michelle had told him. She'd told him that he was such an outstanding musician he should get himself fit and concentrate on his playing. He opened another can. Fuck. It was the last one. He downed nearly half and belched. He took his mobile phone out of his pocket. It was fully discharged. He was due at the session at six o'clock. He scratched himself. He had a rash on the inside of his leg. He pulled his hand from inside his trousers and saw the blood under his nails.

He farted. He'd being doing that a lot more lately. He knew it was something to do with his diet. He must try to get at least one square meal a day. What had Michelle told him? He liked Michelle. But he hated her. No woman worth anything would reject him. She had swarmed all over him like bees on honey when she'd first heard him play. He was going somewhere in those days. They'd had sex that first night on the top deck of the Highgate bus.

It was nearing four o'clock. Two hours to go. Thirty minutes' walk to the studio. He'd just rest his head and have a short sleep. He'd not forgotten the 'final warning' he'd been given earlier in the week.

"Wow. Dress circle. Sixty-four pounds fifty."

"How do you know that?" asked Adrian.

"It's on the ticket."

"Ah. Come on then, Helen. Drink up. Time to get to the theatre."

They left the Charing Cross Road bar with their arms around each other. They reached the Prince Edward theatre, deposited their coats, bought a programme and took their seats, all the while continuing to hold hands.

Adrian felt inside his jacket pocket and produced a long, slim box of deluxe plain chocolates. Helen's eyes lit up at the sight of them and she took one with a smile.

The curtain rose and the jukebox music of Bob Gaudio filled the auditorium. The story of Frankie Valli and the Four Seasons was reaching its fourth birthday and as a performance it was simply getting better and better. When the end of Act One was nearing and the lyrics of 'Walk Like a Man' rang out, Helen wept tears of joy.

They dashed for a drink at the interval and Helen managed to grab an ice cream on the way back.

"How come you are so beautifully slim?" he asked as they took their seats.

"We don't know each other well enough for you to ask such highly personal questions," laughed Helen. "But just wait until you see the real thing."

Adrian groaned and sank back into his seat.

The climax of the show came and the final songs rang out. The audience were cheering and dancing in the aisles. 'Rag Doll' brought an ovation and finally, 'Who Loves You' closed the show.

As they stood up, Adrian bent forward and gave Helen a passionate kiss.

After leaving the theatre, they meandered slowly away down the street.

"I don't want the evening to end," Helen said.

Adrian stopped and put his hands on her shoulders.

"Well, it needn't end, Helen," he said.

"What does that mean?"

"I've booked a hotel room, in Holborn."

She looked at him.

"Shouldn't you have asked me first?"

"What would you have said?"

She grabbed his hand.

"Come on. Not far to walk."

They soon reached the Chancery Court Hotel in High Holborn. The four hundred and twenty pound fee that Adrian had paid earlier in the day secured them a luxury double room.

On entering their suite, Helen's eyes opened wide. She had never been in such a large, exquisite hotel room. Adrian opened the cocktail bar and poured them each a drink. Their eyes met and they raised their glasses, clinking them together. Helen thought that it was a promising start to their growing relationship. She smiled inwardly.

She then put her glass down and went into the bathroom. When she returned, she was wearing one of the fluffy towelling bathrobes. He followed her example. They stood in front of one another.

Adrian reached across and tugged at her belt which came smoothly away. The sides of the robe parted and she stood there, naked.

His eyes opened wide. She was near perfect. Her skin was slightly tanned but naturally and without blemish. Her legs seemed to go on forever.

He ripped off his robe and they tumbled backwards on to the bed.

Sonja Redmaine gasped as the final stitches were inserted. She had been trying to concentrate on the azure-coloured sky that she could see through the surgery windows. Now she was lying on her front. The nurse was wiping her forehead with a damp flannel and she was gripping the iron framework of the bed. Each of the lacerations had required seven stitches. The doctor had given her several injections but the pain from the original brutal attack, and the surgical process that followed, combined to make her body shake with anger and resentment.

"You still refuse to let me go to the police for you, Mrs Redmaine?"

Sonja shook her head. "No police, please."

"It will take us another treatment to complete the healing process. And I will need to check your stitches in ten days' time. I've given you some strong antibiotics, which you must take for five days. They should prevent any infection. If you have any problems, please, come straight back to see me."

"Dankie," Sonja replied, as she tried to convince the surgeon that she was fine. She shook her head again and looked up.

"He will be punished. I'll do it my way."

"Pas jouself op" replied the doctor.

The needle went in deep again and she clenched her teeth together. She was focusing on her revenge.

The Friday morning sunshine cascaded through the window and lit up the bedroom. Adrian was already up and making tea. Helen was slumbering and resisting his prods. She finally sat up, rubbed her eyes, and took the cup he was offering.

"How are you?" she asked.

Adrian sat at the side of the bed and took her spare hand.

"I'm not sure that it gets better than that."

She looked at him, put down her cup, and leaned across and kissed him.

"It was special," she replied.

"What happens now?"

"We make love again."

"We go to work too," he laughed. "But I'm sure the world of corporate finance can wait for me a little longer."

This time it was different. Last night they had been nervous. At one point she had guided his hands as she felt him hesitate and, on several occasions, he had misunderstood her directions and apologised. But still they had reached climax and collapsed into each other's arms before falling asleep.

But now he took charge and she loved it. She was naked and let him see everything he desired – and, when he wilted for just a few moments, she took him in her mouth. Their mutual lust was intense.

Afterwards, she watched him getting dressed.

"So, back to the office. Where does your wife think you are?"

"Yes, it'll be a long day in the office. I've got a merger to make work. My wife? She thinks I was at a client's party last night. I'll be back home this evening."

"Have you cheated on her much?"

65

Adrian stopped in his tracks. For reasons that were not quite clear to him, he didn't think of this as a matrimonial blemish.

"We have an arrangement," he said.

"Ha! That's what they all say."

"You do this often?" he responded.

"It's my first time since…"

There was a knock on the bedroom door and room service arrived with a full English breakfast for both of them. They settled down and started eating. Helen chose decaffeinated coffee, while Adrian preferred to start the day with Earl Grey tea.

As they ate her robe slipped open and Adrian realised that she was showing her femininity.

"Can you close your legs please, Helen?"

She looked at him in complete amazement.

"You were down there a few minutes ago!" she said.

"But we're having breakfast."

"What difference does that make?"

"Helen," groaned Adrian. "We're having our breakfast. I think we should try to maintain certain standards. It seems reasonable to me to ask you to show some modesty at the breakfast table."

"We've been screwing most of the night!" she laughed. "Where are the standards in that?"

"Close your legs please, Helen. I won't ask again."

"Bloody right you won't, you pathetic old man."

She stood up and stormed into the bathroom. He could hear her taking a shower. She re-appeared and dressed. She slipped her coat over her shoulders and paused at the bedroom door.

"I'll tell you something, Helen." Adrian paused before speaking again. "You don't want to do what you're doing."

She took her hand off the door handle and turned and looked at him. She slipped off her coat and walked back across the room.

"Promise me you'll never speak to me like that again."

"I only want standards, Helen."

"It's not about standards, Adrian. It's about that tone of voice. My father used to speak to me like that. I'm one of the few female managers in our firm and the regional executives come and address me in exactly the same way. There's no such thing as female equality. We're still treated as second class citizens."

"I didn't mean any of that, Helen. I was just trying to set the scene between you and me."

"But there's only you here."

"That's not the point. We must start off with the right standards between the two of us if we are going to overcome the difficulties of having an affair."

"So, we're having an affair?"

"Well, we've been seeing each other, we went to the theatre, we've spent the night together and now we're having breakfast…"

"Define an affair," she said.

"What we're doing," he replied, without hesitation.

"Sex. Just sex. That's all."

"Do you believe that?"

"No. It was a stupid thing to say."

She stood up and opened the balcony window. She breathed in the fresh air. Early morning cab drivers were scouring the Holborn area for trade from the law courts.

"I miss him," she said. She paused and wiped the corner of her eye. "I can't get used to the lack of contact. I've had a few men but I've hated it. Last night was lovely. You held me close. I felt wanted. When I fitted your glasses I sensed your arousal. I've so wanted to be with someone."

Adrian remained silent. He wanted her to carry on talking, but she fell silent. Who was she missing?

"We have to go to work," he said.

"Yes, I know."

"Shall we see each other again soon? Will you text me?"

"I want to think about things," she said.

"What is there to think about?"

"How old are you, Adrian?"

"You know the answer to that question. You've looked at my records. I'm fifty-nine."

"And how old do you think I am?"

"I think you're about thirty-four."

"Not bad. Thirty-seven. So there's twenty-two years between us."

"You wouldn't have known that when we were in bed together!" laughed Adrian.

"No. That's true. You look great for your age, Adrian."

"So what do you need to think about?"

"Affairs. Somebody always gets hurt."

"Just a minute, Michelle, please. I've only just arrived at the office."

"You're late, Adrian. You always arrive before eight. Been out on the town have you?"

"Why do you say that?" he asked in amazement.

"Your shirt is creased. You don't look your immaculate self and you seem knackered. A few too many with the boys, hey?"

He breathed a sigh of relief and gave a brief nod.

"So. Mark Appleton," she said, as she sat down in the chair on the other side of his desk. "Did you put him up to it?"

"Has he phoned you?"

"No, he took me out for a coffee. I walked out on him."

"You did what?"

"What's behind it, please, Adrian?"

He poured them both some coffee.

"I should have spoken to you. I've been distracted. The Silicon Capital team is relatively young, and Mark himself is in his thirties. As you know, in MXD I've been a bit slow in bringing on a younger group – and so I see you as rather important in making the merger work."

"That's fine Adrian, but try telling me first in the future. I had no idea why I was meeting with Mark."

"Sorry."

"Now I know, I suggest I go and work there for the next few days. Let me get to know them."

He nodded, already picking up the phone to call Silicon Capital.

The text arrived at around three o'clock in the afternoon.

Can we meet? Six at theThreadneedles bar. H x

Three hours later, he placed a glass of wine in front of her. The tables around them were quickly filling up with early evening City drinkers and their guests. Adrian had managed to secure a discreet table in the corner.

"Everything at work alright?" he asked.

"I want to have an affair with you." It came out in a rush, almost as if she had been rehearsing what to say.

He noticed she'd changed her outfit from the morning. She was now wearing a trouser suit and looking very attractive. He also sussed that she'd had her hair done: it was glowing in the subdued lighting of the Threadneedles bar.

"I think you are already," he said.

"I want you to commit."

"What does that mean?"

"I need to know that you're mine."

"In the sense of having an affair?"

"Yes. You're married. I'm talking about us outside that."

"I can't leave my wife."

"I don't want you to leave your wife. I want you to have an affair."

"Why?"

"Because when we woke up this morning we were together. There was a closeness I've not known for ages. I accept that I have to share you – but that's enough for me."

"You nearly walked out on me this morning."

"I've yet to knock you into shape," she laughed. "No, seriously, just don't patronise me and we'll be fine."

"And where will it lead?"

"Does it matter? Let's enjoy the journey."

"How do you know that I want an affair?"

She looked at him and smiled.

"I know."

"What if we fall in love with each other?"

She lifted her glass to her lips and drank slowly.

"Can I suggest that we don't do that? It'll just complicate things."

Adrian sat back and took a deep glug of wine. He ran his hand through his hair and straightened the knot in his tie.

"I can't believe how quickly you've become part of my life."

"Sentimental rubbish," she responded, rather quickly. "It's about sex. I've got a great body and you're enjoying it. Don't complicate the issues, Adrian. You're a fifty-nine year old man and you've landed yourself a young mistress. That's what all this is about. We're going to have some marvellous fun and you're going to pay for it all. You are rich, right?" she laughed. "Don't worry – I won't turn up on your doorstep with my suit-case!"

He leaned across and took her hand; he was struggling to cope with her mood swings. He wondered if she was hormonal.

"Tell me this is a bit more than just sex," he said.

"What? Of course it's about sex. You're a horny chief executive looking for some fun. You're also a flirt. You've just watched that woman walk across to the bar."

"You made the first move. Remember? Dropping the glasses in my lap."

"I like men who select designer frames," she smiled.

"Did you do that deliberately?"

"I never discuss trade secrets." She laughed.

"What if you meet somebody else?"

"I'm not looking for anybody else. I've got you."

"How do I know you're not going to drop some frames into someone else's lap?"

"Well, you'll just have to take my word that I've never done it before and I doubt I'll ever do it again."

She suddenly stood up, walked over to the bar and returned with two glasses of champagne.

"Adrian," she said, sitting down, "I want to give you a piece of advice."

"Change opticians?" he grinned.

"Stop talking and thinking about us. Please Adrian. No more debate. I don't want to analyse us, think about our relationship, discuss your wife or any other personal stuff. Let's just get on and have fun, an affair, whatever you want to call it. Hotel rooms, meals out, theatre trips, the whole shebang! And then we go to bed and I'll make your dreams come true…"

They left the hotel together and went their separate ways. Adrian was left bemused by Helen's strange mood swings and yet – whatever she did, she continued to tantalise him.

When Adrian arrived home, Annie was already in bed. He went into his study and put on 'Elgar's Variations'. As he imagined himself looking out on the Worcestershire countryside, he saw Helen romping around the fields in a summer dress.

He then noticed he'd received a text message.

Sorry. Been bit under the weather. What's your news? Still love you. S xx

He realised that, for the first time in days, he'd completely forgotten about Sonja. He guiltily texted his response:

Are you ok now? All well at MXD. Any news on NdeG? Miss you. A x"

She did not reply for over an hour. Adrian was unaware that Sonja was having a meeting with two men at her home in Johannesburg. He was not to know about the contract being agreed.

He was slumbering in his chair when another text arrived.

Missing you already. Wish your body was near mine… H x

He smiled and replied immediately.

Thought I wasn't to think or talk about it? A x

He read her response and groaned.

You've been granted a special exemption never to stop thinking about my body. H xxx

The red light flashed again.

NdeG facing an accident. Love you S x

He didn't know what she was talking about, but he was too tired to think anymore and so he decided to go to bed.

Helen was safely in her flat. She wiped the man's mouth and squeezed his hand, and then stayed with him until he closed his eyes and the drugs took effect.

She then went back into the lounge, lay on the sofa and allowed her thoughts to wander.

"He's simply perfect," she said to herself.

She thought back to when they first met at the opticians and the almost electric charisma he exuded. She was used to attending to City people, usually dressed immaculately and wearing expensive aftershave. They were polite and fussy in choosing their designer frames; many were vain and affected by their wealth. They lived on their mobile phones and she was skilled at fitting glasses while her client was discussing share prices with a third party. Although their time together was brief, several attempted to further the contact, and she had been offered either coffee or a drink on a number of occasions.

Adrian was older than many of them and better looking – his skin was healthy and he dressed particularly well. When she'd started fitting his glasses she'd felt a flow of energy between them. There was just something about him; it was as though they were predestined to meet. She knew all about father figures and had loved her own parents, but she'd never dated older men before. Matt was her own age.

Things with Adrian just slotted into place. She had never begun a relationship so quickly in any of her previous liaisons. When she was in her early twenties she had ended up living with a man she'd met at a theatre group, but it had taken them over six months to begin co-habiting.

Yet Adrian had seemed to become a close confidant and a lover almost at once. The events at the Davy's Wine Bar certainly propelled them forward. Even now she swallowed hard as she remembered taking off her shirt and wrapping it around his arm. She was staggered by his actions – the bravery he had shown. She could still recall, however, how he had held her tightly and was shaking immediately after the incident.

And the night they went to the theatre and ended up at the hotel... everything had seemed so natural. He was always in command.

She felt herself beginning to fall asleep. Her final conscious thoughts confirmed that, almost by a miracle, she had found the answer to her prayers.

Chapter Five

May/June 2012

"Pollett, no."

He had been pleading with her for almost half an hour. Michelle gently kissed him on the cheek.

"You know my terms. You get help before I give you another penny. You say you want the children back – but they're better off with her. You know that really, Pollett. You've got to get yourself straight. The band will have you back whenever you sober up, but never in your current state. And you're just lucky the police have said they'll leave it at the caution they gave you."

"They were never going to make a drunk and disorderly charge stick," Pollett sneered.

Michelle just looked at him.

He held his arms to his stomach.

"What do I do then, babe?"

"You go and climb some mountains."

Pollett laughed.

"Great thinking, sis! How the hell does that help?"

"It will help in ways you can't imagine. You need to go and find yourself."

"Where are these fucking mountains?"

"Please repeat the question without the swearing."

His eyes were hot, but he did as he was instructed.

"The ones I'm thinking of are in the Lake District, at a place called Eskdale."

"So how do I get there? Hitch a lift?"

She handed him an envelope.

"The train leaves Euston in two hours. I'll run you there."

She went on to explain that he would be staying at the Outward Bound School and that she'd paid for him to spend a month there as a trainee supervisor. She'd made a real impact when she'd visited the school and the principal had listened

73

carefully to her request; he'd immediately recognised Pollett's needs and promised to commit his efforts to helping him.

"I haven't got any money," said Pollett.

"Here's your food for the journey. It takes three hours to Oxenholme Station at Kendal, and you'll be met there by somebody from the school. It's an hour by car. Mr Mathias, the principal, will receive some money from me by post. He'll allow you five pounds a day. If he sees you drink it you'll be thrown off the course. There's also enough for your return ticket in due course."

"How long, babe?"

"Four weeks, but if you want to stay on I'll send more funds."

"But what if I…?"

She slapped his face very hard indeed, sending him reeling backwards across the floor.

"That hurt me far more than it'll ever hurt you, Pollett."

She then pulled him up off the floor and gave him a tight squeeze.

"Time to get going, brother."

Adrian was now really feeling the heat from the proposed merger between MXD Capital and Mark Appleton's corporate finance business. The root cause of the tension was that, following the receipt of the tip-off from Sonja, he had faced a tight time schedule as he defeated Nigel de Groot at the board meeting. He had yet to tell Annie that he had used the one million pounds she had given him for his small business trust to buy the South African's bank's 22 percent shareholding – but that was the least of his problems.

Lord Singleton, his chairman, was on the phone to him on a daily basis. Whilst it was right and proper for the head of the board of directors to take such an interest in the transaction, Adrian was surprised when the peer asked, numerous times, when he was likely to receive his one hundred thousand pound bonus.

On top of that, Michelle had been unsettled by her brief coffee meeting with Mark. Although she'd enjoyed her time at Silicon Capital she was frequently coming in to Adrian's office to ask about the progress of the deal. And she was becoming more impatient with his unsatisfactory answers.

Adrian had several meetings with Mark, who offered the increase in new business opportunities that Silicon Capital was experiencing as an excuse for their lack of preparation. On one occasion their conversation drifted towards his increasingly turbulent relationship with Cate.

City deals which are not completed usually fail to do so for one simple reason. While teams of advisers, lawyers and accountants incur significant fees as they check every single detail, the root cause of failure, often at a high cost to share-holders, is down to one obvious and often overlooked factor: the willingness of two groups of people to merge and get on with each other.

The first meeting between Adelene Mathias and Chrissie Williamson was volcanic. Both were finance directors in their respective companies, but Chrissie had assumed she was the senior, as MXD Capital was the larger of the two firms.

"I'm sure that we'll be able to find a position for you, Adelene," she had said.

"I don't think so. I'm far more experienced than you and I can assure you that Mark will not complete this deal unless I'm finance director."

The two women had looked at each other. Their mutual dis-like was set to unsettle the whole transaction.

Nigel de Groot was taken by two burly white men when he left the Indaba Hotel, situated on the outskirts of the city. As he stepped out into William Nicol and Pieter Wenning Street he was thinking about the young secretary who had stayed behind to tidy up their room. The weather in Johannesburg was a little cooler, but he was comfortable in his open-neck shirt and off-white jacket. Her husband knew about their liaison but he would be nervous about challenging the adulterer. They had spent two blissful days exploring the hundreds of shops in the Fourways Mall.

The hit from behind took him by surprise. Before he knew what was happening he had been thrown into the back of a black BMW people carrier. He was given an injection and within seconds was lying unconscious on the back seat. A blanket was thrown over him and the driver instructed to press the gas.

After about seventeen minutes the vehicle, having left the Magaliesview area, turned off the main south-west road and into a side street. There were derelict buildings on either side of the road and it was by one of these that the car was parked. The slumbering man was carried into the warehouse and the doors closed. He was handcuffed to a metal frame. He was now beginning to wake up. There was a gag in his mouth. His eyes were wide open with abject fear.

A new man came up and used a knife to remove all his clothes; he then threw a bucket of freezing water over his naked body. He pulled the cloth out from De Groot's mouth, but told him to remain quiet. A table was positioned in front of his legs and a television screen was brought in and placed about ten feet in front of him.

He started to speak and was hit in the stomach with a cosh.

There were now three men with Nigel de Groot in the otherwise empty buildings. Somewhere high above them an extractor fan was whirring round.

"Welkom Nigel," she said.

Sonja Redmaine had appeared from nowhere, dressed in a black one-piece track suit. At the end of his punishment she would take it off and have it burned, along with all the other items of clothing worn by the men.

"Hoe gaan dit met jou?" she asked.

She laughed when she saw the expression on his face.

"But let me guess. You're not feeling too good are you?"

"Waar is die toilet?" he asked.

"Yes, you seem to be leaking something down your legs, don't you Nigel?"

She nodded to one of the men, who approached the captured man with an oak box. He pulled the table up closer to him, placed the box on top and then casually placed his penis on the wooden surface.

"You like taking photographs of people making love if I remember correctly, Nigel."

"Please, Sonja. Please. I'm sorry. I was upset. I was worried that I might lose my job and my money. I was wrong to blame you. I'm sorry. Please let's be friends again."

"You said that you were going to give me five lashes with the sjambok. My doctor said there were six lacerations. Did you get a bit carried away Nigel?"

"It was five. I know it was only five. It was just a warning. That's all."

"Yes it was five, Nigel. I'm just testing your powers of recollection."

She went up close and spat in his face.

"I think about it every day. I'll be having treatment for at least three months. I'm having nightmares and it hurts to sit down." She chuckled. "So I did some research. It seems that if I'm able to, shall we say, retaliate, the therapy will help me." For a few moments she seemed lost in her thoughts. "You must have forgotten that my former husband worked for the Special Forces."

"Sonja. We're work colleagues."

"The obvious course of action was to kill you, but that didn't appeal to me. So I have chosen something much more effective."

"No, Sonja. Please. Not the sjambok."

"No. I'm only going to apply pain to you once, Nigel. Isn't that thoughtful of me?" She patted his head. "Lashing your buttocks would not matter enough to you. You'd recover. I had to work out what could do the most damage. It was not difficult."

She nodded to one of the men, who used a remote control to turn on the television set. To De Groot's complete amazement, the screen was filled with the writhing bodies of a couple making love.

"We thought we'd start with some soft porn, Nigel, and then we'll have a threesome for you. The group video at the end is really vile but by that time you'll be out of control."

"What are you going to do?" he pleaded.

Sonja went over to a cloth bag lying on the ground. She took out a wooden-handled hatchet. The blade gleamed in the artificial light.

"What do you think I might consider doing, Nigel?"

He was violently sick. The vomit ran down his chest.

"I think that it's time that you left women alone. Enjoy the videos."

He fought with all his willpower, but he could not stop his erection growing as he watched the action on the screen. When he tried to close his eyes he was pierced in the side with a knife. He bellowed with rage and anger.

"Teef!" he shouted at Sonja, who smiled. "Fokken kont!" But his resistance ran its course and he slumped down as far as the constraints allowed. His manhood remained fully erect.

Sonja walked up to him and raised the small axe.

For some unaccountable reason De Groot laughed out loud.

The blade flashed and the tip of his penis flew off the top of the box and onto the floor.

"Pas jouself op!" said Sonja.

One man applied a tourniquet to his wound, which was pumping blood. He was joined by the second kidnapper who untied the restraining handcuffs and wires and, as he slumped forward, wrapped a towel around him. He was bundled into a van and taken to the Milpark Hospital in Parktown West, where he was dumped on the steps. Sonja did not want him to die; she wanted to imagine and enjoy his future suffering. Her ex-husband had told her that he thought it unlikely that De Groot would consider retaliating, such would be his fear of any further punishment.

She walked out of the building, stripped off her clothes, changed into a dress and got into the waiting car.

By the middle of June, London was recovering from the Queen's Diamond Jubilee and was anticipating the start of the Olympic Games. Adrian and Helen had agreed to meet for drinks in the upstairs bar of the Royal Exchange café.

Although the lighting was subdued, he knew instantly that something was different. As she approached him, it was not just her immaculate appearance that caught his attention (blue was her favourite colour and her summer dress was perfect for the evening), but more the expression on her face. She kissed him and sat down as he poured her a glass of champagne.

"We're celebrating?" she laughed.

He put his arm around her shoulders and kissed her again.

"It's nine weeks since we first met. The day I collected my glasses."

"When I dropped the frames in your lap!" she chuckled. "Funnily enough I haven't done that since." She became a little more serious. "No regrets?" she asked.

"I've never been so happy," he responded.

"Why?"

Adrian pulled back and sipped his drink.

"That's a good question," he said.

"Is it because I'm so good in bed?" she teased.

"Well, that goes for all the women I've been with!" he laughed.

She poked him in the ribs and pretended to be offended.

"Anything else? My sparkling personality, for instance?"

The drink flowed. Helen and Adrian both felt positively adolescent in their happiness.

"You really do love me don't you, Adrian?" she asked.

"Love," he replied, "what does that mean?"

"It means that you're going to be thrilled by my news."

"Let me guess. You're now regional manager of ten optician shops!" he smiled.

"Be serious," she said. "This is *our* news I'm talking about."

It was, at this moment in time, that Adrian realised something unexpected was about to happen.

"What news?" he asked. His stomach turned over as he sensed a change in her attitude.

"I'm pregnant."

He picked up his glass and slowly sipped at his drink.

"You're pregnant?" he asked, bewildered. "Who's the father?"

"You are."

Adrian looked at her with a mixture of surprise and anger. He downed the rest of his champagne.

"Nonsense, Helen. We've only just started seeing each other. There's no way I'm involved."

79

"It must have been our first night in Holborn," she said in a quiet voice.

"Has the doctor confirmed it?"

"The home testing kits are very reliable. I've not been feeling quite right, so I took a test this morning and it was positive."

"You've been seeing someone else. It's not mine."

"It's ours. I haven't had sex with another man for months."

"But how could you allow this to happen? Surely you're taking the pill?"

"If you're so bloody correct why didn't you use a condom? It's not all my responsibility! You remember our first night at the Chancery Court Hotel after 'Jersey Boys'? You booked the hotel without asking me. I missed my pill for two days but I didn't think it would matter…"

"How can you be sure it happened then? You can't know your dates until the doctor examines you."

"It's the only possibility. There's no other logical explanation."

"You'll have to terminate it."

"No way," she said. "There's a life inside me which you and I made together. I am having our baby."

He looked around him as though he was having a panic attack. He felt his heart rate quicken and his palms were clammy. She grabbed his hands and looked closely into his face.

"Adrian. It's our baby. I'll bring it up on my own as long as you'll support me. You'll see it whenever you wish. It'll have two parents. Only its father will not live at home. You'll stay the night on occasions. This can be the happiest night of our lives."

"The happiest night of… what the fuck are you talking about, Helen? Have you gone mad?"

"You're the father, Adrian. I suggest you get used to the idea."

"It'll have three step-sisters. What do I do about that?" he asked.

"I agree – there's a lot for us to talk about. I just want you to be as happy as I am."

"When will you see the doctor?"

"Tomorrow morning."

"Where?"

"At my local surgery."

"I'm coming. I'll pick you up. What time's your appointment?"

"There's no point. He'll want a urine sample and he'll send it off for testing. Utter waste of your time."

"But you just said that it's our baby. I want to be with you."

"I'm going to need you by me a great deal. But tomorrow I can handle on my own."

"I really think I should come with you."

"No Adrian. There's no point." She held his hand tightly. "You remember that I'm off for three days on a management course. I'll leave for Birmingham after I've seen the doctor. I'll text you when I know the result. Not that there's any doubt."

Two days later he received the following message:

Wonderful news. It's positive. H x

Annie was having lunch with Honeysuckle in the Landmark Hotel in Marylebone. She was telling her daughter about her growing tiredness and her doctor's diagnosis that it was a stress-related condition. Honeysuckle was astute enough to know that eventually her mother would confide in her and sure enough, when the tears came, they arrived in a torrent.

Annie knew that her husband's mind was elsewhere. She was aware of the difficulties over his firm's merger with Silicon Capital, but she was also aware that he usually took these pressures in his stride.

She already knew, too, that there was a woman called 'S' who sent him text messages. She'd read one once when he'd left his mobile phone charging overnight and she'd come downstairs for a glass of water. She'd been alerted by the flashing light. The message meant nothing to her, but 'S x' suggested something else.

But in the last few weeks her husband had changed. Outwardly he showed his usual concern and attention towards her; but he was distracted and seemed to prefer the solitude of his study over her company. He had declined an invitation to a

81

dinner party thrown by their friends, when usually he was the first through the door.

Honeysuckle put her hand over her mother's palm.

"Mid-life crisis, Mum. All men go through it. I'm sure there's nothing to worry about."

"At the age of fifty-nine?" asked Annie

They met again on the Saturday morning in Lincoln's Inn Field, the largest public square in London. They sat down on a park bench and watched the gardeners cutting the grass.

"So, when's it due?" he asked.

"The doctor thinks around the middle of January."

"How are you feeling?"

Helen breathed a sigh of relief that he was showing concern about her condition.

"I'm great," she said. "The doctor gave me a full examination. I'm in full working order."

"Except in that you're pregnant."

"With your baby, Adrian."

"Do you feel like walking round the park?" he asked.

They held hands as they strolled in the sunshine.

"I still find it strange that you became pregnant the moment we started sleeping together."

Helen stopped and pulled him round to face her. A deep concern was etched on her face.

"You don't want our baby?" she asked.

"I've accepted what's happening, Helen. But we didn't know where our relationship was going, did we?" He stopped walking and they sat down on a bench seat. "We'll work together to make sure that it has the right upbringing."

"You'll never be my husband, Adrian. I know that. But my baby and I will share you."

"Yes. Somehow we'll make it work. There's a bond between us now."

She kissed him on his cheek.

"I like that word Adrian. Bond. That's where we are, I guess."

Helen was wearing a short summer dress and already showing a slight bulge. She threw her arms around him.

"Tell me you want our baby, Adrian. Please."

He kissed her.

"It's been a shock, Helen. I never thought this would happen. Now we're in this situation... well, we'll have our baby."

"Have you finished reading it then?"

The atmosphere had been tense ever since Mark arrived home late after another demanding day at the office. He found Cate lounged on the sofa, wearing a shirt and panties. He thought carefully about how he should answer her question. He'd finished *Fifty Shades of Grey* in the early hours of the morning and had found it a real page turner. He thought Christian was a total misfit, but was seduced by the innocence and growing strength of Ana as she dealt with the ever increasing demands of her lover.

"You seem to be absorbed by it," he said, eventually.

"What did you think about their relationship?" she asked.

"I wanted to find out how Ana would deal with his ever-increasing demands."

"Yes. I thought so. You completely missed the point."

"Which is what?"

She came over and sat on the kitchen chair. She was drinking herbal tea. He had poured himself a beer.

"Most relationships start with sex. Right?"

"Well, I usually allow a few days for the chatting up," Mark said with a smile.

Cate threw her hands up in the air.

"You are just incapable aren't you, Mark? I'm trying to have a serious conversation and all you can do is make silly jokes."

"Most relationships start with boy meeting girl, Cate. Sex may come next and that's often what both are after. What's your point?"

"What comes after the sex?"

"More sex?"

Cate slammed her mug down hard on the table.

"I'll tell you what happens in your case, Mark – just more and more sex! But what happens then?"

"What happened in *Fifty Shades*...?"

"That's my point. Nothing. That's the thing about the book. They never get past sex."

"What's wrong with that?" he laughed.

"But surely every relationship has to develop! No two people stay together purely for sex. There must be a growing something between them."

"I think we're doing ok."

"Are we, Mark?"

Chapter Six

July/August 2012

She had cut out the article from a magazine earlier in the day. She gasped as she read the contents.

Intracytoplasmic sperm injection (ICSI) is a specialised form of IVF. It involves taking a single sperm and injecting it directly into each egg rather than mixing semen in a dish with the woman's eggs from her ovaries. It can counter a male's low sperm count and increases the chances of a pregnancy by 5 percent.

A report published in the New England Journal of Medicine in the summer of 2012 found that women who undergo the most popular form of IVF treatment in Britain are unlikely to suffer any higher level of birth defects than those who have conceived naturally. Those using ICFI are likely to suffer the risk of ten out of every hundred births having defects against five in every hundred in natural births.

She put her hand to her mouth. She had a one in ten chance of giving birth to a baby with birth defects. She wished she had somebody close to her to share this with.

As the Olympic Games dominated the summer months, the proposed merger between MXD Capital and Mark Appleton's business continued to be delayed by the hostility of the two finance directors. Lord Singleton's daily phone calls to Adrian became increasingly strident, until he met with his bankers and signed over further substantial family assets as security for his personal borrowings.

Throughout this time Adrian and Annie never talked about personal matters. She knew that her husband was distracted, but his continual references to the delays in the proposed merger initially convinced her that his stress was work-related. He remained considerate and concerned and regularly asked about his family. But, deep down, Annie remained convinced there was something else going on. Her own nerves were increasingly troublesome.

Meanwhile, Adrian was seeing Helen almost every day. She continued to resist his attempts to visit her flat and so they became regular visitors to the Chancery Court Hotel in Holborn. Adrian had taken the precaution of booking ahead and managed to squeeze a room out of their system throughout the Olympic Games. Helen seemed in the best of health and approached their love-making with a youthful relish. Her stomach was growing, but she was careful with her diet and tried hard to control her weight. She had stopped drinking alcohol.

Despite their growing closeness, however, Helen talked little about her personal life and rebuffed any attempt Adrian made to discuss the mysterious Matt. She remained adamant that she had only been sleeping with Adrian at the time she conceived.

Yet the one thing about which there was no doubt was her joy at being pregnant. She was almost thirty-eight and confessed that she had just about given up hope of being a mother. When he tried to find out why she and Matt hadn't succeeded, she changed the subject and made it clear that she wasn't prepared to discuss the issue.

Despite Helen's reticence, Adrian told her about Annie and his family. Helen had shown an amazing amount of concern about Annie's nervous condition and told him that he was to devote all his energy to looking after her. Adrian was already committed to doing so – when the situation had arisen with Sonja in South Africa he had decided that his wife was a completely decent woman and that he'd stay with her forever.

"I'll look after our little one," Helen had said.

One night, while he was in the bathroom, a text message came through on his mobile phone. Helen spotted the red pulsating light and read the message.

So much to tell. NdG badly damaged. Am healing. Love you more and more. When are you coming? S xx.

Adrian came out of the bathroom and knew immediately that there was a problem: Helen was lying on the bed sobbing. He made a pot of tea, handed her a cup and wiped her eyes with some tissues.

"Whatever is wrong?" he asked.

"I'm sorry, but I read that message that came in. I thought that it might be urgent. Who is 'S'?"

He realised later that he'd felt a very sudden sense of relief at being able to tell her the whole story. Helen had taken it relatively calmly; the only stumbling block came when she'd queried Sonja's question: "When are you coming?"

He explained that Sonja was living in the hope that he'd return. He also felt somewhat obligated because of her role in telling him about Nigel de Groot's attempted boardroom coup and the subsequent events. Helen struggled to digest De Groot's violent assault on Sonja.

"Do you usually mix with people like that?" she asked.

Adrian brushed her question aside and kissed her on the lips.

"Promise me you'll never go back to her," she said.

He leaned over and hugged her.

"Of course not – especially now that I have another person to consider." He laughed out loud. "Two more people to think about, I mean."

"So, we'll always be together?" said Helen.

"Yes," he replied. "Soon I'll tell Annie about the situation."

Helen looked thoughtful.

"You've mentioned her family wealth."

"Yes. But I'd prefer we don't talk about that."

"I agree," said Helen. She stood up and walked towards the window.

"So when are you going to tell Sonja about me?" she asked.

The river Esk rises in Cumbria in the Sca Fell range of mountains at around eight hundred meters, just below Esk Hause. This is a mountain pass between the fells of Great End and Esk Pike. The name comes from the old word 'Isca', meaning water. The river flows south and then west through the farming land of Eskdale before joining the Irish Sea at Ravenglass.

Pollett loved the river's raging torrents as it poured down the valley floor. He was now into his second month at the Outward Bound School. He missed his children and relied on hurried phone calls with their mother to check on their safety and wellbeing. He had spoken to Michelle only once but she was being kept informed by the principal.

Following a difficult first week, during which he broke curfew twice and spent his allowance furtively at the local pub, Pollett began to enjoy the activities. He had quietly started to build relationships with those around him and, after four weeks, was asked if he wanted to become involved with a group of ten teenagers from Liverpool. He'd jumped at the opportunity and took his duties seriously. It was now eleven o'clock in the evening and the group were spread along the river bank, sleeping alone on their ground sheets and learning survival techniques. Pollett knew that two of them were co-habiting further up but decided to turn a blind eye.

He was beginning the process of reassessing his life. He knew he loved his jazz and the night life the London clubs offered him. He also realised that his children were better off with their mother. All he had was Michelle, and little else; he was penniless and possessed few assets. But for the first time he felt able to escape his demons and think inwardly.

The problem was he had reached a mental block. He was more at ease with himself, but he knew he had to return to London before the end of the summer. He needed something to happen.

The August sun was blazing down on Regent's Park and Adrian sensed that Helen had some news for him. She seemed tense but not nervous. She told him how she'd been forced to make two members of staff redundant as trading conditions deteriorated.

"I do wish they'd stop blaming it all on Gordon Brown. If we'd won the election and Alistair Darling had implemented his spending plans the economy would now be showing a recovery." Helen was a paid-up member of the Labour Party. "We haven't got any growth, Adrian. Quantitative easing isn't working. It's just the printing of money. It's inflationary."

She stood up suddenly and spun around in a circle.

"What would make you really happy?" she asked.

"Is this a serious question?"

"Yes. Serious."

"I hate seeing Annie suffering, but I don't think that's what you have in mind."

"She's lucky to have you," replied Helen. "No. I'm thinking about us."

"I'm more than happy."

"So nothing could make you happier?"

Adrian sat up and ran his hand through his hair.

She opened her bag and took out an envelope.

"That's for you," she said.

He extracted the contents and looked at the scan she had collected from the hospital earlier in the day.

"That's our baby," she said. "Notice anything?"

He looked closely at the five month old child inside her.

"When did you have this taken?" he asked, in a raised voice.

"This morning at the hospital. Why?"

Adrian asked angrily why she had not told him and why he hadn't been allowed to accompany her to the clinic. She dismissed his questions and told him to look at the medical report.

"Is everything ok?" he asked at last.

"Very ok," she replied. "In fact, Daddy Dexter, he's very, very ok."

He missed it. He was so concerned with checking that the baby was healthy that he missed the significance of her words. She let them hang in the summer air. There were people all around them, but at that moment their whole world was a scan showing a baby. Their child. Their future.

"You said 'he's ok': that's what you said?"

Helen smiled. "You're going to have a son, Adrian."

He wrapped himself around her and vowed never to let her go. She was carrying his son.

In the end it was Michelle who broke the impasse between the two corporate finance houses. She proposed to her boss that MXD Capital should host a drinks party for the senior staff of both companies. Adrian understood its potential impact and within days had organised drinks and canapés in the upper lounge area of the Royal Exchange café. Mark Appleton immediately accepted the invitation on behalf of his colleagues.

The big breakthrough came within the first hour. Adelene asked Mark, Adrian and Chrissie to move to the adjoining lounge section where they found a bottle of champagne and yet more pastries. It was Adrian who asked Michelle to join them.

"Time for some female power play," announced Adelene, at which Mark laughed and Adrian looked perplexed.

"You, Adrian, are staying on as chief executive for six months when Mark takes over. You then ride off into the sunset and save the nation's small business community with your new trust and a probable knighthood."

There were chuckles and an increasingly friendly atmosphere. Adrian thought about the million pounds that Annie had given him and that he had used to buy the South African bank's stake in his company. Meanwhile, nobody seemed to notice that Michelle had edged her way around the chairs and was now sitting by Adelene.

"As always with you men no thought has been given to who will actually do the work and make the new business prosperous," Adelene started. "If we leave it to you the project will fail." By now Michelle and Chrissie were closer and Mark was pouring glasses of champagne from a second bottle, which had been quietly served by the Polish waitress.

"So this is what we propose..." Chrissie shook her head vigorously, Adelene smiled and Michelle seemed to be deep in thought. "We think that Mark will be an excellent chief executive and should take over now."

Since, at that moment in time, Mark was thinking about Cate and the atmosphere she had created as they were dressing earlier in the day, he missed the reason that everybody was applauding. He was disconsolately remembering what she'd said. "I don't think we should have sex for a month." He was certain that she did not mean it.

"We also feel, with great respect, that Lord Singleton should move on, since he appears to have lost interest as our chairman. We propose that you, Adrian, stay on as our non-executive chairman."

Michelle congratulated herself on backing the right man. She also realised that this was the warm-up act. Now it was time for the more substantial matters.

"That, however, if we may say so, is quite a dilution of senior strength, so we have decided... er... sorry... subject to your agreement... that I should be deputy chief executive." Michelle made a mental note to get to know Adelene better. "Chrissie will hold the key position of finance director."

The discussion continued for another twenty minutes. It was accepted that further thought was needed but the key decisions had been made and, over the next two weeks, the details would be hammered out, mainly by Adelene, Chrissie and Michelle.

Later that night, around nine o'clock, Adrian found himself at home in his study. As usual, Annie was in bed. He was in a slightly dark mood, so he put on a CD of music composed by Mahler. Some critics feel that 'Symphony No. 5' best reflects the Austrian composer's split personality. As the music filled the room, so Adrian experienced brief moments of tragedy and joy, depression offset by mania, pain and pleasure.

He opened some letters and found a further report from Annie's consultant. As he started to read, his mobile phone buzzed.

Your son's had a lovely day. Love Helen x

He sent a message back and confirmed the details of their lunch the next day. He then studied a message from Sonja that caused him some concern; he replied asking for further information.

By the second week in September, the application for the merger of MXD Capital and Silicon Capital was completed and submitted to the Financial Services Authority. Lord Singleton had gone, following a surprisingly lively lunch with Adrian who was not to know that the severance payment agreed allowed the peer to make peace with his bank.

The working relationship between Adelene, Chrissie and Michelle was flourishing and, anticipating regulatory approval, they wrote an operation plan which was both thorough and complete. It was, however, Chrissie who realised the threat posed by the gathering storm clouds. Michelle had brought to her notice the growing concerns in the market place over the deteriorating economic situation. The Coalition Government was finding it difficult to stimulate the economy; European matters were dominated by the currency crisis, and America was already thinking about voting in November for its president.

"Contrary thinking," said Michelle.

"What's that?" asked Chrissie.

"Going in the opposite direction of the herd," laughed Michelle. "Chrissie. Just think about it. It's doom and gloom everywhere. Retail sales are down, government borrowing is just as high. Unemployment is under three million but far too high. But, and this is the point, we've been in recession a long time. Since 2008, in fact. It has to turn – and I think we should be looking at the oil price."

"What's oil got to do with it?" asked Chrissie.

"It's about inflation. The CPI, sorry the Consumer Price Index, what we're always hearing about on the news, is around 3.2 percent. Most of the factors which made it rise, like the increase in VAT, have worked through and the most likely factor to destabilise the rate of inflation is the price of oil. That's falling because of lack of world demand. It's under a hundred dollars a barrel. Therefore our rate of inflation will fall. That relieves the pressure on interest rates." She was not to know that further energy price rises lay ahead.

"So what are you suggesting, Michelle?"

"Simple. It's about the next period of expansion. If I were in your shoes, I'd be preparing for better times. There are good market conditions ahead."

Chrissie thanked Michelle for the coffee and left the office. That night she started reading everything she could find about the economic outlook. She went on the internet and downloaded a number of European and international newsletters. She read the *Financial Times* from cover to cover and, the following day, she telephoned a journalist friend and took him for lunch.

Two days later she asked to meet with Adelene and Michelle.

92

"Here's a ten page summary I've prepared together with supporting documentation. I propose we go for growth."

Mark arrived back at his flat and realised immediately that Cate's body language was again indifferent. But, after some coaxing, she allowed him to undress her and take her into the shower. She soaped his body and gave him a hesitatingly brief massage.

After they'd had sex, Mark lay back. He had brought home an evening's worth of files to review. He was unprepared for her question.

"Don't you think we should have a contract?"

"A contract for what?"

"Us. Our relationship. You seem to think that you can have me whenever you want. Don't I have some rights as well?"

He remained still as he pondered her question. What was this all about?

"I asked you a question, Mark."

"I've a lot of work to do tonight, Cate. Let's open a bottle of wine later and talk this through."

She leaped out of bed, snatched her towelling robe, and stood with her arms wrapped around her stomach.

"No! You'll just want sex again later. That is all this relationship is about. You never ask me about my day! I've had a difficult time on Skype with my Australian client. They're questioning our fees and refusing to pay our last invoice to them."

"But you have a signed contract with them. They can't do that."

She pulled her robe round her even more tightly.

"That's typical of you! What about my feelings? How do you think I reacted in the office when I was told that my next trip to Sydney has been cancelled?"

He got out of bed and put his arms around her shoulders, but she pulled away.

"Go and read your bloody files. I'm going out." As she reached the door, she turned and looked at him angrily.

"I meant what I said, Mark. That's the last sex we have for a month."

Chapter Seven

Late September 2012

In the United Kingdom today there are thought to be around thirteen million CCTV cameras watching everyone's movements. An individual may be on over six hundred separate databases; many people have their own websites and Facebook pages; business operatives use LinkedIn and millions Tweet on a daily basis. Most residents are PIN-numbered somewhere; GPS systems circle the earth looking down on us.

But each year it is estimated that two hundred and fifty thousand people go missing. That is one person every two minutes. Most are found and many return of their own volition. Some are never seen again.

Helen disappeared off the streets of London in the third week of September. She simply vanished into thin air.

Adrian was contacted by the police following the discovery of his mobile telephone number on her latest account supplied by the operators. Their enquiries, initiated by the staff at her place of work, led first to her flat in North London. They also told the investigating officer that she was thought to be five months pregnant. At her flat they met with Matt. He was housebound and decidedly unwell. He had been the victim of a stroke the previous year and was home again following a three week spell in hospital recovering from a bout of pneumonia. He knew all about Adrian and seemed pleased that he offered Helen a long-term future. He told the police that he had been warned by his doctors that his life expectancy was marginal.

Matt had last seen her on the previous Friday. He hadn't been concerned by her absence from home, although he was surprised that she had not returned on the Sunday evening to prepare for work the next day.

The police initially questioned Adrian at his home. This resulted in Annie being told the whole story. Initially she cried and then she seemed to accept the situation with a surprising calmness although this was, to some extent, because of Adrian's unshakable commitment to continuing to look after her. She also felt some relief because she had known that Adrian was seeing somebody else. She could smell the perfume on his clothes. On a number of occasions he had returned home with his tie knotted in a different position from where it had been at the start of the day.

The problem for him was that the police did not believe his story and suspected that they may be dealing with a murderer.

Detective Chief Inspector Sarah Rudd had been surprised at the speed of her move from Ealing to Islington Police following her recovery of Tabitha Harriman, the four year old child taken from the streets of the town. She said in her letter requesting a transfer that she was keen to understand the policing requirements of a diverse cultural community. Had this been the real reason, her time at Paddington Green and Ealing might have been considered sufficient experience in this area.

It was one of the few occasions that Nick Rudd had seen his wife cry. She had been told that she was due to be promoted to Superintendent and they had assumed that the source of the information was so reliable that it was definite. No further reference was made to this situation and when DCI Rudd raised the issue of her future it was made clear that she was staying where she was. She left for Islington four weeks later. She silently vowed that she would discover who had blocked her promotion. It was nearly always a male colleague and she had her strong suspicions.

Detective Superintendent Khan had no hesitation in asking her to look into the case of the missing woman. DCI Rudd had quickly settled into her supervision of the crime team, which comprised three detective inspectors, six detective sergeants and nineteen constables. There were also ten investigation officers. Together they dealt with serious acquisitive crime which covered both the investigation and detection of house burglary, robberies, vehicle offences (both 'from' and 'the taking of'), and serious violent and sexual offences.

"So how are you settling in, Sarah?" asked the detective superintendent.

"Much to learn, sir."

"Such as?"

"Well 'honour-based abuse' is new to me. We had a sixteen year old Pakistani girl who ran off after being told she was being put on a plane. The parents reached her before we did."

"It's hard to control. In those cases, the family think they are in the right."

"I find hate crimes difficult, of course – but it's the same everywhere. We had a gay man badly beaten last night."

"Well, it's time to test your detection skills, Sarah. We have a missing woman who's also pregnant. DI Blake will brief you on the details. There's something funny about this one. See what you can do but get it out of the way as soon as possible please. Possible murder, I reckon."

As Sarah approached the interview room, and despite her extensive experience, she went through the 'structured inter-view model' she had been taught many years earlier. She whispered the word 'PEACE' to herself.

Plan and prepare, Engage, explain and, if appropriate, cau-tion, Account, Challenge and Evaluate.

DI Blake met her outside the room and briefed her fully. They entered together.

Adrian, who had agreed to attend an interview at the police station and was accompanied by George Merrydew, a City lawyer specialising in criminal law, was nervous. DCI Rudd announced all their names for the benefit of the tape recorder, including DI Martin Blake who, she explained, had conducted the initial enquiries.

She then issued a caution:

"You do not have to say anything but it may harm your defence if you fail to mention when questioned something you later rely on in court. Anything you do say may be given in evidence."

Adrian was then asked to begin his statement.

He detailed again his first meeting with Helen and the devel-opment of their relationship. After thirty minutes, and when Sarah Rudd picked up the situation with Annie, she reached 'C' in 'PEACE'.

"So you're telling me, Mr Dexter, that you consciously began a relationship with a younger woman when, at the same time, you are married with three daughters, hold a responsible position in the financial markets and your wife has been showing signs of illness. You are clearly a selfish man. Is that fair?"

Adrian whispered into the ear of his lawyer who nodded in agreement.

"It wasn't like that," he said. "I've been, and remain, totally committed to Annie. Please ask her yourself. I'll never leave her and I told Helen exactly that from day one."

"Oh, that exonerates everything does it, Mr Dexter? You are a saint because you'll never leave your wife. That gives you licence to roam the financial streets of London preying on the young women who are, without a doubt, dazzled by your position and your wealth."

She sipped at her glass of water.

"I'm sure you're aware that you're very handsome. A young manager of an optician's shop was simply putty in your hands. You get her into bed. You get her pregnant. And then you murder her."

"Detective Chief Inspector Rudd," interrupted his lawyer, "with all due respect, you have not a single scrap of evidence that Helen has been murdered. She is missing. Surely your efforts should be spent on finding her! That is why my client is co-operating fully with you."

"Does your concern for your wife include getting involved with a younger woman who you managed to get pregnant?" continued DCI Rudd.

Adrian exploded with anger.

"It was not deliberate!" he shouted. "I needed some new glasses. I met Helen. It just happened!"

DCI Rudd slammed her fist down on the table, rattling the coffee cups and spilling a glass of water.

"So why didn't you take precautions? Why is she pregnant? I'm not going to sit here listening to your impassioned pleas of innocence, Mr Dexter. You're a dirty old man. You get the chance to have sex with a naive young shop manager. You take her to your posh bars and hotels. You treat her to the theatre.

You take her to bed. You take no precautions and get her pregnant. You're a selfish man. End of story."

DCI Rudd paused, looked down at her note pad and continued.

"You find out she's pregnant. You let it go for some weeks, and then you realise you'll have to tell your wife. So what do you do? You kill her. Where's the body, Mr Dexter? Stop messing me about. What have you done with her?"

Adrian looked at Sarah Rudd and raised his hands to his head.

"She's carrying my son. The thing I've always wanted more than anything else is a son. I love my daughters but, for a father, a son is the dream." He stopped and wiped an eye. "Please DCI Rudd. I did not kill her. She's alive and she's out there. Please find her."

For Pollett, certain things happened unexpectedly and surprisingly quickly.

He was called to the principal's office on the Tuesday morning to find Michelle sitting there and drinking coffee. Less than an hour later he was packed and driving in her two-seater Mercedes sports coupe to the town of Cockermouth, on the north west edge of the Lake District.

Having booked in at the Trout Hotel in Crown Street, they spent the afternoon idling around the town and watching the fast-flowing waters of the river Derwent joining the Cocker. They went to bed early, before nine o'clock, Michelle through choice and Pollett because he was told to in view of their early start the following day. As they parted company, Michelle finally told her brother that they were going to climb Great Gables and to dress accordingly.

"It'll take about five hours," she said.

At six o'clock the next morning they drove from Cockermouth through Lorton Dale and over the Honiston Pass. They left the car near to Seathwaite Farm.

"Most climbers will be heading for the Scafells. We're ahead of them and climbing a better mountain," she told Pollett. "Final check. Right shoes: yes. Map and compass: yes. Change

99

of clothes: yes. GPS: yes. Provisions: cheese and oatmeal bars: yes. Kendal Mint Cakes: yes. Water: plenty. Let's go!"

They left the farm and walked westwards following a gravel path to the foot of Sourmilk Gill. Pollett began to increase his pace up the path.

"No, Pollett. Slow down. This isn't a race. You must pace yourself. We've six and a bit miles to cover. It's nearly three thousand feet high."

She smiled as she watched her brother trying to restrain his natural instincts to rush ahead.

"Just think of the views, Pollett!" she yelled, as he took the lead again. "You'll see Ennerdale and Crummockdale to the north west, Haystacks, High Crag and…"

His response contained some expletives but again she just laughed and breathed deeply. She had forgotten about her angry exchange with Adrian when she'd announced that she was taking three days off. She'd reminded him that she had put the merger of the two firms back on track, but she sensed that her boss was a worried man.

As they climbed, the terrain became more demanding and they were forced to concentrate on their footholds. They reached Seathwaite Slabs, rested, drank deeply from their water bottles and ate some Edam cheese.

"Why Edam?" asked Pollett.

"Milder milk. It digests better. Time to go."

They could see a party of three climbers about five hundred feet below them and they could hear the ravens in the cloudless skies. Their path ahead levelled off as they rounded Base Brown; now they began the ascent to Great Gable.

"I trust there's a McDonald's at the top," laughed Pollett.

Michelle groaned and checked her compass. She knew they would need to drop down and cross Windy Gap. Conditions remained calm and she told him that they were now beginning the final stage of clawing their way onto Great Gable itself. An hour later, they reached the summit. Pollett did not seem impressed when Michelle announced she could see the Solway Firth and the start of the Scottish Hills.

They sat down amongst the rocks and the small boulders. Michelle distributed the provisions and turned her back as Pollett went for a pee.

He returned and smiled.

"Well, it's never dull with you, sis."

Michelle was silent for a moment and then began to speak.

"As I told you yesterday, she never wants to see you again. The girls are fine and I've been to their school. You can see them once a month, but I promised I'd be the one to make the arrangements."

"They're my daughters, Michelle."

"You drank that right away, Pollett. No court in the land will allow you custody."

He became lost in his thoughts and over five minutes passed before either of them spoke. It was Michelle who broke the silence.

"What happened to you at Outward Bound?" she asked.

"I stopped drinking," he said. There was a gust of strong wind and he reached across to stop the map blowing away.

"Go on," she instructed.

"I'm not going to say it was easy, but now I'm enjoying not drinking," he said. "I feel better."

"Go on."

"The kids from Liverpool. Do you have any idea what sort of lives they lead? Three of them have fathers in jail. Drugs are everywhere. Violence is the only way they settle things."

"Did you like them?" she asked.

"They're great lads. One has serious problems and I fear for him, but generally, give them space and they're fine. We did a lot of leadership exercises. This one lad was called Hector. Yes – Hector. He has a West Indian mother and a Colombian father he's never seen. He was timid and scared. Then he went canoeing and he loved it. He eventually won the race down the Esk!"

"So, what did you discover, Pollett?"

He looked at his sister and frowned.

"I want to be part of something again. I want to come home."

"What does that mean?"

"London. It's where I belong. Sorry to sound emotional, sis, but I guess I want to start again after two fucked-up careers, one rotten marriage and two lost daughters later."

"Where did you work all this out?"

"Sleeping rough on the banks of the Esk. It's one of the first exercises we organise for the kids. They're actually only fifty yards from each other but we space them up the river for the night. It's amazing how honest you can be with yourself at four o'clock in the morning."

"So you want to be part of something? You want to start afresh?"

"You make it sound like a John Le Carré novel: *The Fool Who Came In From The Cold!*" he laughed.

"You're no fool, Pollett. It's just been a hard road."

She stood up and stretched her muscles, looked around at the panoramic views and sat down again.

"I've had an idea," said Michelle. Over the next fifteen minutes she told him about her plans. Pollett could hardly contain himself – to her joy. He understood the concept.

They began the descent and return to Seathwaite Farm. Two hours later they had still not stopped talking.

Pollett turned to her as she loaded the boot of her car with their luggage. He was going to ask if she was sure he would be able to play his part in her plans. He then remembered Michelle's temper and decided the question was simply not necessary.

Annie struggled to drink from the cup that Honeysuckle was holding. Her daughter wiped the spilt liquid and kissed her mother. She hated watching her hands shake.

"I believe what he's telling me, darling. Your father's a good man. He's not the first to stray – and he must be finding my condition very frustrating."

"Well, I think you're taking this rather calmly, Mum. I've talked it over with Clare and Victoria. What worries us is what we don't know. How can you be sure that there aren't other women?"

"Honeysuckle, I've been married to your father for a long time. He's spent much of that time building his business and being a really good father to you all. He's always given me total commitment. I could not ask for more. I've listened to how this Helen woman came about. It wasn't planned. It just happened. Your father is a very handsome man, Honeysuckle."

"Well, I wouldn't take it the way you have. I'd simply tell my husband to get out."

"You don't know how you'd react until you're faced with an actual situation."

"Not me. He'd be out." She paused and again straightened up her mother's nightdress.

"Have you spoken to the police again? Apparently they're placing a lot of importance on what you're saying."

"Yes. And I think they're beginning to realise that your father is not a murderer."

"What do we know about Helen?"

Annie remained thoughtful. This was the issue that she was having trouble rationalising, but she wasn't going to tell her daughter about her concerns. Outwardly Adrian had told her all he knew about his lover. The gaps were what worried Annie. There was little background information and Adrian's lack of understanding about where Helen lived, the vague details about Matt – whoever Matt was – and her own family left her feeling empty and unsettled.

"She's carrying your brother," replied Annie.

"In your dreams, Mum. We want nothing to do with the baby. We think it should be put up for adoption."

Annie shuddered at her words. She then indicated that she wanted to go back to sleep, so Honeysuckle kissed her and left the bedroom.

Over the next few weeks Annie would recover her health to some extent. It was as though a weight had been lifted from her mind.

Adrian's mobile phone rang at seven minutes to midnight. He recognised the voice immediately.

"Good evening, Adrian."

"Nigel de Groot," said Adrian. "I thought you were in hospital?"

"You've been speaking to Sonja. I recover quickly. From your position I would suggest far too quickly. My mobile's linked to some associates of mine in London. They're with a friend of yours. Would you like to hear from her?" Adrian listened and heard a loud scream.

"Now, that's just for starters."

He realised with horror that Helen had been kidnapped by his South African adversary. His mind raced against time. De Groot's phone was linked, suggesting that he was in South Africa, almost certainly Johannesburg. He referred to his 'associates'; Adrian decided they must be in England and almost certainly London.

"She's pregnant, you bastard!"

"They're taking good care of her. And they'll continue to do so, providing you meet my conditions."

"Screw your demands, Nigel. I'll come and find you."

"You're upset. Of course you are. She's safe and being well cared for providing you do as you're told."

Nigel de Groot then explained to Adrian exactly what he was required to do if Helen was to be released safely.

He listened in total amazement.

"Never. There's no way I can do that. You know yourself it's impossible."

As he held the phone to his ear he heard another piercing scream and then the line crackled.

"Contact the police and she dies." The call was then shut off.

He texted Sonja immediately, asking if she was awake. There was no response. He sat back in his chair and evaluated his options. He knew what he must do and it required instant action.

He phoned a mobile number. It took only three rings before it was answered. DCI Rudd said she'd meet him in one hour's time at Islington Police Station.

At one-thirty in the morning he was facing three police officers in an interview room. The atmosphere was tense.

"DI Blake is in charge of the search for Helen. He's reporting to me," explained the senior police officer. "PC Mitchell is working with Helen's partner Matt."

"I saw him last night, ma'am, but he's not at all well. His doctor has now prescribed stronger anti-depressants which seem to be knocking him out." She drank some coffee. "I'll go again in the morning but I don't think Matt is going to be much help to us."

"He knows Helen better than anybody. Please see the doctor. We must understand how she'll withstand the trauma. How pregnant exactly is she, Mr Dexter?"

"About twenty-seven weeks," he replied.

"Shit! That's a worry," said Sarah. She turned to her colleague. "What has this Matt said about the baby?"

"Surprisingly little," replied PC Mitchell. She ran her hand through her blonde hair. "He's said very little at all. He's in a trance most of the time. A nurse comes in twice a day to check up on him."

"Tell me about Nigel de Groot and then explain the demands he's making," ordered the investigating officer. DI Blake prepared to take notes.

Adrian summarised the background from the time that the South African bank made their investment into MXD Capital. He stumbled when he came to Sonja Redmaine. He tried to brush over their relationship but survived less than thirty seconds. Sarah Rudd slammed her fist on the table.

"Why are we hearing this now, Mr Dexter? I've a good mind to arrest you for wasting police time. How many other women are you involved with?"

He told the whole story in lurid detail. Within an hour DCI Rudd would be speaking to the South African police in Johannesburg.

"Tell us about his demands," she ordered.

"He's being investigated for taking bribes in connection with a company called Zambian Goldfields. He negotiated a settlement with the authorities. He's told them that the money, about eight hundred thousand pounds, was passed to me – that I've been his partner in the scam."

"So what does he want you to do?" asked DI Blake.

"He wants me to sign the confession that I'm going to receive from his solicitors and to repay the money." He paused. "And if I don't, Helen will be killed."

"Were you involved with this Zambian Goldfields, Mr Dexter?" asked DCI Rudd.

Adrian hung his head in frustration but did not reply to the question. He had not been involved with Zambian Goldfields but he was being forced by Nigel de Groot to sign a document saying something else. A few minutes later he left the police station and drove home. When he entered, the chimes of the hall clock said it was six o'clock in the morning. He was therefore surprised to find his two older daughters waiting for him.

"Dad," said Honeysuckle. "We were going to come and speak with you today, but then Mum phoned me to say you had gone out in the middle of the night."

"I'm tired, Honeysuckle. I'm going back to bed."

At that moment his other daughter, Victoria, entered through the back door. She gave him a kiss on the cheek and before he knew it, Adrian found himself sitting with his daughters around the pine kitchen table.

"Dad," began Honeysuckle, "what do you think of Mum's health at the moment?"

Adrian looked at his eldest daughter and her flame-red hair.

"Honeysuckle, Dad's tired. Dad, do you want some sleep…"

"Victoria! You agreed over the phone that we need to understand what's going on!" snapped Honeysuckle.

"Your mother is suffering from her nerves. It's been a problem all her life," said Adrian wearily.

"It would help her nerves if you didn't go around screwing young girls!" said Clare.

"Have you even told Mum everything?" Honeysuckle fired. She was ablaze with indignation.

"The police think you've murdered this Helen woman, Dad!" yelled Clare. "Tell us the truth…"

"Everybody, stop it!" said Victoria as she went over and put her arm around her father. "You haven't murdered anybody have you, Dad?"

"So why have you just got back from the police station?" said Honeysuckle.

"Earlier this morning I had a phone call from a South African called Nigel de Groot. He has kidnapped Helen and is demanding a document and money from me. The police are now treating Helen's disappearance as a 'missing person' case."

Victoria kissed her father again and ran her hand through his hair.

"That's not enough for me," said Honeysuckle.

"Shut the fuck up, Honeysuckle. There are two big things about you - your chest and your mouth!" Victoria spat.

She was now kneeling beside her father.

"Dad. We need to know everything. For Mum's sake."

As he explained the whole series of events, all three of his daughters were trying to work out Helen's dates. Victoria was ahead of her siblings.

She was strapped to a bed in a building in Clerkenwell on the northern boundaries of the City of London. Three people were taking care of Helen. The woman was a trained nurse and was monitoring her carefully. She was taking her blood pressure on the hour every hour.

"What are you doing?" asked the taller of the two men suddenly.

"Her binding is too tight. I think we should take it off altogether. She's hardly going to run away."

"No. Our instructions are clear. She remains tied to the bed."

"If her blood pressure remains this high I'm calling an ambulance."

"I don't think so. Since you are not welcome in any doctor's practice, I suggest your position would be rather difficult."

"Do what you want. I'm untying her."

She wiped a flannel over Helen's forehead and untied the straps.

"I'm just going to listen to your baby, Helen," she whispered.

"It's a boy," Helen stammered.

In a wine bar, near the offices of MXD Capital, Michelle seemed very excited.

"The idea is that we form a corporate research agency!" she said. "The whole drift of the 'Know Your Customer' regulations is that financial concerns must be certain about their customers. Adrian should have looked much more closely at Nigel de Groot before accepting the investment from his bank."

"And you say you've acquired the capital?" said Adelene.

Michelle indicated that Pollett would answer the question.

"Michelle," said Pollett, "is putting in a hundred thousand pounds and we're raising a hundred and fifty thousand pounds from a new government scheme. Investors get big tax breaks, so it's pretty attractive."

"But we're an unproven business…" interjected Adelene.

"That's the beauty of the system. It's called SEED/EIS. It applies to new companies and those up to two years old. The important point is that we'll have two hundred and fifty thousand pounds which, as you'll see from these cashflows, will pay the bills for two years even if we don't earn any income."

"You're proposing that there are three of us," continued Adelene. "You'll run it Michelle, Pollett will be the scavenger, to use your term, and I'm the client liaison manager."

"Yes, to start with."

"Why me?" Adelene continued.

"A hunch. You're going to have problems with Chrissie when the merger is completed and I've watched you in recent meetings. You handle people as well as any of us. You'll be great at getting the best from our clients."

"So where does the business come from?"

Michelle took a sip from her wine glass before answering the question. She explained that her contacts with London-based law firms would provide some initial leads. She advised her colleagues that she had spoken at length to several of the brokers at MXD Capital. They were of the opinion that, although the news from Europe was still worrying, there were signs that the markets were beginning to believe that western economies were picking up, which should be reflected in more active stock markets. Michelle stressed that this would lead to an increased number of companies seeking public trading facilities for their shares. Each of those applicants would then need to be fully investigated and Michelle was banking on the concept that law firms and company advisers would be pleased to outsource the process.

Pollett then asked Michelle to explain the term 'due diligence' again.

"All it means is that the advisers to a company which is applying for its shares to be admitted to a public stock market must ensure that all the information given to potential investors has been thoroughly researched," she answered. "It includes financial accounts, the history of the company and information on the directors."

"That sounds fairly straightforward – and you've said that solicitors undertake most of this work?"

"Yes. The opportunity lies in the fact the system is conventional. Solicitors and accountants follow standard lines of enquiry. The risk for companies like MXD Capital and Silicon Capital is that the crooks are usually smarter than the advisers. They know the systems and use this to their advantage. They ensure that all the information provided meets the regulatory criteria. But we'll go outside the usual channels to really understand the directors. If they're crooked, we'll find out. You must remember that one bad deal can wreck an advisory business."

"Don't we need a licence to act as a detective agency?" asked Adelene.

"There are several legal loop-holes, including data protection, to get through. Leave that to me." She sipped her drink. "One other small matter. We need a name."

"Rochford Research," said Pollett instantly. "It's my sister's business. It's the right name."

"That sounds like it could be a health clinic," said Michelle. "A name is best when it conveys what the business does."

"City Detective Agency," said Pollett.

That suggestion was rejected unanimously. Over the next few minutes various ideas were proposed and dismissed. Pollett looked across the table at Adelene.

"Are you going to say anything?" he asked.

Adelene sniffed and stared back.

"Cyberforce Investigations," she said.

"The 'CI' would make a great logo," enthused Michelle.

And so the business of Cyberforce Investigations was born that night, although in time it would become shortened to 'Cyber'. In due course, perhaps a chief executive would say "we need Cyber on this one" – and they would pay well for the services provided.

"So, what exactly will Pollett do?" asked Adelene.

"He'll work with you. He'll ferret. He'll travel. He'll find out about people."

Adelene looked at the subject of their conversation.

"Are you a good ferreter?" she laughed.

Pollett just smiled.

DI Blake thanked DCI Rudd for seeing him at such short notice. She had managed three hours sleep.

"He's here, Gov. He came through Stansted from Europe two days ago. The Johannesburg police returned your call. They'll help in any way they can but apparently he's plea bargaining. They made it clear that they don't want any publicity about the problems with Zambian Goldfields."

"What about his medical condition?"

DI Blake laughed. "Sorry, Gov. Apparently the penis heals reasonably quickly. It was a clean wound and he needed stitches. He was detained for less than thirty-six hours. He'll be on penicillin tablets but he's unlikely to have any problems."

They looked at each other and silently decided to avoid the next obvious comments.

"He re-routed his mobile phone call through South Africa to Adrian Dexter. He's bought a unit in London and we think the call probably came from the West End. We've no way of tracing it."

"Have you spoken to the solicitors?"

"We know who they are. The senior partner at Bailey Mayhew spoke to us earlier today but he's stonewalling. We're awaiting the written confession to arrive at Dexter's home."

"So we're agreed, no warrant at this stage."

"Helen's life is in grave danger. We're quietly checking the hotels and we have a photograph of De Groot which MXD Capital has supplied. We're awaiting his next call to Mr Dexter."

"Thank you, DI Blake. Please keep me informed."

"One other thing. We're having trouble with Ms Greenwood's doctor. PC Mitchell has interviewed him and he was rather defensive. He kept referring to patient confidentiality. As you know she's spending time with the partner, Matthew Rogers. He's unwell and PC Mitchell is getting little out of him."

"Why is the doctor being evasive?" DCI Rudd mused. "She's pregnant. He knows that. He should be co-operating. What reason could he have for not helping us?"

"When we asked if he'd met the father his phone rang, and somehow he never answered the question."

"Do you think you'd better see him?"

"Yes. I'll go with PC Mitchell, Gov."

The plain brown envelope arrived at Adrian's home at six-twenty that evening. The confession, written on Bailey Mayhew headed notepaper, covered two pages and detailed the business relationship between him and Nigel de Groot – how they'd met in Johannesburg, and how they'd become friends and socialised regularly in London when Nigel flew in for MXD Capital board meetings. They were both involved in the Zambian Gold-fields transaction and Nigel had agreed to pay Adrian the eight hundred thousand pound incentive that he'd received from the company, in return for providing references and help in introducing the business to the London markets. The money had been paid in cash two months earlier. Adrian admitted that he was wrong to accept the funds, that he'd encouraged Nigel de Groot to press ahead with the transaction and he regretted the actions he had taken. He now admitted to the offence and agreed to repay the money.

As he was reading the document for a third time his mobile rang. He answered it immediately.

"You'll not trace this so don't bother trying," said Nigel de Groot. "Please listen carefully."

A scream pierced the silence of his study.

"You will sign the confession and put it in a bag with the money in used fifty pound notes. You will leave this in Finsbury Square. There are seats on the north side overlooking the bowling green. Do this at 7:00 a.m. the day after tomorrow. Helen has a nurse looking after her. She will die unless you comply. I'll phone you tomorrow night."

The line went dead.

After an hour and several drinks later, Adrian climbed the stairs and went into Annie's bedroom. She was reading her book and drinking a cup of tea. He read out the whole document to her and explained the phone call.

"It's not difficult," she said. "It's your son's life we're talking about. Nothing else matters."

Adrian looked at her in surprise.

"I've discussed matters again with the girls. They're angry with you - well, Honeysuckle and Clare are. Victoria is more supportive. But they'll support whatever I decide. You're a good man, Adrian. She seduced you and you were vulnerable, but you've stayed with me every inch of the way. Now we stay with you. If we lose the money, so be it, but we must try to get Helen and the baby back to safety. This Nigel de Groot is a very nasty man. No police. I'll arrange with my bank in the morning for you to collect the money tomorrow afternoon."

"We must tell the police. DCI Rudd will murder me herself if we don't!"

"That's my only condition," replied Annie. "No police."

He hesitated before speaking.

"I think that's a mistake, Annie."

She lifted herself up in the bed and frowned.

"Adrian, I'd rather not read in the papers that my husband has taken a mistress."

He returned to his study dazed and anxious. And then he received a text message from Sonja.

Chapter Eight

Early October 2012

Michelle smiled confidently at Mark Appleton as he began to react to her explanation of their proposed new venture.

"The thing is, Michelle, what you're proposing does make a lot of sense. It's impressive. I can't think why we shouldn't outsource our due diligence work to you. You can take responsibility for checking up on our clients."

He paused and drank some coffee. "It's something we discuss at our board meetings because we all know that the real crooks will always find their way around the system." He hesitated. "In some ways, regulation is simply a charter for the fraudsters. They get to know our rules, make sure they tick all the boxes and plan their investment scams accordingly."

He stood up and ordered two more drinks at the counter. He held up a small packet of biscuits but Michelle shook her head. As he waited for their coffees, he felt an ache in his groin. It was now six days since Cate had imposed the 'no sex' stipulation. Last night she had prepared for bed early. The weather was particularly warm and her skin had tanned to a golden glow. She had re-appeared in the lounge of their flat wearing a silk dressing gown, which she'd continually wrapped and unwrapped around herself. When he had suggested they sleep apart she had become angry and demanded they went to bed together.

"But, remember, no touching," she had said.

"Surely," he continued, on his return to Michelle, "the lawyer boys are unlikely to sit back and let you take their business. The bigger firms have strong links with the criminal and security investigation companies."

Michelle put her cup down.

"But we have one big advantage, Mark. As you know, lawyers are obsessed by chargeable hours. Time and again at MXD we get invoices detailing charges that are way above what's

113

been quoted, and then we have to go and argue it with the client who can see no reason why they should pay!"

"True. But where do you score on that?"

"We'll operate on fixed price contracts. You'll know exactly where you stand."

"But you'll lose money on the more difficult assignments."

"Probably, but think as a decision-maker. You'll use us because we'll build our reputation on delivery at the agreed price."

"That could be a winner."

"And I'm taking Adelene with me."

"I suspected as much. You and she seem to have hit it off. We do need to reduce numbers as part of the merger deal, so this will actually help. What does Adrian think?"

"He's been busy for the last few days. I'm hoping to see him later this afternoon. How are the merger plans going, by the way?

"We're getting there. Have you thought of a name for your business?"

"Cyberforce Investigations."

"Cyberforce Investigations," he repeated. "Wow! Good name."

As they rose to leave the coffee house Michelle's skirt rose briefly up her legs.

Mark groaned. He took out his mobile phone and sent a text. *Cate: we need to talk.*

DCI Rudd was concerned about Helen's wellbeing.

"Where's PC Mitchell?"

"She's sitting with Matt Rogers. She phoned me earlier. The nurse came in and said he needed a stronger sedative. She called the surgery and they sent a locum. PC Mitchell phoned the surgery again but the doctor was too busy to speak to her."

"Nothing else from the usual sources?"

"I called in at the London Wall opticians and spoke to several of the staff. Helen is popular and considered to be a good manager. But nobody seems close to her. And none of them have ever been to her home."

"A loner," mused DCI Rudd. "That makes things more difficult."

"We're tracking her mobile and landline number; there's been no action on her credit cards or bank account and the father of her child is not saying a word."

"He's too quiet," she said. "He's not telling us what's really happening."

"He's saying he's still awaiting the call from De Groot," replied DI Blake.

"When did we last speak to him?"

"He's had his mobile off for most of the day, Gov. I last contacted him early this morning. He promised to phone me the moment he heard from De Groot."

"Try him again now, please."

DI Blake made the call and again indicated that the phone was switched off.

"Adrian Dexter is not somebody who has his phone switched off for any length of time," she said.

The journey from St. John's Wood to City Road, passing both Euston and King's Cross stations, took him less than thirty minutes. The traffic would become heavy and impatient just before seven o'clock in the morning, with road users wanting to cross into the Congestion Charge zone before the cameras recorded their entry and they became liable for the ten pound charge.

He reached Finsbury Square and parked his car in one of the vacant bays. He watched as the early morning commuters hurried towards their offices and coffee bars. He walked into the recreational area and noticed that there were two gardeners on the far side sweeping the paths clear of the falling autumn leaves. He walked up to a bench and deposited a canvas bag containing the signed confession together with the required sum of money, as he had been instructed. He walked quickly back to his car and began the return journey which would take him through Holborn and Regent's Park to his home.

He stopped his engine, parked his vehicle and walked back into the gardens. He could see across to the bench where he had left the bag. The seating area was clear: the ransom had already been collected. There was nobody in the vicinity. He looked around but could not identify anyone other than the office workers and the street vendors. He then realised that the leaf sweepers had disappeared.

Less than an hour later he was back home and had taken Annie a tray of tea. She seemed on edge. Her hands shook as she took the tray.

He went down to his study and checked the calls on his answerphone. He would have to ring DI Blake within the next hour. At a few minutes past eight o'clock he received a call from Nigel de Groot.

"Thank you. You're being sensible. We've yet to count all the money – but you're not that stupid. Your woman is in good hands. We're going to hold her for two more days so that I can return to South Africa. You have my word that she's well and we're caring for her properly."

"Two more days!" gasped Adrian. "You never told me that! You said once we paid the money we'd get her back. I've followed you to the letter. 'No police,' you said. I want her back right now!"

"And you will have her back soon, safe and well. You'll get a call within forty-eight hours and that'll be the end of the matter. Goodbye, Adrian."

"No! Stay on the line, you bastard!"

He told Annie about the call. "Now we have no option. I must contact the police."

Annie nodded her head in agreement and lay back on the pillows.

An hour later, in Islington Police Station, DCI Rudd exploded with rage when Adrian told her about the events of the previous two days.

"You stupid man!" she exclaimed. "What gives you the right to play with people's lives in this way? You know you should have told us."

He decided against telling her that it had been Annie's stipulation, and simply stared at the irate officer.

"Take me and DI Blake through the events EXACTLY as they happened."

After Adrian had spoken for a few minutes, the police officer knew where Helen was.

Cate looked at Mark and decided that he needed to talk. She went over to the stereo and put on some Bob Dylan.

"Heavy day?" she asked.

"It's about the milk bottle, Cate."

"Excuse me?"

"Is it half full or half empty?"

She put her arms around his waist. "If you are assessing your chances of wild, uncontrolled sex, yours is half empty."

"I was thinking about the economy."

She stood up and refilled their glasses with a cold, white wine.

"I think the worst is over. We've had a long period of hardship as spending has been contained, but there are signs in the City that we might be at the start of an uplift in our levels of new business."

"Your magical City!" she laughed. "What do you know that the rest of us don't?"

"Money flow. It's as simple as that."

"At least I can understand your words for once! None of this 'bull market' stuff. Ok, tell me about money flow."

"In periods of excess… oh Cate, I do love this track: 'The Times They Are a-Changin'. He wrote it as a protest song. Civil rights and the 1960s movements."

"Money, Mark. You're telling me about it."

"It's really about cycles, Cate. In periods of excess – which we now know took place in the Blair and Brown regimes – money lost its value because there was too much of it. Then the Coalition Government overreacts and suddenly there's too little of it. That's what recession is all about. The economic cycle simply balances these periods out and now I think we're beginning a period of stability. Inflation is falling, and perhaps next year wages will start to improve and we'll begin a consumer-led recovery."

"Fascinating. Ok, would you like to hear my news? I'll tell you anyway." She sipped at her wine. "I'm making a career change. I've left the agency. I walked out this morning. They were being funny about paying me my bonus for the Australian bank deal. Told them to stuff it up their…"

"How much do they owe you?"

"I've decided to become a nurse."

"A nurse!"

"Yes, no need to shout."

"A nurse. They don't earn very much."

"You do, though. And money isn't everything. You know my mum died last year in hospital. During her last few days I watched the nurses look after her. She died with a smile on her face. She was so ill but they sent her off to heaven happy. I want to do that. I've already enrolled. I start in January. Three years' training and then I'll specialise in geriatric nursing."

"So, you're giving up the bright lights for bedpans?"

She looked at him and then put her arms around his shoulders.

"I've been wanting to talk to you about something else, Mark."

"Wow. My Cate a nurse. When do you… where are you… fantastic… "

"Do you really mean that?"

"I'll work with you, Cate. It'll be ten times as hard as you think."

"Would you like to see the uniform?"

A few minutes later she came out of the bedroom wearing her white trainee outfit.

"Of course normally I'll be wearing underwear, but I thought I'd save you the bother of taking it off."

DCI Rudd put down the telephone after completing a long call with a senior assistant at The Royal College of Midwives. Her instinct was that the individual she was after would be a member of the Royal College. If she was affiliated to the Royal College of Nursing she would be an Associate Member. The question of disciplinary action, however, proved more complicated and the representative of the Midwives College finally agreed to send a list of the members who had been removed from the list in the last two years.

She then telephoned the Royal College of Nursing where the spokesperson tried to deflect all her questions back to the Royal College of Midwives. After a long conversation it was finally agreed she would be sent a list of all nurses who had been disciplined in the last two years. There was a further delay while the data protection form was authorised.

By the early afternoon she had made no further progress. Only one list had arrived and that proved so detailed she had little idea where to start. She then thought of an alternative course of action and made a phone call to a health centre in Highgate.

An hour later she was in a doctor's surgery.

"It's been a long time, Sarah," said Martin Redding.

"We made a mistake, Martin. How's your wife?"

"Not good." He answered his internal phone and immediately left the room. He returned a few minutes later.

"Mums and rashes," he said. "We have to check. You look well, Sarah. And Nick?"

"He's fine. He never found out or, if he did, he never said anything."

"It was a wonderful three months, Sarah."

"We have a missing woman. She's pregnant and she's been kidnapped."

Sarah explained the circumstances surrounding the abduction of Helen Greenwood.

"How pregnant is she? How many weeks?"

"We think about twenty-seven."

"How old is she?"

"Thirty-seven."

"You need to find her as soon as you can; the baby could be in danger. My worry, assuming it's a normal pregnancy, would be high blood pressure. She'll be very scared even if she's being looked after properly."

Sarah then told him that there had been mention of a nurse looking after Helen. She related her conversations with the two nursing colleges and her thought that the nurse in question, if working with a kidnapping gang, could well be a disgraced or struck-off midwife.

"If you're right, the good news," said Dr Redding, "is that I suspect there are not many of them. Leave it to me. I'll talk to my partners. There's an unofficial grapevine between doctors and I'll see if we can use it."

As she left the surgery he went to kiss her, but she turned her head away. She turned back at the door.

"Martin. There might be a South African connection."

"Tell me more about Pollett, Michelle."

Adelene had bought them a bottle of fizzy water and they had settled down in the lounge of the Threadneedles Hotel.

Michelle was glowing. She was wearing her favourite blue business suit.

"Pollett?" repeated Adelene, as she refilled their glasses.

Michelle told Adelene the whole story and, in particular, about his period in the Lake District.

"I've always felt with Pollett that there's a good man inside him waiting to burst out. Many men are in their thirties before they mature. I thought the children were having a good effect, but the marriage broke up."

"And his drinking?"

"It depends how much he wants a future. Cyberforce has given him a focus."

"But we're gambling with him?"

"Yes, Adelene. We're gambling."

Sarah Rudd returned to her office in Islington and caught up on the early evening reports. An extensive questioning in the Finsbury Square area had produced no leads and there were no CCTV cameras covering the drop-off point. She telephoned Adrian but he'd heard nothing more from Nigel de Groot.

She decided to stay on at the station. At around seven-fifty, her mobile rang.

"Sarah. I have a name for you. No guarantees. Try Annalie Visagie. She's a South African nurse who was dismissed from a practice in Fulham about a year ago. There were no charges but she was forced out by the doctors. You need to find the pregnant woman as soon as you can. Bye, Sarah."

She put the phone down, picked it up and called a detective in West London she knew well. He replied an hour later.

"We've got her. I'm sending you a photograph. She's got two convictions for drug offences and there were issues over an abortion. I have three officers watching outside the building. We'll need authorisation."

An hour later, DCI Rudd arrived from Islington with the search warrant and six officers. They positioned themselves about fifty yards from the entrance. DI Blake had arrived earlier.

"She came out about twenty minutes ago, Gov. She had a cigarette and went back in. It was definitely her. Here's the photograph."

"So what do we know?" asked Sarah Rudd.

"They're on the second floor in a two-bedroomed flat at the back of the building. There are now only three of them. The nurse, one other man and, of course, the hostage. We've used the sound direction equipment. As you go into the entrance lobby there are two doors facing you. They're in the left-hand one."

After a conference between the senior officers and a phone call to the Metropolitan Police Headquarters, the area of Clerkenwell, within a two hundred yard radius, was cordoned off.

The building was rushed by an armed unit who stormed up the stairs and broke down the door of the flat. The medical team were held on the ground floor until it was safe for them to proceed. DCI Rudd was unarmed and was held back from entering behind them. They opened the first door, where they found the nurse cowering in the corner. Meanwhile, Sarah had slipped in behind them and opened the other door. A thickset man was holding a shotgun to Helen's head.

"Shut the door and lock it," he said. "Come over here."

Helen was tied up on a mattress. Her eyes were red. She had a blanket pulled over her but her pregnancy was evident.

"Hold me but let her go. She needs medical attention urgently," hissed DCI Rudd.

121

"Actually I think I'll keep both of you," he said. "You're my passport out of here. Use your phone. Call them off. Then go over there and park yourself."

Sarah spoke over her radio and immediately the hammering on the door stopped.

"Everybody is to leave the building," she ordered. "Take the nurse to Islington."

"Good. Let's discuss my demands," the man said. "I said sit down, bitch!"

"Fuck you," said Sarah calmly. She went over to the bed and undid Helen's bonds. Her wrists were red and so she gently rubbed them to encourage the blood supply to return.

"Helen. My name's Sarah Rudd. I'm a police officer. We know all about you. Adrian Dexter has paid a ransom for your release but they refused to let you go. We'll get you out of here. How are you feeling?"

"I need a drink of water and I need to go to the loo," Helen rasped.

"She needs a drink," Sarah snarled at the gunman.

He went over to a bag on the floor and produced a bottle of water which he threw onto the bed.

"Thank you," said Sarah.

She looked around the room and then stood up and went over to the wardrobe. She pulled it out from the wall and dragged it over to the corner, where she created a makeshift cubicle.

"Use that, Helen. I'll occupy James Bond over there."

Helen mouthed "thanks" and climbed off the bed. As her feet hit the floor she groaned and stumbled. Sarah caught her and held her as she regained the feeling in her legs. She managed to reach the temporary facility just in time. Sarah addressed the gunman.

"My name's Sarah. She's urgently in need of medical attention. You'll be guilty of murder as well as a number of other crimes unless you let her go."

"Fuck you."

"We're not going to get anywhere unless you start talking to me properly."

He was around six feet tall, in his thirties, with fair hair and a bruised face. He was heavy and unfit and had terrible body odour.

"I want a car and I want some money."

"Why not let me get you a helicopter?" said Sarah.

He held the shotgun to Sarah's throat but was distracted as Helen returned to the bed and lay down.

"Give me your name for heaven's sake."

"James."

"Right, Jimmie, thanks. How are you feeling, Jimmie?"

He looked at her in surprise. "It's James and I ain't that fucking stupid! You don't care a bugger how I am."

"Well, you're about to begin a long holiday at Her Majesty's expense."

"Get on that radio of yours. I want a car and money."

Sarah picked up her mobile and called out.

"DCI Rudd. I want all police officers out of the building." She paused. "Good. Nothing happens without my agreement. I need a car at the front of the building. On the left-hand seat I need five thousand pounds in used notes. When you've done that, take a photo of the car and send it to me."

She turned to James.

"You can see, James, that I'm going to get you away from here but it will take a little time. Please let me call a doctor in to see Helen. I promise you there'll be no funny business."

"No."

"I'll make it a female doctor. She'll just carry a bag."

"Are you fucking deaf? I said no!"

"What harm can it do, James? She'll simply check Helen over. Have you got children James?

"A boy and two girls."

"What are their names?"

"Jack, Velvet and fuck you, bitch. I know what you're doing."

He moved over to the police officer and lashed the butt of the shotgun across her face. Sarah collapsed to the floor and Helen screamed, but she leaped back to her feet almost immediately and used her mobile phone.

"DCI Rudd. No problems here. I fell over. I'll call you back."

Superintendent Martin Parsons had now taken over the police operations.

"DCI Rudd does not normally fall over, sir," said DI Blake.

"She shouldn't be in there. This is a disciplinary matter."

"Let's hope it's not a posthumous hearing, sir," said DI Blake.

"I'll ignore that, DI Blake. When will the car and money be here?"

"In ten minutes, sir. I'll take the photograph and send it to her. What then, sir?"

"We wait, DI Blake. We wait. We have no choice."

Her cheekbone was badly damaged and there was blood trickling down her face.

"Lovely name Velvet, James," she said.

"Bloody stupid name. My wife wanted it. At least I got 'Jack' for my son."

"Let us go, James, and after you come out you can see your children again."

"Where's the car?"

Sarah Rudd picked up her phone and made a call. She told the abductor that the vehicle would be there in twenty minutes. She then asked again if a doctor could attend to Helen. To her surprise, this time he agreed.

"DCI Rudd. I want a female doctor up here now. She's to come alone. She must only carry her bag. She is to knock on the door twice and then wait. She must come alone."

Chapter Nine

October 2012

Five minutes later there were two knocks on the door. The gunman positioned himself in the centre of the room and nodded to Sarah. She went over and opened the door.

"Remember I have the gun."

The doctor entered and nodded to the police officer.

"I'm Clare Fisher. I'm a gynaecologist."

She went over to the bed. She put her bag down and began to examine Helen. She took her blood pressure and looked at the readings. She was whispering all the time to her patient, who continued to lie motionless. She took the blood pressure again and administered an injection. She set up a drip via a needle into the back of Helen's hand. She called Sarah over and told her to stand close and to hold up the bag of saline. She checked Helen's hand to make sure it was safely attached and that the fluid was passing through into the vein.

"She's seriously dehydrated," the doctor said. "Please stand as still as you can. I want to listen to the baby's heartbeat."

The doctor looked over at the gunman.

"Will you turn your back, please?"

"Fuck you."

She laid a blanket over Helen and pulled her dress up to give her access to her stomach. She spent some time examining the abdomen.

"Helen. How many weeks are you?"

"Twenty-eight, I think."

"No, you're not. Your baby's nearer thirty-two weeks. The heartbeat is strong and it's moving around. I've got a good idea of the size."

"Perhaps I might have my dates wrong…"

"We'll worry about that later. Your baby's fine. Do you know the sex?"

"It's a boy."

Dr Fisher looked at the Police Officer and mouthed one word: "hospital."

DCI Rudd quietly passed the bag of saline to the doctor, moved away from the bed and walked over to the gunman.

"She needs to go to hospital now. She has high blood pressure. There's a real risk of a premature birth. If the baby comes here, he could die without immediate attention."

DCI Rudd looked intensely at the gangster.

"James. Did you say your son is called Jack?"

"What? What do you mean, 'she'll die'? Just look after her!" he yelled at the doctor.

"And your daughter's called Velvet?"

"Shut the fuck up about my kids!"

The doctor moved a pace towards him.

"She could give birth at any time. The baby could die."

DCI Rudd drew her fists together and lashed them into his face. He stumbled backwards and dropped the gun. She went down on top of him. Dr Fisher was on her phone calling for help, but he had already managed to turn Sarah over and had pinned her beneath him. He hit her fully in the face beneath the left eye, the blow landing on her damaged cheekbone. Sarah cried out and used her free hand in a futile attempt to push him away.

Then suddenly, her armed colleagues came through the door and pulled him off her. She struggled to her feet and watched as he was handcuffed and led away. A medical team had reached Helen and she was being lifted onto a stretcher. Dr Fisher was speaking urgently to a male colleague.

"She says twenty-eight weeks but it's longer than that."

DI Blake rushed into the room and focused immediately on his boss. He leaped forward and took her in his arms.

"Hold on, Gov! They're just coming for you."

"It's just a scratch," she said, as she lost consciousness.

Adrian put down the phone and exhaled slowly. He went upstairs and told Annie the latest news.

"Where have they taken her?" she asked.

"St. Bartholomew's Hospital in West Smithfield."

126

"Did they say…"

"They refused to answer any questions. I've phoned DCI Rudd but her mobile's switched off."

"You better go and see her."

Without further ado, he turned round and ran back down the stairs.

At four-eighteen the following morning, Helen Greenwood gave birth to a baby boy weighing just three and three-quarter pounds.

Adrian was not present at the birth, which took place in an operating theatre, but he was asked to give a blood sample as a precaution in case either Helen or the baby needed further help. Helen was returned to the ward early in the morning and reunited with Adrian, though he was only allowed to remain with her for twenty minutes, and he wasn't yet able to see the baby. He told her he would return at midday.

Later that morning a consultant visited Helen. He checked her physically and then told her that the baby was doing well and she would be able to see him shortly. He would be in an incubator in the Special Care Baby Unit for a few weeks, until he was bigger and properly developed. The consultant added that the baby stood an excellent chance of survival, despite being eight weeks premature.

"At just under four pounds the lungs are not fully developed and he needs help with his breathing." He coughed and then looked at Helen.

"You were thirty-two weeks pregnant when you gave birth. But your partner seemed to be confused and kept saying something about twenty-seven weeks."

"I must have been uncertain," she said quietly.

"In my experience, women rarely get their dates wrong, Ms Greenwood." He stood up and looked down at his patient.

"You know we have a problem don't you? We've spoken to your doctor," he said.

Helen shook her head and tears began to trickle down her face.

"When will you tell him?"

"He's coming back at twelve. I'll tell him then."

"You realise that..."

"I'll handle it," she said.

Honeysuckle arrived to see her mother just after her father had left for the hospital.

She insisted her mother get up and have a shower while she tidied the room and changed the sheets. She held up the bed-covers as Annie settled back in.

"So what about the money?" she asked.

"I'm sure the police will recover that."

"And Dad's gone to St. Bartholomew's?"

"Yes. That's where Helen is. She gave birth during the night. A boy. Three and three quarter pounds."

"That's big for twenty-eight weeks."

"Yes, Honeysuckle. That's exactly what I've been thinking."

He arrived at twelve-twenty. He'd been held up in Holborn due to road works and had struggled to find a parking space. He reached the ward slightly flustered, found Helen with relief, and put a huge bouquet of flowers on the bed.

"Sorry," he said as he kissed her. "The car park was full. Too many new-born babies!" he laughed.

She kissed him back and then suggested that he pull the curtains around the cubicle. She asked him to sit down and grasped his hand tightly. She looked into his eyes and put her right hand tenderly on his cheek.

"You know that I love you very much, don't you, Adrian, and I wouldn't hurt you for the world."

"The baby. What's wrong? Is something wrong?"

"The baby's fine, Adrian."

He looked at her. She was pale with worry.

"Helen. Please – what is it? You're scaring me."

She then told him that it was not his baby. She'd conceived by IVF and Matt was the father. She explained that he had only a short time to live. Adrian stood up.

128

"I need to go and get some fresh air," he said. "When I come back I'll have several questions for you. It's important you answer honestly." Helen nodded meekly in agreement.

Adrian left the ward and went down in the lift to the ground floor. He found a wooden bench in the hospital courtyard where he sat down in a daze, head in hands. Half an hour later, he returned to Helen's bedside. He sat down and felt his heart sink as he looked at her pain-filled face. He took her hand in his.

"When did you begin the IVF treatment?" he asked.

"Early February. Matt's condition was deteriorating and I wanted a baby so badly."

"And we began sleeping together in April."

"Late April." She coughed into a tissue. "That's why I was in a muddle over my weeks. I had to take off a month because otherwise you couldn't have been the father."

"So you always knew it wasn't my son?"

"Yes. I also knew that Matt was going to die. I decided you'd make a wonderful father. It could have been your son."

"Because I'm wealthy. You'd talked to me about wanting a bigger flat."

"I never thought that you'd find out." She paused. "I so wanted it to be your baby, but my doctor said there was no chance of that."

"You must have given a lot of thought about telling me, Helen." He was no longer holding her hand.

"Hours and hours."

"DCI Rudd told me you were amazingly courageous."

"Is she alright?"

"She's had an operation on her face to repair her cheekbone."

"I was not very brave, Adrian. I just wanted our baby."

"But it's not our baby. It belongs to you and Matt."

"I never loved Matt. My relationship with you was the first time in my life that I'd made love with a man I truly wanted. It so easily could have been your baby."

"What happens if I walk out? What happens to your baby?"

"Our baby. We'll survive. I'll bring him up in your memory."

He paused and drank some water from a plastic cup on the bedside table.

129

"Yes. You will. You'll be a wonderful mother."

She watched as he stood up and walked away from the cubicle. She closed her eyes and groaned. She should have told him. She had never meant to deceive him. Although her doctor had told her it could never be his conception, she had felt his sperm swirling around inside her. It was a matter of weeks. Matt was dying. He could never be the father. Adrian was the father of her child. Adrian was the man with whom she had fallen in love. He was everything she had ever wanted. She knew that she had to share him with Annie – but perhaps one day they'd be together with their child. Everything that her baby would know would come from Adrian. She should have told him... but how was she to know that she'd be abducted? If it had been a normal birth Adrian would never have known and her baby's future would have been secure. Was she wrong to do what she believed was best for her child? Was she at fault when all she was trying to achieve was a union with the man of her dreams?

He so wanted his son. He loved his daughters. Of course he did. But he'd admitted that for him a son was everything. A few hundred yards away a son, his son, was lying in wait for them.

The curtains were drawn back and he was holding her dressing gown open for her.

"The nurse says we can go and see the baby."

She climbed slowly out of bed and allowed him to tighten up the buttons of her robe. She clung to his hand as he pushed her in the wheelchair to the Special Care Baby Unit. There were several incubators in the room.

There he was, with tubes for breathing and liquid, and wires for monitoring his vital signs attached to his tiny body. He seemed at peace.

"Are you feeding him yourself?" he asked.

"No, not yet," replied Helen.

"He needs a name," said Adrian.

"Definitely not James."

"James?"

"That's what the gunman was called."

"Perhaps William or Harry. They all seem to be called after the royals at the moment."

Helen pushed her hand through a hole in the side of the incubator and tickled her baby's cheek. She then turned and looked at her lover.

"Adrian," she said. "We've always wanted to be together, haven't we?"

He kissed her.

"I have one request," he said.

"Seems fair. What is it?"

"Do you mind if we don't call him Nigel?"

"Not at all. Why not Nigel?"

"I don't think your son should be named after a South African gangster!"

"My son, Adrian?"

He took her in his arms and kissed her.

"You need to help me, Helen. You're now saying we're in love. Yet time after time at the hotel you insisted we were having an affair. I can't help feeling that you used me. I could have spent the next twenty years believing he was my son. It's Matt's baby, Helen. Why did you not simply tell me the truth?"

"And risk losing you?"

"Risk losing me as a father to your baby, a wealthy godfather or a lover?"

"I thought I was going to die at that flat, Adrian. The gunman was crazy and scared. He lashed the police officer in her face. I knew my baby was alive and active inside me. But the thing I wanted more than anything else was to see you."

"Because of what I represent, Helen – your security and your future."

Helen rolled her eyes.

"I've no more to say, Adrian. Go away and back to Annie. You can always fly off to see Sonja."

"And you and the baby?"

"Don't patronise me, Adrian. I'm not Michelle. I don't want your bonuses. I have a baby and I'll give him all my love and care. We don't need you."

She turned her face away from him so that he wouldn't see that she was crying.

"Well, I suppose he'll need to know one day that I'm not his father, but I think for the time being we'll concentrate on giving him a proper start in life."

Helen turned to face him and wiped the back of her hand across her eyes.

"And us?"

"Well, once I've sorted out Annie, Honeysuckle and Sonja it should be plain sailing."

Helen then kissed her fingertips and put her hand into the incubator, touching her son on the top of his head. They then returned to the ward, where she combed her hair and changed her nightgown.

"He needs a name," she said.

"You've already decided."

"William Adrian Greenwood."

"Bill."

"William. It will always be William."

"The initials spell 'WAG'."

"Oh."

"How about William Matthew Greenwood?"

"Would you mind Matthew instead of Adrian?"

"It would certainly mean one less row with Honeysuckle," he laughed.

"Ok. That's decided. I need some sleep now. Will you come later?"

But her eyes were already closing and she didn't hear his answer.

As he left the ward he asked the nurse if he could go back to the Special Unit. There he watched through the glass as William Matthew Greenwood slumbered peacefully.

Chapter Ten

November 2012

Annie's health deteriorated again as the cold winter winds began to blow in from the continent. However, she supported Adrian's decision to buy Helen and her son a flat in North London (William Greenwood seemed destined to become an Arsenal supporter), and was growing surprisingly fond of a woman she was starting to think of as a surrogate daughter.

Honeysuckle took a rather different view and continually criticised her father. She refused to meet with Helen and said that, as far as she and her sisters were concerned, Adrian had behaved appallingly.

"One evening, Adrian found himself six hundred feet high at the top of Tower 42 off Old Broad Street. The champagne bar Vertigo 42 was the location for the leaving party for Michelle, who was joined by Pollett. Cyberforce Investigations would be starting business from their offices in Moorgate the following Monday.

Over thirty people attended the party, which was surprisingly subdued. Michelle was a popular member of the office and her departure was seen by some as regrettable. The news that the regulatory authorities had now agreed the merger and that the new firm would start trading in early December also dampened some people's enthusiasm. When the time came, Adrian gave a short and moving speech. It was almost inevitable that they would end up together in a separate bar.

"Changing times," he said as he raised his glass.

"Though you're still flirting, Adrian," she laughed, "even now you're a father again. How is Bill?"

"William. His name is William, and he's fine."

She leaned across and put her hand on his leg. She kissed him on his cheek.

"I'll miss you," she said.

An hour later he was back home in his study. Annie was fast asleep. His phone buzzed in his pocket.

He's not in South Africa. There's a warrant out for his arrest. I spoke to my ex. He says he's dangerous. How's William? S x

"He had a special skill."

"What was that?" asked Adelene.

"He used scat singing, when you vocalise using sounds and syllables instead of the lyrics."

"Don't get that."

Pollett sighed. He was enjoying himself on a November Sunday night in a Drury Lane pub. There was a tradition of improvised jazz sessions, and he had played himself on many occasions. This time he was focused on Adelene, his new colleague at Cyberforce Investigations. A few gold bangles jingled on her wrist, and she was smiling broadly.

At around nine o'clock Adelene announced she'd had enough of the jazz and proposed that they go and have sex.

"Just like that?" said Pollett. "Don't I even get a chance to chat you up?"

"Let's cut to the chase. You've been eyeing me up since we first met," she said. "And you're pretty hot and you don't do convention. I like that."

"So where do we go?" he asked, slightly flabbergasted.

A few minutes later they caught the Central Line to Bank, from where they walked down to the Tower of London and her flat nearby.

She opened the door and invited Pollett in.

"My partner's away," she said. "We're private here. There's wine in the fridge. Pour me a glass." She pressed a button on the CD player which, to Pollett's surprise, started playing the theme music from 'Four Weddings and a Funeral.' She reappeared about five minutes later, wearing just an open shirt and pink panties.

"Your turn," she said.

Pollett disappeared into the bathroom and returned wearing a blue dressing gown.

"Ok. Time for our game," announced Adelene.

"What are the rules?" asked Pollett.

"I know that you want me to take everything off, don't you, Pollett?"

"There's not much more to remove," he said. He was six foot two inches without his shoes and she was almost a foot smaller.

"You won't find it easy," she said. "Men are so predictable."

She went back to the CD player and replaced the disc with one offering classical violin pieces. The haunting sounds quickly enveloped the room.

"I'm going to make it last a long time, Pollett," she continued. "Can you hold out?"

"I could lose interest," he said.

"Unlikely. I just let my shirt open a bit more and you couldn't take your eyes off me. You're dreaming of me removing my panties, aren't you?"

She drank some more sauvignon blanc and went back to the fridge for a second bottle. She left it on the table as she suggested it might be needed later and she did not want to be disturbed.

Pollett did not understand what she meant.

"It's the greatest weapon we have, you and I, Pollett," she continued.

"Don't know what you're ranting on about."

"Course not. You're totally focused on my body. I can do what I want with you while you think there's a hope that I'll have sex with you." She drank some more wine. "I'm talking about Cyberforce Investigations. We'll be different because we'll use predictability when we investigate people. As I'm demonstrating now with you, I'm able to find out anything I want because you'll do anything to have sex with me. So, Pollett, I'll take my panties off if you'll tell me the password on your computer."

"Good example. I see what you mean." He laughed. "I like this game."

She stood up and moved in front of him. She thrust out her hips and gently opened her legs. She ran her fingers down her legs and tilted herself towards him.

"I mean what I said – I want to know the password on your computer."

"You're fucking joking. Michelle would sack me if I revealed it. Come on, Adelene, you've made your point. Please stop teasing me."

"Pity, there goes your sex," she said. "I was looking forward to it."

"You know I can't tell. We've signed confidentiality agreements."

"I won't tell if you won't. What's happening, Pollett? Are you enjoying watching me take my shirt off? What are you staring at?"

She had firm, compact breasts, each with a prominent dark peak.

"Would you like to suck my nipples, Pollett? Just tell me the password. It'll be a secret between us. Michelle will never know."

He was aching like never before. Her body was glistening with sweat and her panties were clinging to her buttocks.

"Put yourself out of your misery, Pollett. Tell me your password and I'll take them off for you."

"I can't!" he shouted.

She put her fingers inside her pants and slowly edged them downwards.

"Think, Pollett. Just a few more centimetres…. Do you like seeing shaven women?"

"You've stopped, Adelene. Please. Take them down."

"The password, Pollett," she smiled demurely.

"Armstrong7!"

She slapped him across the face.

"The correct password if you please."

"Eskdale1." He put his face in his hands. "Eskdale1, you bitch."

She moved over to the table and picked up an envelope.

"Open that," she said.

He did so and took out a piece of white card. Written on it was 'Eskdale1'.

"You knew all the time!"

She came over to the sofa and put her arm around him. She kissed him gently before telling him to go and get dressed. When he returned, he found her in jeans and a sweater.

"What was that all about?" he asked.

"You need to read *1984* by George Orwell. He explained that you can wreck any human being if you can find their weak spot. In the book they break a man because of his fear of rats."

"How exactly does that relate to Cyberforce?"

"We'll be dealing with some pretty horrible people, Pollett. It's all fairly new to me, but already I've grasped that stock markets attract some absolute cretins. They're smart and clever, but we'll be smarter. We'll earn our fees by getting behind their veneers. What I've just shown you is that every person has a breaking point."

She poured some more wine for each of them.

"Just think, Pollett. I've just managed to get you to reveal something that was absolutely confidential. Michelle would sack you on the spot. And for what? A quick fuck."

Pollett shook his head. "But you knew the password?"

"I know all the passwords. That's not the point. I'm trying to get you to understand that the success of your ferreting will depend on your ability to establish the other person's weakness. It can be as simple as a good lunch and a decent bottle of wine. But the clever ones... that's much more difficult and it's unlikely to be sex. They're too streetwise for that. But don't underestimate it."

"Me?"

"Of course. There are women out there desperate for a relationship. You're good looking and sexy. Add it to your armoury."

"How's that weapon doing at the moment?"

"It's failing." She looked down at her mobile. "My partner's ten minutes away."

They said their farewells. He was exhausted, but genuine in his thanks.

"I should thank you, Pollett," she said, waving him goodbye.

"Why?"

"I'm feeling pretty horny."

On Monday 31 December 2012, Adrian found himself pushing a pram down The Mall.

"Excuse me asking Helen, but you've insisted I park the car in Northumberland Avenue, you feed William early, and that we have an early morning walk… any particular reason? It's a beautiful day, I'll give you that."

They were nearing Buckingham Palace. The traffic was light and the absence of the flag indicated that the Queen was not in residence.

"Sorry, William," said Adrian. "Grandma's not in."

They found a park bench and Helen checked on William's breathing before sitting down.

"The reason is New Year. I want the three of us to bring in 2013 together. It's an important twelve months ahead."

"What's this really about, Helen? You know that I won't leave Annie."

"I've never asked you to do that. You know I'm getting on well with Annie."

"But you're looking for something, I can tell."

She paused and checked William again.

"Reassurance, I suppose. I do spend a lot of my time alone."

"Have I let you down?"

"No, you've been fantastic, Adrian. Of course you know that I dream of us being together, but I'll wait."

"Annie's not too bright at the moment, but she'll get better. And I'll give her my all for as long as she needs me."

"I'll support that. But please can I just have a little bit more of you?"

Adrian put his arms around her and looked at the pram.

"That's our son, Helen."

She turned and kissed him. She felt the sense of warmth and belonging she had been craving. She was not prepared to evaluate the chances of them remaining as close in the coming year. She had her baby and William had his guardian. His actual father was at his home almost beyond communicating. She would try to bring Adrian and herself as close together as their circumstances would allow.

Adrian was surprised at how loud his heart was beating. The blood must be flowing through his clear arteries. He was fit for the coming year. He decided to ignore his breathlessness which he attributed to the stress of the kidnapping. He would improve his diet in the New Year and cut out the increasing amounts of fatty foods that he'd been consuming. He'd return regularly to the gym although his session on the running machine the previous week had been worrying. As his calf muscles had pleaded for him to stop he'd noticed the sign on the wall: 'Cholesterol kills: get it checked – TODAY!'

Not him. He'd had a scan and did not need to be assessed for perhaps four years. The corpuscles were rushing through his arteries and veins and back into his healthy heart. That was one worry that did not concern him. All he needed to do was to moderate his drinking, lose some weight and exercise regularly: 'piece of cake' he said to himself without realising the irony of his inner thoughts.

He became aware that the sensation he was experiencing was his mobile phone vibrating in his inside pocket.

He took it out and saw that he'd received a text. As he read it he refused to panic, but at that moment in time he wondered what part Sonja Redmaine would play in his life over the coming months.

He looked at Helen who was leaning over the pram and singing softly to the baby.

"Please keep him safe," he said quietly to himself.

"No, Sarah. Now is not the time. Please give it some more thought."

They were walking hand in hand in the bitter cold outside their house. It was a few minutes to midnight, nearly the start of a new year. They had refused several invitations and were oblivious to the laughter coming from their neighbours' homes.

They could only walk a few yards away from their front door, which they watched continually. Their children were fast asleep upstairs. But they'd needed some fresh air.

"I've been overlooked for promotion and I've been beaten to a pulp by a crazed gunman."

"You saved the life of an unborn child, Sarah."

"Maybe. It would have survived anyway."

"Is that really what you think?"

"Nick, I spend all my time with horrible people. Do you know how many people Islington has on its sex offenders' register?"

"They say that the problem with doctors is that they only ever see sick people."

"And school teachers, Nick? What do they say about you?"

"Oh, Michael Gove thinks we're all crap."

"Ooohh! A show of temper from Mr Nicholas 'I'm always calm' Rudd," she laughed.

"Seriously, Sarah, we had an assault just before term ended. They're becoming more frequent. A girl of ten stabbed a boy of fifteen. The world's going mad."

"So what does the world hold for our children, Nick?"

"Never lose faith. Give them everything we can. They'll make out."

They started walking down their drive. There was frost on the tarmac and the car windows were covered with ice.

"Let's decide to make 2013 the best year of our lives," he said.

Sarah stopped and faced her husband.

"Nick, when I saw the gun coming down on my face... for the first time ever I was really scared."

"I'm not bloody surprised."

"No, Nick. You're not getting it. I've faced danger before. As a police officer you become detached. It's your job. But this time..." She paused and wiped a tear away from her eye. "This time it was personal. It was a new kind of fear."

"Why not ask for compassionate leave? They've offered you counselling and you've been paid compensation money."

"That's not what's worrying me, Nick."

"What's worrying you, my darling Sarah?"

"What happens, Nick," she said very quietly, "if next time I fluff it? What if I'd been responsible for that woman losing her baby?"

"That would have been very unlikely," he said.

"But what if the unlikely had happened, Nick? My whole career would be wiped out in just a moment."

"Too many 'ifs' and 'buts', Sarah. You're a fantastic mother, a great wife and a dedicated police officer. And I have a gut feeling that 2013 is going to be your..."

Down the road, a window was thrown open and somebody yelled a 'happy new year' to the world at large.

Sarah had reached the front door. She just wanted to hug her children close to her.

"But what if you're wrong?" she said, under her breath. "What if next time I lose my nerve? What if I cost somebody their life?"

Annie had prepared a supper for the two of them but had gone to bed well before the year ended. So, as the new year arrived, Adrian was listening to a Mahler symphony in his study. He read a text message from Sonja and, after a long, considered pause he responded.

Sonja. Happy New Year to you. How has he been found 'not guilty'? A x

The reply was almost instant.

Money. He has so much influence. Your police gave up trying to tie him into the abduction. S x

He hesitated before replying.

You're sure about what you are saying? It's important. A x

The red light flashed a few minutes later.

My ex checked it out. He's already left. He'll arrive in Ireland tomorrow. S x.

Adrian put the phone down and thought back to that board meeting earlier in the old year.

"Nobody crosses Nigel de Groot and survives," he had said.

PART TWO

Chest Pains

Chapter Eleven

January 2013

Pollett's artistic instincts were in evidence as the three founding partners of Cyberforce Investigations huddled together in their rented office in Old Broad Street, near to Liverpool Street Station. They had decided to limit their time off to the Christmas period and were starting work on the second day of the New Year. While the London markets were operating, few other City workers were returning to work until the following Monday. Train and tube services were restricted due to staff illness (drivers with hangovers) and overhead line damage (administration staff hadn't turned up). It was cold, damp and depressing. Poor retail sales had marred the holiday season, and the rate of inflation continued to rise. Pensioners, many of whom were struggling to feed themselves properly, were crouched around electric heaters which they could hardly afford to run for more than two hours a day.

"Pollett, that's so cool!" cried Adelene, looking at the logo her business partner had designed for the new company. He had somehow combined a futuristic capital 'C' with a vapour trail 'I' and given it a global perspective.

Michelle nodded and picked up her papers from the table that represented their meeting room. There were two adjoining but rather small rooms. An office manager would be starting work with them at the beginning of the next week. Meanwhile, their computers were now online and a coffee machine had been installed.

"Our business is going to come from personal recommendations," she said, "but the brochure needs to exude confidence. Pollett's artwork really achieves that."

"Confidence?" said Adelene.

"Yes. We are paid a fee and we achieve results. Right – these are the investigations I think we should offer." Michelle sipped from her mint tea and then talked them through the 'CI Menu of Services'.

The first was 'Cheating Partners', likely to be a lucrative source of income in the City. Then came 'Teenagers', as parents often wanted to find out if missing items at home were being sold by their offspring to pay for their drug use. This was followed by 'Location', which would largely consist of executives wanting to know about an area before committing to moving house. Then came 'Missing Persons', followed by 'ID Checks'.

Michelle laughed at this last category.

"When I was researching the competition I found out that there is quite a demand from online dating users wanting to be sure that Mr Wonderful is quite as wonderful as he appears."

"Married with three kids, a huge mortgage and credit card debts is my guess!" said Adelene.

"So, I've divided our services into 'Personal' and the following 'Commercial' options," continued Michelle.

She quickly went through 'Employee Checks' (bosses trying to avoid recruiting troublesome staff); 'CV Vetting' of job applications (which contain, with the support of realistic certificates, such academic achievements as 'Masters in Economics from Bangalore University'); 'Fraud' (when cash is disappearing and there is no obvious source, false invoices being the starting point); and, surprisingly, 'Partnership Fidelity'.

"This came as a jolt," she said. "A lawyer friend told me that they spend a lot of their time dealing with business partners who have simply fallen out. They start the business with mutual trust and communicate well during the build-up period, but then they start arguing. They'll defraud each other and worse."

The three partners looked at each other warily.

"Of course," Michelle hurried on, "our real business is corporate due diligence, when we check out the directors of companies proposing to apply for a share trading facility on one of the London markets." She sipped more of her tea. "I was talking to Mark at the MXD Silicon Capital Christmas party and he was saying that there are signs of a pick-up in levels of new business."

"So the merger is done?" asked Pollett.

"Yes. They're all housed together in Cornhill. Their only problem is that their chairman is distracted by outside matters."

Adrian had spent the afternoon with Helen. She had asked him to look at a one-bedroom flat in Clerkenwell. The transaction was agreed without much discussion. The accommodation was ideal for the two of them and the location convenient for Helen, who had worked out that she needed to return to work in July to maximise the financial benefits of her maternity package.

"Unless we decide that William needs a sister!" she had joked with Adrian.

She had also told him that Matt was now in hospital and was expected to last no more than four to six weeks. He was seeing William nearly every day but was finding it difficult to maintain his interest for more than a few minutes.

Adrian had asked her how she would feel when Matt died.

"I've taken a picture of him with William," she had answered.

Adrian arrived home and hurried upstairs to sit with Annie, who had gone to bed at around six o'clock. She wanted to hear about William's progress, his weight and feeding habits. Adrian told her he now weighed ten pounds and was sleeping fitfully. She went very quiet when she heard about Matt's condition, but thought the flat in Clerkenwell was a sound choice and asked if she could visit the area. A little later, as they were discussing a letter they had received from Clare, she fell soundly asleep.

He had moved into his study and put on a Chopin CD when the red light on his mobile started to flash. He read the text message.

NdeG has links with IRA. Ex has rec'd tip-off. Still love u. S x

As his study was filled with the playing of the 'Concerto for Piano and Orchestra No 1 in E minor, Opus 11', Adrian mulled over this new information.

"Fuck. Of course," he said suddenly and out loud, "of course fucking Nigel de Groot is in Ireland and is going to come for me!"

He re-read the message. Why would he want to involve the IRA? Although there had been some minor problems in Belfast over the flying of the Union Jack, generally Ireland was at

147

peace. He tried to assess his options but he was already very scared. He wondered about speaking to DCI Sarah Rudd but he had no concrete evidence that Nigel de Groot was a serious threat to him or anybody else.

He knew Sonja would not alarm him unnecessarily. He wondered whether to engage the help of a private detective agency, but where would they start? He suddenly felt incredibly isolated. The music composed by Chopin played on as he read from the CD cover notes.

The finale takes a nationalistic turn, a Polish folk dance, with martial strains mixed in.

The concerto ended and he decided it was time to go to bed. He went upstairs and checked that Annie's door was closed before entering his room. He climbed into his cold bed. As he dropped off to sleep, he wondered whether he should buy Helen a two-bedroom flat. He decided that perhaps he would discuss this thought with Annie at the weekend.

Nigel de Groot settled back into the soft cushions of the large leather sofa in the penthouse suite of his Park Lane hotel. He laughed. The other man did not join in. He knew better than that.

"Hulle het werklik geval daarvoor," he said, satisfied that they had fallen for his deception.

"Completely. They think you're in Belfast."

He stretched out to give his still aching limbs the chance to recover from the eleven hour journey from Belfast by ferry to Holyhead and then down the A5, joining the M6 and then the M1 into London. Throughout the whole journey he had remained hidden under a blanket on the back seat of the black BMW.

"So Mrs Redmaine seemed pleased to take her ex-husband's tip-off at face value?"

"Yes. We bribed his colleague who convinced him by giving false information."

"Why not simply kill Dexter?" asked the diminutive planner.

"Because I must shoot him myself. It's a matter of honour."

"So when do you plan to do that?"

"Not yet. I need some medical treatment. I'm booked in tomorrow for a minor operation. I'll meet you back here next Monday at three p.m. Now get out."

As the door closed he downed a glass of vodka and tonic water. He picked up the file on the table in front of him. The surgery was annoying but necessary. His penis had become sore and the antibiotics had failed to clear up the infection. His doctor promised a swift and certain recovery within days of the operation.

He was happy to have some thinking time because, before killing Dexter, he intended to ruin MXD Silicon Capital. But he knew he needed to recruit a top class partner to help him achieve his objective. The British Financial Services Authority was based in Canary Wharf. He knew that they were to become the Financial Conduct Authority and report to the Bank of England but there was time enough to fuck them and MXD Silicon Capital.

He read his papers once more and completed a risk assessment of his plan. What could go wrong? Absolutely nothing because, if anything is certain, it is the probability that the system is wholly predictable. He knew exactly how the FSA would react. He laughed out loud as he remembered his own 'De Groot law of probability': the higher the salary and the pension, the more certain the behaviour.

Cate sat patiently while Mark secured a bottle of Frascati and two glasses. He sauntered over and placed their drinks on the table. She poured each of them a rather generous measure.

"Your starter for ten. Where is Frascati from, Cate?"

"Germany."

"Correct continent."

Covent Garden was busy as early evening theatregoers hurried towards Drury Lane down icy streets.

"Oh, I know," she laughed and at that moment Mark realised why he was so hopelessly in love with her. Even when sullen she was very pretty but if she smiled her face radiated happiness and she exploded into a bundle of sheer passion and spirit.

149

She was the woman with whom he wanted to spend the rest of his life.

"It's a trick question! Frascati is the grape. Can't fool me, Mr 'Cleverclogs' Appleton."

"Frascati is a town about twenty miles south east of Rome."

"Oh."

"So what's with the file of papers?"

Cate explained that she was preparing to enrol on a diploma course in pre-registration nursing. She had her degree in marketing but was pleasantly surprised when she had read that, from September 2013, nursing would be a graduate-entry profession. She had completed the 'personality quiz' on the NHS website and was thrilled when she discovered she fitted well into her chosen category of mental health.

"But I thought you had already secured a position?" asked Mark. "Otherwise, where did the uniform come from?"

Cate put on her 'naughty little girl' look.

"I bought it off Ebay," she confessed. "I know you can't resist girls in…"

"I'm tempted to put you over my knee and…"

"Don't let a wine bar full of people stop you, Mark."

"Oh, all in good time, nurse."

"Seriously, that's at least three years away, Mark. It's going to be a long, hard slog."

They finished the first bottle within twenty minutes, so Mark ordered another as he began to tell Cate about developments at MXD Silicon Capital. The staff had merged well together, helped by the departure of Michelle Rochford. He was excited by the uplift in new business opportunities and especially by the client agreement secured by one of the newer team leaders. The new agreement had slipped in during the height of the merger, despite the fact that Mark had checked that the 'take-on' procedures had been correctly followed.

"It's a bit strange, Cate. Alan Joyce is probably the weakest member of the team according to Adrian, but he's landed an investment company opportunity that will make us over a million pounds."

"Sounds too good to be true, Mark."

They left central London by taxi and arrived home forty minutes later. Cate had whispered that she wanted to take a bath as soon as they arrived. They kissed as they moved towards the bathroom and, with them both still in their clothes, Mark turned on the shower and pulled her into the powerful jet cascading down on them. He reached out and grabbed an atomiser of perfume, which he sprayed in the air over her, the exotic fragrance filling the air as he reached behind her to release the catch on her skirt. As it fell to the floor he kicked it away. He stopped and removed his trousers before ripping off her blouse. He decided to leave her bra in place as he liked the way the silk cloth clung to her breasts. He then took a bar of soap out of the side tray and began to lather her near-naked body. She bent forward into the position she knew he loved. He pulled her panties off her buttocks and slowly ran them down her legs. She kicked them away. He simply couldn't wait and penetrated her deeply. The warm soapy water acted as lubricant and the pleasure of skin on skin brought her to a screaming orgasm. Mark was desperately trying to hold back and make it last longer for her. He thought about the rate of inflation and, if Uzbekistan is only one of two completely landlocked countries in the world, which is the other? But her bra had now disappeared and he felt her nipples in his fingers. He went deeper into her – how had she managed to enable him to do that? – and he knew he was close. The water flowed over them, hotter than before. He increased his pace before exploding with a cry of satisfaction.

They slumped down onto the floor of the shower, wrapped in each other's arms.

The new office manager had failed to turn up for her first day of work at Cyberforce Investigations and they were deciding whether to give her a second chance.

"Let's save ourselves future problems and tell her not to bother," suggested Adelene.

"She seemed genuine in her excuse," said Pollett. "Her little boy has a rash and she's trying to get an appointment at the doctors."

"No. I had a thorough interview with her," said Michelle. "She'll be here tomorrow." She tapped the table with her knuckles. "We have our first case."

"Great," said Adelene. "Is it fraud? Or an infidelity?"

"I have an acquaintance in Grey's Inn Road. He runs a legal practice and specialises in employment law. He has a case on at the moment and he's asked us to help."

"How did he hear about us?" asked Pollett.

"Word of mouth. I've been putting myself about." She sipped some water. "Here's the file. In a nutshell, he doesn't trust his client. It's a simple situation. The business is a group of greeting card shops in the Home Counties. There are nine outlets in all. Despite the recession and competition from internet companies trading is good and they had a reasonable Christmas period. Eight increased their turnover by between 7 and 16 percent. The shop in Hampton fell by 11 percent. The manager is a divorcee who has been with the group for four years. She says that a new competitor opened up a few doors away in September last year and has taken away much of her trade. She also questions the statistics. The tills automatically record the takings centrally and she is questioning the downturn. She says she has carried out a stock check and she's 3 percent up."

"So what are we supposed to be looking at?" asked Pollett.

"Patience, brother. My lawyer friend says he has been asked to prepare a dismissal notice. His client is Mohammed Khalifa. He says he thinks his manager is playing the stock trick. The manager allows her friends in and then pretends to take their money for the cards and other goods sold. With their luxury range of accessories, such as cuddly toys, the amounts can build up quite quickly. Mr Khalifa believes the proceeds are probably being split half and half. A divorcee short of money. The rest follows.

"The law firm have investigated Mr Khalifa and he appears to be squeaky clean on all the usual checks. They have acted for him on several of the shop purchases. He always pays cash for his premises. My friend says he is worried that the case is weak and the manager will counter sue. Mr Khalifa insists that she's dismissed immediately. Adelene went to the shop yesterday. Adelene?"

"If she's fiddling she's clever, Michelle. To be fair it wasn't busy but there were about twenty customers during the time it looked like I could not find the right card for my sister's birthday. The manager was really helpful. I also noticed that she was keeping a close watch on her shop all the time I was there."

"Ok. Apparently Mr Khalifa prays four times a day at the mosque in Richmond. After the late morning session he has lunch at the pub by the bridge. He's thinking of buying a boat and watches the traffic on the Thames. My friend knows that because they met there before Christmas. Pollett, I think you should take a trip to meet Mr Khalifa. Here's a photograph taken from his Facebook page."

Pollett stared at a good-looking man in his mid-forties.

"I wonder if he likes jazz."

Michelle asked Adelene to run credit checks on the manager and to find out all she could about her. Pollett left the office shortly afterwards, having first studied the Transport For London journey planner closely for the best route.

Two hours later he arrived in Richmond and entered The White Cross pub overlooking the tow path. He was unaware that on occasions high tides can mean that access from the river is restricted. He bought himself a glass of orange juice and ordered a sandwich. He settled down at the bar and quickly became absorbed in a local paper. He spotted Mr Khalifa about twenty minutes later. He wandered over to the window table and pretended to look out at the view.

"High tide later?" he said.

Mr Khalifa ignored his remark and carried on eating a salad and reading the *Financial Times*. Pollett persevered.

"I've promised my girlfriend we'll have a boat by the spring."

During most of his adult life people had immediately warmed to Pollett: he was good-looking and had an engaging smile. Mr Khalifa proved no exception and soon they were engaged in an animated conversation about river boats, tides, locks and all things nautical. Two glasses of orange juice later, Pollett asked him what he did. The flood gates opened and Mr

Khalifa talked at length about his business. He was lucky and had repeated the increase in trade for each shop over the final quarter of the last year.

"Do I recall that you have a superb shop in Hampton?" suggested Pollett as he sensed the opportunity had come to press home his investigation.

Mr Khalifa did not reply.

"You did not say what their trading was before Christmas."

"I must go." Mr Khalifa jumped suddenly to his feet and left the table.

Pollett scratched his head and watched him disappear up the steps and out of the pub.

"What do I do now?" he asked himself.

"Why two bedrooms, Adrian? That's going to be another sixty or seventy thousand pounds."

Annie was sitting in the lounge of their North London home and had a blanket wrapped around her legs. She was having afternoon tea but was not eating any of the cakes which he had bought for her earlier in the day. She took a sip of tea from her cup.

"Well, one bedroom is very small for the two of them."

"The baby will be with her most of the time, Adrian. She only needs one bedroom. There's a nice lounge and kitchenette. She should realise how lucky she is. It's a safe location for her."

They both knew the real reason for this discussion. Annie realised that her husband had every intention of sleeping with Helen again in the future and, strangely, she was relaxed about this development. Her belief was that once Matt died their relationship would regain its intensity. Her own libido was now extinguished and she struggled to cope with her periodic outbreaks of depression. It would so help if Honeysuckle would stop phoning her and repeating yet again how her father was to blame for Annie's condition. Meanwhile, she decided to make him work a little harder for the eventual concession that she would grant him.

"When is she going back to work and what are the child care provisions. Has she been signed off by the hospital?"

Yet again they went over the arrangements being put in place. Helen would be returning to work in late summer.

"She enjoyed bringing William to see you, Annie. You were so warm towards her. I appreciated that more than I can say."

"He's lovely. Mind you all newborn babies are gorgeous. She let me hold him for longer than I was expecting."

"She's alone, Annie. She never mentions her parents and Matt is very ill."

"She has you, Adrian."

"She knows that's not true. I'm with you, Annie."

"While I keep writing out more cheques, you mean?"

"Is that what you really think, Annie?"

What did she really think? She secretly blamed herself. She had allowed her three daughters to dominate too many of their years together. Her mind drifted to Adrian's extended visit to South Africa and his increasing tendency to spend more time alone in his study. She sighed.

"No. You're a decent man, Adrian. Go and buy her the flat she needs."

"What the hell, Pollett? What happened?"

"What could I do, Michelle? He stopped talking and walked out of the pub!"

"Cyberforce Investigations has to achieve results, Pollett. You failed to get him connecting with you."

"Adelene to the rescue, guys!"

They both turned to look at their partner, who put pieces of paper in front of them with a smile.

"She tweets. The Manager. She only has seventy-two followers but she gives herself away. She's troubled. Just read her last two messages, both from last night."

Pollett read down the page.

In my home safe. Cooking lamb chops. Son with father. Watching TV #love

"That's meaningless, Adelene. Why's she sending this rubbish out? And why are you telling us about it?"

"Read it again, Pollett. She's saying she's safe; her home's safe; her son's safe. Safe from what?"

"How do you know that?"

"It's a cri de coeur. She's scared. Read on."

"Tomorrow is tomorrow #friendship"

"What are these hash tags about?"

"They tell us something. I'm not sure she understands what a hash tag does, she's simply copying other people, but it's the words she's using – love, friendship. She's reaching out to her followers."

"Reaching out for what?"

"My first guess is that she's being harassed and my second guess is that it's Mr Khalifa who's making her shit scared. She's saying 'no' to him and he's retaliating in the only way he knows."

"That's a bit wild isn't it, Adelene?" Pollett drank some more of his coffee.

"We're only a third of the way through our checks on her but so far there's nothing to indicate money problems. The utility bills are being paid on time and we've found only one late payment on a credit card."

"I want a result," interrupted Michelle, "and frankly I don't care how we get it. If she's being harassed in some way by Mohammed Khalifa we must find out."

"There is a way, Michelle," Adelene said. "Pollett, you and I are working late tomorrow night."

The world of MXD Silicon Capital came crashing down at the end of the first week of January. As Mark Appleton was contemplating a surge in new business opportunities, and his colleagues in the merged firm were beginning to work well together, the Compliance Director would have benefitted from reading the home page of one of London's most respected firms of solicitors.

Under the heading *Financial Services Authority Investigations & Enforcement*, the following warning was given:

The Financial Services Authority has the power to make rules that businesses offering financial services have to follow. It also has the power to investigate if a business is accused of breaking the rules and to take businesses to court to enforce the rules if necessary.

Amongst the powers that the Authority has is the one that allows it to investigate and sanction firms and those working within the industry; to force people to attend interviews; to obtain documentary evidence and to prosecute wrongdoers.

The home page also contains the following warning:

Being investigated by the FSA is often traumatic and can lead to a huge strain being placed on your business and private life. It is incredibly stressful to have every detail of your financial dealings looked at by someone else. It can disrupt your business and be difficult for you, your loved ones and your employees to cope with.

The FSA does not have power of entry. So on Friday, at exactly seven o'clock in the morning, a police vehicle, together with a personnel van and two civilian cars, screeched into Cornhill, stopping outside the building that housed the offices of MXD Silicon Capital. Two shaven-headed officers, armed with tasers, rushed into the reception and ordered the night porter to stand aside. They knew exactly where to go. They took the lift to the third floor followed by three other police officers, two civilians and three members of the FSA Enforcement Division.

Having reached the floor marked with the name of the business, they hammered on the door, shouting "Police! Open up immediately!" A member of the sales team heard the commotion and went to investigate.

"What the fuck is going on? I'm on the phone to Hong Kong."

She was ordered to stand in the corridor and not to move, and then to tell them where the office in which Mark Webster worked was located. She was scared. She indicated a door further down the passageway. The police officer in the lead found it was locked and so he called up a companion who broke it down using one of his heavy boots. The two civilians rushed in and turned on the computer on the desk. To their surprise, access was unrestricted and they began to download the files for an investment client. Elsewhere the FSA officers were taking the names of the staff already at their desks, and that of each staff member who arrived for work.

An hour later, in the boardroom of MXD Silicon Capital, the three Enforcement Officers commenced the first interview with the Directors. Their target seemed to be Mark Webster, the

Compliance Director. Chrissie, meanwhile, was on her mobile phone, desperately trying to speak to their legal advisers. Mark Appleton had sauntered in with his mind on planning the weekend ahead with Cate.

The senior FSA Officer read out a long statement explaining the powers under which they were present, with the police, and which allowed them to carry out an investigation into the firm. He explained that they would be reviewing all the current cases, but that they wanted to start with Medoc Wines Investment Limited.

Mark Webster's heart sank. Alan Joyce had been so persuasive and, with the Christmas break and the strains of the merger, he had allowed a process that he knew was dangerous. He had tried to talk to Adrian about it, but the chairman had rarely been around. He had been nervous about starting off on the wrong foot with the chief executive – and he so wanted to be able to report earnings of perhaps a million pounds in the first month of the New Year.

He had been staggered at the terms the directors of the client had offered. They agreed to pay fees of four hundred thousand pounds plus a success bonus of three hundred thousand pounds when the company joined a London market. They were to receive free shares with a potential valuation of over one million pounds. He had not quite understood at the time why the first million pounds had to be passed through their bank account, but was reassured that the following nineteen million pounds would be coming in from Hong Kong.

By ten o'clock, the FSA officers had completed a first review of the Compliance Files. They looked at the documentary information on the three directors of the wine investment business. One was a London-based businessman and two were Chinese residents in Macao. To his horror, Mark Webster realised that the solicitors had not yet completed their investigations into the two foreign directors.

"So tell us about Simon Ruffles-Forsythe, Mr Webster. Where are your due diligence papers on him?"

He had never met him. Alan Joyce, himself an Old Harrovian, had told him that he had an impeccable pedigree and had produced a photocopied passport and utility bills as evidence of his background. The file showed that Companies House and credit agency searches had proved clear.

"So explain to us why you allowed over one million pounds to pass through the bank account of MXD Silicon Capital?"

"We were told that it was the directors' own money and there was a delay in opening the company bank account. They wanted to pay our initial fees so we agreed to accept the funds – and we paid them out as instructed less our costs."

"To whom did you pay the net amount, which I think you'll find was a little over nine hundred thousand pounds?"

Chrissie looked daggers at Mark Webster. She had strongly opposed the transaction but, what with Christmas and the merger, when she had tried to talk to Adrian he had been distracted and had just told her to make sure Mark was happy with the details.

"It was paid out to three companies with bank accounts in Madrid," said Chrissie.

"Why?" asked the FSA Officer. "Why was it not paid into the account of Medoc Wines Investment Limited? Why did you not wait for the bank account to be opened?"

"Good question," thought Chrissie. She looked at Mark Webster.

"Alan Joyce said that Simon Ruffles-Forsythe wanted to pay out some commissions he owed for the raising of the twenty million pounds."

"When can we meet Mr Joyce, Mr Webster?"

"I'm afraid he always takes the first week of the New Year for his skiing holiday."

"Mr Webster, have you heard of New Territories Brokers, Westminster Discount Brokers and Zurich International Capital?"

The Compliance Director shook his head.

"They are all boiler room operations run by Simon Ruffles-Forsythe, whose real name is Archie Abrahams. He has homes in Essex, Barcelona, Hong Kong and Australia. The shares were sold in the last two months from offshore locations to doctors and dentists in the United Kingdom. They're making so much money from their NHS contracts and the new Clinical Commissioning Group's purchasing arrangements, in the case of the medics, that they are being targeted by the fraudsters. We're starting to receive complaints that no share certificates have been issued."

The FSA Officer did not reveal that the FSA had received an anonymous parcel containing the full background to Simon Ruffles-Forsythe, as well as details of the money laundering sting.

Chapter Twelve

January 2013

Pollett arrived outside the greeting card shop in Priory Road, Hampton, at five-fifty in the afternoon as instructed by Adelene. He had travelled by train and knew that Twickenham Rugby Football Club and Kempton Park Racecourse were to the north-west of the hamlet.

He gaped in amazement at her appearance. She was wearing a blonde wig and a floral tracksuit beneath her open coat. She was ensuring that she would not be recognised from her previous visit.

"What the hell's that?" he exclaimed.

"Shut up, Pollett. And you're now my brother Paul. Come on."

They entered the shop and Adelene went over to the birthday section. She busied herself, pretending not to be able to choose a card. She carefully watched as the remaining member of staff closed the door, reversed the 'open' sign, and walked over to them.

"Can I help you?" the manager asked.

"I hope so. It's our father's sixtieth birthday and my brother here has forgotten to get him a card."

"You're looking in the wrong place. The relations cards are over here."

As Adelene turned round she allowed her coat to fall open. The manager looked in surprise at her outfit.

"Excuse me asking, but is that a Onesie?"

"Actually, yes, it is. What do you think? Can I show it off to you?"

"Oh, you definitely can! I like it. Where's it from?" She smiled. "I'm Litinia, by the way."

"That's a pretty name," Adelene said. "Litinia. Eastern European?"

"Turkish. I came to this country ten years ago to study and

161

I've now gained British citizenship. Here you are. 'Father: sixty years old today'."

The card had a nautical theme, which Adelene said fitted the bill perfectly. Pollett followed them back to the cash register and was told by his 'sister' to pay for their purchase.

The transaction was completed and, as they were leaving, Litinia asked if she could look at Adelene's Onesie again. She took off her coat and completed a twirl. Her admirer clapped her hands together.

"I read that the London Mayor has got one!" she laughed.

"Yes - in a Union Jack design," said Adelene. "Litinia, you've been so helpful, would you let us buy you a glass of wine?"

"I must get home for my son and I'm expecting a visitor. But... I do want to hear more about your Onesie! Fifteen minutes. No more."

She quickly alarmed the shop and followed them out of the front door. Adelene turned right, since she already knew where the nearest bar was situated. Once they were settled at a table, she told 'Paul' to go and buy a large bottle of something cold and white.

"That'll teach him to forget my instructions!" she said.

Pollett arrived back with the bottle and two glasses. He was sticking to orange juice. Adelene poured the drinks, and it wasn't long before they were chatting like old friends. Litinia told them about her son, her family back home and her work responsibilities. She suddenly revealed that Jos, her son, had never known his father.

Adelene put her hand on Litinia's arm and suggested that, if she purchased a Onesie, the men would come running. Instead of responding, Litinia, in fact, went rather quiet. Adelene sensed her opportunity.

"Are you ok, Litinia?"

"It's nothing. I must go now. I'm expecting a visitor. I'm late."

Adelene knew that she had to pry.

"Who's so special?" she asked.

"Not special. It's my boss, Mr Khalifa. He's insisted on coming to my flat. He says my takings are down. They're not but he has the figures."

"He's coming over to your flat to talk about that?" asked Adelene, feigning surprise.

Litinia shook her head. "I'm saying too much. I have to go now."

"Would you like me to come with you?"

"Why would you do that?"

"Because Mr Khalifa wants to talk about more than the takings, doesn't he Litinia?"

Tears welled in Litinia's eyes.

"He says he'll sack me if I don't agree to…"

"Agree to what?"

"You know."

Pollett announced that he was going to the toilet and marched out of the bar. Just as he left, a man approached them.

"Mr Khalifa!" exclaimed Litinia as her hand flew to her mouth.

"Litinia, your car is still parked behind the shop," he said. "You've forgotten our meeting. It's taken me nearly thirty minutes to find you."

Pollett had seen what was going on and hurried back to the table. He positioned himself behind Mr Khalifa.

"Your meeting is cancelled, Mr Khalifa," said Adelene.

"And who the hell are you?"

"My friend here is going to take you outside and have a little chat. Can I suggest that you co-operate, please?"

"Your friend?" said Litinia. "I thought you said he was your brother?"

Adelene explained the whole story to her. It took time for the frightened woman to settle down but slowly she began to trust her. She said that Pollett would persuade Mr Khalifa to provide a good reference and three months' pay-off.

"You can't stay with the business, Litinia, and sadly we'll never make a charge stick. You just have to get out – but I promise that you'll be safe from Mr Khalifa."

Pollett had the man up against a wall. His eyes flashed in recognition.

"Can I suggest that it's in your best interests that we never meet again, Mr Khalifa?" he concluded. "Now, before I go, there are things for us to discuss."

163

The following day Michelle was beaming.

"What's happened?" she asked. "Our client phoned me early this morning to say that Mr Khalifa was making the shop manager redundant on very generous terms."

"Let's just call it a Onesie moment!" said Adelene, winking at Pollett.

"A what?" asked Michelle.

Dr Raymond Stelling smiled at his patient.

"I meant to ask you last time, Mrs Rudd, how did you hear of me?"

"I'm a detective."

"Yes. Well, as you know, I'm a GP and a sexual psychotherapist. Let's get the GP bit sorted. It's mostly good news. The tests show you are in pretty good condition. Ideally, you should lose seven pounds in weight, but what the hell. My internal examination was satisfactory but you have a minor infection. It's not connected with what we're going to discuss but I've prescribed some antibiotics for you. Please collect those on your way out – and you must complete the whole course of tablets. It's your choice but I'd prefer that you come back and let me check you in a week's time. It's a five day supply: two pills daily. Your own GP can see you if that is easier for you."

"Ok. Thanks."

"Can I also ask you about the operation on your cheekbone? Have you had a follow-up scan?"

"I haven't had time."

"No. I know it's been a difficult period for you. It's not my responsibility, but there is some swelling under the skin. It's almost certainly post-operative and nothing to worry about. In a perfect world…"

"In a perfect world, doctor, I wouldn't have lost my sex drive and I wouldn't be talking to you."

"But you are here, Mrs Rudd, which tells me that you want help."

"I want answers."

"That's what we both want, Mrs Rudd. Now, you're forty-three years of age and I suspect you're in the early stages of the menopause. Very early."

"What does that mean?"

"It suggests that your body is producing less testoster-one. Between the ages of, say, twenty to forty-five or fifty, your body naturally reduces its production of testosterone, although regular sexual activity can counterbalance this. We have another problem in that most medical research has focused on the male production of testosterone and women have been left behind. There are patches I can prescribe that allow your body to absorb mild doses of the chemical through the skin. However, I think we should get to the real reason for your condition before we discuss possible treatments. In your questionnaire, you said that you are taking Black Cohosh tablets?"

"I studied my condition on the internet. I read up on them."

"Are they having any effect?"

"No."

"Throw them away, Mrs Rudd, please. The theory is that the root of the plant was used by native Americans as a medicine because it was believed to possess sedative and analgesic properties. They now seem to be promoted as a counter to the menopause. There is no real research and we can't rule out the possibility of liver damage if taken over a prolonged period."

"So what do I take?"

"Nothing."

DCI Sarah Rudd looked across the table. For a reason she was never fully able to explain, even to herself, she trusted this man.

"Nothing."

He leaned forward and smiled.

"Mrs Rudd. Do you really understand what happened to you when you rescued the pregnant hostage?"

"Yes, doctor. I got smashed in the face by a shit from Liver-pool."

"No, Mrs Rudd, that's not what really happened to you."

"I imagined it, did I?"

"You know that's not what I'm trying to say."

He lifted the phone on his desk and ordered a tray of tea,

which was served almost immediately. Sarah suddenly realised how famished she was and quickly took one of the iced cakes off the plate on the tray.

"I'll start the diet tomorrow," she laughed. "So, what exactly did happen to me, Dr Stelling?"

"You exhausted your body, Mrs Rudd. When an individual faces stress there are a number of protective chemical reserves that rush to deal with the situation. I can only imagine what it must have been like facing the gunman and having the life of a pregnant woman to save. Not only were you physically assaulted, but your body also reached a point where it had no more to offer. Now your body is simply telling you that you must rest and recover." He paused. "You were telling me that you're hoping to return to work to do community policing?"

"That's what I'm thinking about, yes. I'm going back to work in two weeks' time and they want to promote me – but I'm not certain I want that."

"And your husband?"

"He's been a little quiet – and no doubt the lack of sex is a bit frustrating for him. So, no treatment from you, doctor?"

"Quite the opposite. Come back anytime. We can try patches, therapy, black cohosh tablets, and no doubt a few other things. You just don't need them. Trust your body, Mrs Rudd. You are an exceptional woman and, if I may say so, it's been a privilege to meet you."

He paused as he sat back in his chair.

"Go home Sarah, and wait," he advised. "You'll get better. Let your body decide when."

"I love my husband very much," she said suddenly.

"Yes. That's obvious. Just give it time, Mrs Rudd."

"Cate, can I ask you a question?"

"Let me guess. The nurse's uniform or the wet T-shirt?"

He handed her a gin and tonic and took a gulp from his pint of lager. In the background The Rolling Stones were struggling to get any satisfaction, a problem they'd had since 1965.

"Tell me about why you made your decision to become a nurse. You gave up a well-paid job, an international lifestyle and a great environment to empty bedpans for geriatrics."

"Expressed with riveting and dramatic emphasis, as ever, Mark, but that's about the size of it."

"Why?"

"If we carry on with this conversation, we're likely to get serious."

"Answer the question, please, Cate. It's important to me."

She held out her glass and waited for the refill to be pushed into her hand. She drank deeply and sighed.

"It was about sex, Mark."

"No. I want to talk about your decision."

"We are."

The Rolling Stones were now realising that you can't always get what you want.

"It was that book, Mark. Fifty Bloody Shades of Grey. I started to wonder, not only if our relationship was based entirely on sex, but whether I was empty – as a person. Did I go out to work because that's what was expected of me, and was my whole ethos based on clothes, drink and sex?" She finished her drink. "I didn't like the answers I came up with."

"But you've already discovered that the training is going to be hellish. It'll be three years before you're able to begin as a qualified mental nurse."

"But that's the whole point. I'm aiming for something I want. I'll never give in, Mark. Whatever happens to me, I'm going to make it."

"We're in trouble at work."

"I know – I've overheard a few telephone conversations. How bad is it?"

"I suppose it's just down to what the regulatory authorities decide."

"Nonsense. Are you guilty?"

"I'm the chief executive."

"Drop 'the captain of the Titanic' bit, Mark. Where does the responsibility lie?"

"I can't understand how the FSA are so well informed. It's

not certain there is even a fraud." He shook his head. "There probably is – but the shareholder complaints only started coming in during late November."

"But you put a million pounds through the company's bank account and paid it out to this fraudster, Simon Rulling. I heard you shouting at somebody last night."

"Simon Ruffles-Forsythe. They haven't found him yet and our man Alan Joyce has disappeared."

"Is that his real name: Simon Ruffles-Forsythe?"

Mark laughed. "Well done Miss Marple. His real name is Archie Abrahams. I still cling to the belief that there will be an explanation to all this."

"And Santa Claus might re-appear. What's going to happen, Mark?"

"Our solicitors are negotiating with the FSA."

"Plea bargaining."

"In a way." He fetched her another drink but swamped it with ice cubes and tonic water."

"So what happens now?" she asked.

"I'll tell you, Cate. Somebody has to grab this by the balls. I'm damned if I'm going to let them close the business down."

Cate put her arms around her partner's shoulders.

"Let's go to bed, Mark. But can we just hold each other tonight?"

He'd confided in her at last.

Helen wanted to tell Adrian about William's weight increase and Matt's further deterioration, and he wanted to explain about the problems at MXD Silicon Capital. The coffee shop was busy and somebody was smoking a cigarette. Adrian refused to make a complaint to the staff.

To add to the tensions, William started to cry and so his mother took him outside. This gave Adrian time to make a phone call but he was told that Mark, Chrissie and the compliance officer were unavailable.

When Helen returned, he told her that he had some exciting news. He revealed that he was going to secure a two-bedroom flat for her and William.

"But that's what we'd always agreed, Adrian!" she said. "You surely don't expect William and me to manage with only one room."

He sighed. Yet another mood swing. She'd seemed so pleased with the first flat they'd seen and she was now positively underwhelmed by the news of the improved property purchase. He'd return to this later. He moved on to describe events in the Cornhill offices.

"You're overreacting, Adrian. You're the chairman. It's the executive directors who are responsible. Get on that phone and tell Mark you want to see him at two o'clock. You must assert yourself."

"It's not that easy, Helen. When the money went through the company bank account I was the chief executive."

"Mark's had plenty of time to check the files. It's his problem now. Get on that phone to him."

Adrian made the call and this time reached Mark and assumed an authoritative tone of voice.

"Mark. It's Adrian. I'd like to receive a full report from you on the investigation. Please meet me in the boardroom at two o'clock."

"That's better, Adrian. William doesn't want a pussycat Daddy, do you, darling?"

William gurgled in delight and was then sick.

"What did Mark say?" asked Helen.

"He told me to fuck off."

At the end of the following week, the directors of MXD Silicon Capital held a meeting which lasted for much of the Saturday morning. Although the lead was usually taken by the chairman, Adrian seemed content to let Mark run the show. And it was clear from the start that he intended to do exactly that. The first hour was taken up with a presentation by the company lawyers on their progress in resolving matters with the Financial Services Authority. They had now left. Chrissie hadn't said anything all morning.

Russell Warren, the Marketing Director, broke the silence.

"They could have closed us down," he said.

"With the conditions they're imposing, that's rather what they have indeed done."

Mark Webster looked exhausted. As compliance director, he had taken the full force of the regulatory onslaught.

The chief executive tapped the table. The FSA officers had laid down an extra condition and he had no idea how to tell the individual involved.

"We do have choices," he said.

"I beg to differ, Mark," said Chrissie. "Regardless of the process, our reputation is in tatters."

"We were the victims of a fraud. We did not set out to commit a crime. We're going to pay a high price but I, for one, will fight through this."

The discussion continued, despite the fact that everyone around the table knew what was going to happen. Finally the compliance officer made his decision.

"I have no other option but to resign," he said. "The FSA holds me responsible and I accept that. I gather that if I go, and leave the industry, there'll be no fine. Will I get my pay-off?"

"In full," said Mark.

He picked up his file and walked out of the room. As he passed Chrissie, he put his hand on her shoulder.

"We're going to change our name. I want it to go back to Silicon Capital," announced Mark.

"What!" exploded Adrian. "That will send out a clear signal that it was the fault of MXD Capital."

"It was, Adrian. It was your compliance officer and Alan Joyce was a member of your team."

"You were chief executive. You go."

"Technically, no, I wasn't, because the merger was delayed."

"So it was my fault was it, Mark?"

"That's what the FSA officers think, yes."

"But the solicitors never said that," defended Chrissie.

"The FSA said it to me."

"When?" asked Adrian.

"On Thursday evening. I made an appointment to see the chief enforcement director. They went through the whole file with me. I'm afraid, Adrian, that I have some difficult news.

They're going for you. They intend to try and have you banned from the industry. And my guess is that they'll succeed, despite your wife's money."

"Watch me fight my corner."

"That's your choice – but by the time they've finished you'll be ruined. They're prepared to let you off provided you leave the industry completely."

"But it's been my life. Nobody will believe that I was guilty."

"It's the way things are done these days. Everybody's guilty of something."

An hour later, Adrian agreed to leave without compensation. He departed the boardroom rather bemused by this turn of events.

Mark tidied up his papers and strolled quietly back to his office. What he could not understand was why there was a second file on the desk of the FSA enforcement officer that had remained unopened throughout their meeting.

Nigel de Groot had enjoyed his walk down Park Lane. His operation had been a complete success. He returned to his hotel and took the lift to his penthouse suite. He ordered champagne and seafood cocktail with extra lobster. The girl was wearing very little but knew that she was not allowed to touch him. She also sensed that he liked to see her pose in various positions.

He was now on his mobile phone, laughing.

"Ja. I expect they liked the photographs of him and that Sonja woman in the hotel. I chose the one where... Archie... he's in Thailand. It's as we thought. The authorities never really investigated. He was guilty before they finished our file. The money? It's gone into two businesses. The investors may do well. There never was a fraud. The FSA just assumed it was a con. We've now issued the share certificates and Archie will be back next month. The Chinese directors have raised the nineteen million by the way."

He rang off and pressed the digits for another call.

The girl had positioned herself across the sofa and was hiding her modesty with a few strands of lace.

"Is that Adrian? This is Nigel de Groot speaking."

He waited for a few moments. There was a torrent of abuse from the other end of the mobile phone.

"That was for starters, Mr Dexter. I'll phone you back in a few moments."

"Dis nog maar die begin, Meneer Dexter," he repeated to himself.

Adrian slumped back in his study chair. All was quiet because Annie was already asleep, the dog was slumbering in the kitchen and he had no wish to play any music. He had made the decision to speak on the phone to Sonja in Johannesburg. Her report made even more dispiriting news. Her ex-husband had found out that he'd been fed false information about De Groot's movements and had told his former wife that he wanted no more to do with the matter. Separately Sonja had shared lunch with the bank's chairman, who'd told her that their former colleague had completed his plea bargaining and was now clear of all charges. He'd asked her whether she had heard that De Groot had needed urgent medical attention.

His phone rang. He answered it as his forehead creased with worry.

"Good evening again, Adrian. As I was saying. This is Nigel de Groot. I do hope that you've had an awful day. You've been ejected from MXD Capital, I understand? I thought you might like to receive some more bad news."

"If you ever touch my son, you bastard…"

"He's not really your son, is he, Adrian? You're not the father. Managed to get yourself trapped, didn't you? I suppose really I should leave you to your fate."

"What does that mean?"

"You made a bad error of judgement when you went to the police. Now it's time for you to suffer."

"This is England, Nigel. I'll be fully protected."

"Unlikely, Adrian. Anyway, I've already decided what should happen to you."

"Go to hell."

"Ek gaan jou vrekskiet. Dit sal gebeur binne sewentien dae. Kom ek gee jou 'n clue," snarled Nigel de Groot. "Would

172

you like to know what I've just said to you? You don't speak Afrikaans, do you, Adrian? You just fuck our women. What I said was – and please do listen carefully – I am going to shoot you dead. You'll die in seventeen days' time. Let me give you a clue."

"As I said. Go to hell."

"Hierdie webb het nooit bedoel dat jy onstsnap en nie rooi sien nie."

The line went dead. A few minutes later the button started to pulse on his mobile. He read the text message:

This webb never meant you to escape but don't see red.

Chapter Thirteen

February 2013

Adrian decided to book a breakfast table in the West End. He knew that she'd be late but he was there promptly at eight o'clock. She left her coat with the cloakroom attendant of The Meridien Hotel in Piccadilly and visited the bathroom. It was bitterly cold as the easterly winds swept in across northern Europe from the Russian Tundra. She removed her boots and slipped on a pair of black shoes. She looked in the mirror and sprayed a hint of perfume on her neck. She undid the top button of her blouse and then remembered it was her former boss she was meeting. As she was shown to their table, he was peering at his mobile and a text message that had just arrived and which read:

Sixteen days to go. This webb never meant you to escape but don't see red.

From the start of their conversation, he was rattled. They ordered fresh fruit and a cooked breakfast and were soon served English tea. Michelle answered questions about the progress of Cyberforce Investigations and summed up the success of their first case. She sensed he was not really listening to her. He launched into an outspoken criticism of the people involved with recent events at MXD Silicon Capital.

"You must fight the ban, Adrian. It sounds like Mark Appleton has railroaded you into resigning."

"We've heard that there was a package sent to the authorities and my solicitors are certain it originated from Nigel de Groot. There were some photographs which I'd prefer they'd not seen."

"What photographs?"

"I've resigned, Michelle, and now I have another problem."

"Not another woman, Adrian, for Pete's sake."

"No. Nigel de Groot is in the UK."

"So tell the police."

"Tell them what? I've heard from South Africa that he's been cleared of all charges arising from Zambian Goldfields."

"He kidnapped your girlfriend!"

"The police have charged three men over that but they can't tie in De Groot. Annie is refusing to allow me to press charges for reasons best known to herself. And there's also the small issue that nobody knows where he is."

"So what's this other problem?" she asked as her breakfast of scrambled eggs, bacon, black pudding, grilled tomatoes and granary toast was placed in front of her. She indicated that she wanted another pot of tea and was still waiting for her fresh orange juice.

"Nigel de Groot has contacted me. He called me last night and also sent a text message. I received another text this morning."

"Saying what, Adrian?"

"I suggest you read it."

He handed her his phone.

Sixteen days to go. This webb never meant you to escape but don't see red.

"It reads like a Harlan Coben novel. For god's sake – this is London, Adrian. This sort of thing does not happen to people like you."

"Well, my son's been kidnapped and I've been ruined by a South African fraudster. It is happening, Michelle."

She decided not to correct the inaccuracies in his statement.

"Sixteen days to go until what?" she asked.

"He's going to shoot me in sixteen days' time."

She started to laugh and then remembered that the text message was real. This Nigel de Groot had already caused havoc at MXD Capital, kidnapped a pregnant woman and blackmailed her breakfast companion.

"What on earth does 'This webb never meant you to escape but don't see red' mean?"

"He said it's a clue."

"A clue to what?"

"He linked it to the threat to shoot me in seventeen days' time – which is now sixteen days."

He drank some tea and then looked across the table miserably.

"What should I do, Michelle?"

"Have you told Annie?"

"She's not well."

"Helen?"

"Matt only has a few more days to live. I don't want to add to her worries."

"Your daughters?"

He laughed. "I think Honeysuckle and Clare would encourage him to shoot me."

"Go to the police, Adrian."

"To achieve what exactly? I've no evidence. They'll say it's scare tactics. They won't be able to find him. They were none too impressed when I didn't tell them about the ransom monies either…"

"That was Annie's stipulation."

"Try telling the police that."

"I'll arrange for you to have personal safety guards. I have a friend who can supply ex-forces personnel."

"Not yet, Michelle. Nearer the time perhaps. Right now we need to find him."

"We can try, Adrian, but he's smart. Truthfully he's almost certainly too clever for Cyberforce to find him. Go to the police."

"Not yet."

He rested his hand on hers. It was the first occasion that she could remember that he didn't try to look down her cleavage.

"I need your help, please, Michelle."

DCI Sarah Rudd was finding life difficult. The problem was that her husband was struggling to understand the lack of physical contact between them. She had returned to full-time police work in Islington and the second X-ray of her facial injury confirmed that the healing process was on schedule. She had been invited to attend several meetings with her senior officers and the file on the kidnapping of Helen Greenwood was now closed, pending the trial of the three accused men from Liverpool.

She found the sessions difficult. She was being patronised by the most senior members of the force. She knew that it was because she was a woman. She had seen her male colleagues perform a number of heroic acts but, because the hostage had been pregnant and Sarah badly assaulted during the rescue, they were trying to put her on a publicity pedestal. They were trying to show her off and Sarah did not like it. She just wanted to get out and about on the streets of North London again with her colleagues and continue their attempts to maintain a civilised society.

At home their two children were enjoying school life, and her husband was happy as a teacher. There was, however, an undercurrent of uncertainty in their household. As a couple they were usually able to talk over any issue but, on this occasion, neither seemed willing to break the ice. When it came to bedtime, Sarah was turning her back on her husband. For his part, he was nervous about initiating any increased contact because he knew that Sarah was going through a troubled period.

She had talked openly about the events in Clerkenwell and had refused all offers from her employer of counselling services. But when they received an invitation from her sister to join them for Sunday lunch, unusually, Sarah turned it down. She busied herself in housework and in playing games with the children, and watched more and more evening television. They went to a parents' evening at their elder child's school. Nick felt that, during the meetings with the teachers, Sarah was simply going through the motions.

Matt died in hospital, with Helen and William by his side. It was twenty-four hours later before Helen told Adrian. She brushed aside his words of solace and told him that he would be cremated at a private service and that she did not think it would be appropriate for Adrian to attend. She added that she'd decided against moving and had renewed the rent on her apartment for another year. She also said that she did not fully understand why Adrian was no longer chairman of MXD Capital.

When Adrian insisted that he felt he should attend Matt's funeral, she expressed her anguish.

"Matt was William's father, Adrian. My son has lost the most important person in his life. We want to be left alone please."

He couldn't see the point in trying to discuss matters further and returned home to St. John's Wood, where he discovered that Honeysuckle and Clare were visiting their mother.

Later in the evening, Honeysuckle entered his study and asked whether her father realised that Annie's condition was deteriorating.

"Yes, Honeysuckle, of course I do. And we went together to see the doctor on Tuesday. Your mother is having some further tests. She's receiving the best treatment possible."

"I sense that even if I was to put on my briefest nurse's uniform it wouldn't have the slightest effect."

Mark took her in his arms and hugged her close.

"Sorry, Cate. Life's not much fun at the moment."

"I thought the investigation was completed."

"It is. I'm now trying to repair the office atmosphere. We've had two resignations and Chrissie is sulking. But it's just a matter of time. A few good deals and we'll be underway again."

"And Adrian's gone?"

"He left the board meeting and none of us have seen him again. There have been some emails and I had to write to him formally, but otherwise it's as though MXD Silicon Capital never happened."

"Is the team leader who brought in the investment deal still absent?"

Mark put a glass of wine down in front of her.

"He'd broken his leg skiing. He's now happily hobbling round the office." He paused. "You won't believe this but I want him suspended because of the fraud but, legally, the solicitors are saying there's no proof that he did anything wrong. The FSA case was more about procedures."

"There are times, Mark, when I really don't understand the work you do."

"Cate," he said, kissing her, "there are times when I don't think I understand it myself."

179

She returned to her study books and asked him to listen while she read aloud.

"Prostate cancer is classified as an adenopcarcinoma, or, in other words, glandular cancer. It starts when normal semen-secreting gland cells mutate into cancer cells."

"Why are you telling me about prostates? I thought you were training to nurse old people?"

"I am, but we were told that around 70 percent of men will die with some form of prostate problem."

He put his arm around her shoulder and placed the other inside her shirt.

"And did you know that regular sexual activity is considered the best way of preventing prostate cancer?"

Cate pretended to fight him off.

"Do you think I should look that up in my books?" she giggled.

She was unable to say anything else, as he was now carrying her into the bedroom.

The office manager had settled down well into her role at Cyberforce Investigations, partly because she was both friendly and efficient, and partly due to her understanding that the three partners lived on percolated coffee.

"Right," said Michelle. "We've started the hunt for De Groot and I'm hoping we'll hear from the agency later today."

"We're on day fifteen, right?" said Pollett.

"Yes. I saw Adrian yesterday and spent the rest of the time deciding on the best people to ask to help find our South African gunman."

"So, in theory, he shoots him two weeks from tomorrow."

"Yes, assuming he's real, and everything is telling me that he is. So, let's start by asking ourselves the question, 'why did he give Adrian a clue?' assuming that's what it is," said Michelle.

Fresh coffee arrived together with chocolate biscuits.

"To scare him?" suggested Adelene.

"He's certainly achieved that, but if I'm right, the phrase offers us something else. He's arrogant and playing games with us. Read it out again for us, Adelene, please."

She pronounced each word in a clear and loud voice.

"This webb never meant you to escape but don't see red."

"The obvious meaning is a spider's web and anger," said Pollett. "Bastard can't even spell the word properly." He paused. "It must be a reference to being ensnared in a spider's web, which in turn will make him cross. He's going to be led to a place where he can be shot."

"If we simply follow the obvious, we'll be wrong," said Michelle. "Mr De Groot is a clever man and that tells us this is a riddle that can be solved. He's going to shoot Adrian and he's telling us where and when."

"So how do we solve it?"

"We think laterally."

Sonja Redmaine lay back on her lounger in her extensive garden in the neighbourhood of Houghton. She knew that less than half a mile away Nelson Mandela was recovering from the removal of gallstones and a lung infection. Sonja was happy: she adored President Mandela and all he stood for, and she was elated by the improvement in his health since the operation.

She was, however, thinking about fate. It was a word she often used, although without realising, she was referring more closely to destiny. She felt as though there were invisible strands pulling her towards a future happiness.

The news from London was grim and the collapse of MXD Silicon Capital distressed her. Her ex-husband's total refusal to talk to her was also confusing, although she was aware that he had a new girlfriend.

'I'm going to hold Adrian in my arms again one day,' she said to herself, as she drank deeply from the glass of citrus fruits she had blended earlier in the day. As the sun beat down and the oil on her skin absorbed the heat, she imagined seeing him again.

Sonja was right. While fate is unpredictable, she would, much sooner than she expected, be holding her lover in her arms.

On Friday morning Adrian received another text.

Thirteen days to go. This webb never meant you to escape but don't see red.

An hour later he was in the offices of Cyberforce Investigations in Old Broad Street. The coffee was freshly percolated and the three partners settled round the table.

"Pollett, you start, please," said Michelle.

"We're taking everything at face value, Adrian, at this stage. De Groot is going to try to shoot you in thirteen days' time. The reference to 'webb', we think, is either about a spider's web or the internet. Because he uses the word 'escape', it's obvious he wants us to think it's a reference to a spider's web."

Pollett paused and drank some coffee. He looked at Adelene but she was saving her detective work for later in the meeting.

"To be frank, we have no idea at this stage what it means. It could be a reference to London Zoo, but there again there are a number of private collections in the London area. We can visit importers of insects but what are we looking for? It makes no real sense. And if it's to do with the internet, where do we start?"

"So you have no idea at all," Adrian said, deflated.

"At this point in time, no, none."

"Michelle suggested that De Groot is playing games. He's given you a clue which, if solved, will tell you where and when he will try to kill you. In other words, we should focus on time and place."

"Why would he want to warn me?" asked Adrian.

"Because," replied Michelle, "he wants you to suffer. I suspect he could try to shoot you tomorrow but, for some reason, the second Thursday in February seems to be the day he has chosen. The puzzle he has set is designed to tell you the location and the time. He thinks he's superior and that you'll not be able to solve it."

"Have you found De Groot yet?"

"He checked out of his hotel the morning after he had phoned you and now he's disappeared. But we think he's still in the UK."

"So where do we go now?"

"We accept the obvious – that the conundrum will not be solved conventionally – and we feed each word into our computer and see what results we get."

"What are you looking for exactly?"

"The thirty-nine steps."

"And I'm Richard Hannay, I suppose, Michelle?"

"It took him the whole film to find out from where in London the spies would be leaving, together with the British secret military plans," she replied.

"We need to find your equivalent of the steps," suggested Pollett.

Michelle watched while the three other members of the meeting remained quiet.

"Why seventeen days?" asked Adelene.

"That's what De Groot said," replied Adrian.

"I know, but why seventeen? Why not ten or twenty? I think the number of days is significant."

"It's the second Thursday in the month, Adelene – that's all," dismissed Pollett.

"And what's the date?" asked Adelene.

"Er... 14 February," said Michelle. "Hell, it's Valentine's Day."

"In South Africa it's quite a big event. The girls follow the old Roman festival of 'Lupercalia' and pin their lover's name on their sleeve. In recent years men have been doing the same," Adrian said.

"Nigel de Groot is saying he's going to pin something on you, Adrian!" said Michelle.

"There's also the St. Valentine's Day Massacre," continued Adelene. "1929. Al Capone and Bugs Moran managed to shoot dead seven gangsters."

"So where's the connection?" asked Pollett.

"In 1999 'The St. Valentine's Day Massacre' was the name given to a World Wrestling Federation event in Memphis, Tennessee. It was quite famous. I've been checking, but I can't find any events being held in London on that day."

"So where does that take us?" asked Adrian.

"Let's review all we've discussed," said Michelle. "I'll phone you tonight."

He closed his file. He thanked them for their efforts and returned home to his study. He thought for a long time and decided there was only one sensible course of action he could take.

Helen herself was not certain why she wrote the letter that was delivered to Adrian's home, and which he would read later that day. She had found saying goodbye to Matt much harder than she had imagined and the responsibility for a young child was maturing her in a way she had not expected. She was discovering a new lease of life, where each day belonged to her and William. The medical services were unbelievably supportive and she fell asleep at night exhausted and fulfilled. She was making new friends at the baby clinic and she loved swapping tips and stories with them.

She had also received an approach. Her Area Manager had come to see the baby and bring presents from the staff at the opticians. Helen had always liked Ahmed and found him attractive, but the management's attitude was so anti-women that she'd never considered him as more than her boss. But he'd stayed for nearly two hours and at one point held on to William when Helen prepared a tray of tea. As he had left, he'd placed his hand on her sleeve and squeezed her arm. There was no kiss, but it did not matter – there was a clear signal that he might return. Besides, there were several forms for her to sign and why waste a postage stamp.

When she realised that the two-bedroom flat which Adrian was suggesting was priced at over five hundred and fifty thousand pounds, she knew that matters had reached a point where she had to make a decision.

He had been sensational over her deceit in pretending to be carrying his baby. And he was devoted to William – but Adrian was the type of man who would commit to loving aliens from outer space if it suited his purposes. He was also nearly sixty and it was clear that in the last few weeks, as he consumed more alcohol and managed less sleep, his appearance was changing. The sparkle had gone from his eyes.

So her decision was made and she knew it would be impossible to cope with a physical encounter. She began writing her missive: *Dearest Adrian. I am going to hurt you so badly and*

I'm already crying my heart out. But, Adrian, I must think about William, who has just lost his father, and his future. You cannot be part of that…

Earlier in the day, Adrian had met with Detective Chief Inspector Sarah Rudd at Islington Police Station. To his surprise she had read that morning's text message without a murmur:

Ten days to go. This webb never meant you to escape but don't see red.

"Of course you should have gone to the police on day seventeen and not wasted your time with a bunch of amateurs," she had said, before calling for a second tray of tea. She had listened to the whole story without interrupting her visitor.

There was a knock at the door and a few minutes later they were drinking cups of tea and eating hobnobs.

"I shouldn't really have another one. My doctor says I need to lose seven pounds in weight."

"You look pretty good to me, DCI Rudd."

She raised her eyebrows in surprise.

"Have you ever read *The Day of the Jackal*?" she asked.

"The Frederick Forsyth book? I haven't read it but I've seen the film."

"At the start, when he met the terrorists in Vienna, what was the Jackal's main concern?"

"How, where and when to shoot President de Gaulle."

"Good answer, Adrian, but he had one overriding worry."

"The money. The OAS was robbing banks to raise his fee."

"He was paid five hundred thousand dollars and this was in 1973. But it was not the money that took his focus."

"The rifle. He had it specially made."

"He was mostly thinking about how he could get away with the assassination. Do you remember Edward Fox creasing his forehead and saying 'and speaking as a professional that's rather important'? That was the Jackal's main preoccupation and I suspect that's where we should start."

He sat back and pondered her comments.

"Let's cut the crap. We know this Nigel de Groot rather well. He's clever. He's going to try and kill you. He doesn't know

185

where you'll be on 14 February, but he's got a good idea about that, no doubt. My instinct is that he won't try to blow you up. He does not need to give you time to prepare – but he's done just that. My guess is that, given time, we can solve his riddle. What we need to do is to work out how he intends to get away with his crime. He may well return back through Northern Ireland and we might pick him up, but with his connections that's unlikely. So how's he going to get away with shooting you?"

They talked further and DCI Rudd explained that she'd have to pass the case on to the Metropolitan Police. She asked Adrian to relay all text messages from De Groot to her immediately.

Later that evening she broke the rules and told Nick all about the case. It was a relief to have something concrete to talk about. He was particularly interested in De Groot's message.

"We've done spiders' webs, the St. Valentine's Day Massacre and the rest, Nick," she laughed. "Nobody has any idea what it means."

"But it means something?"

"Definitely. I've met a few of the Nigel de Groots of this world. To him this is a game. Adrian's broken his rules and he lost his hostage. So I'm certain he's going to try to kill Adrian and almost certainly in London on 14 February. He knows we'll all be working hard to try to solve the clue and he's loving every minute of it. He'll be holed up somewhere in London and, frustratingly, we've no way of finding him. We have to solve the puzzle and be there when he tries to shoot Adrian."

"So how will he get away?"

"He'll create a diversion and fly out in a private plane from Essex."

"Unless Detective Rudd can solve the puzzle first?"

"I doubt that the Met will even look at it," she replied.

He read her letter once, put on a CD of Beethoven compositions, and then re-read the three pages. He was surprised at how steady and authoritative her handwriting was. He put the correspondence down and drank about half of his glass of whisky. He then turned the music up and tried to lose himself in the sound.

He just couldn't believe some of her reasons. On the one hand, he knew that Annie was going to take more and more of his time and he couldn't escape a certain sense of relief, but, on the other, he and Helen had become very close and he was hoping she might start having sex with him again soon.

The final paragraph contained a plea that he mustn't try to speak to her or see her. It was over.

It seemed his relationship with Helen Greenwood had come to a final and very definite end.

He laughed to himself.

"Where the hell am I going to get my eyes tested now?"

Chapter Fourteen

February 2013

It was a cold Tuesday afternoon in early February when Adrian and Annie left the Harley Street consulting rooms and took a taxi to The Landmark Hotel on Marylebone Road. Once seated, their order for afternoon tea with scones, jam and clotted cream was quickly taken. Neither spoke. As Adrian buttered his scone and scooped out a spoonful of the strawberry preserve, topping it with cream, Annie repeatedly stirred the tea in her cup.

"You know that Honeysuckle and Clare are coming this evening and they're going to want to hear the outcome of today's consultation."

Adrian pretended to be absorbed by his efforts to lift the crumbling food. He finally gave up and used a fork.

"What do you think we should tell them?" he asked.

"The truth."

"Which is, Annie?"

"We both know that when they open me up they're going to find a bit of a mess."

"Mr Spooner didn't quite say that, did he?"

"We'd need to be medically qualified ourselves to understand all the details from my blood tests. Did you hear anything beyond 'cell structure', because I didn't?"

Adrian cut her scone in two and lifted a piece with his fork towards her mouth. She shook her head.

"I've lost over two stone in weight," she said. "I can look in a mirror, Adrian."

"Mr Spooner did seem apprehensive, I must admit."

"I think I'm going to refuse the investigative operation. I know what's wrong without them cutting me open. I can feel myself getting weaker by the day."

"If only you'd eat more, Annie. You were rather short with Mr Spooner. He was merely suggesting that you should try and eat regular meals."

"That's easy for you to say, Adrian. I have no appetite at all. I think it's the body's way of telling me that I've had my allotted number of years. I've been reading up on pain management: it's quite a precise science these days. We need to discuss what will happen to you. You know, after…"

He looked at his wife who was also the mother of his three daughters. His hands edged towards the side of his chair and he held on with all his strength.

"When's Helen bringing William to see me?" she asked.

"Where in the human body would you find the Eustachian tube?"

Mark paused as he completed the washing-up and decided to let the plates drain. He made a cup of coffee for each of them and returned to the sofa where Cate was sitting surrounded by books and print-outs.

"No idea," he said, "but I'm keen to find out." He placed his hand on her inner thigh.

"Even you, Mark, couldn't find anything sexual about this part of my anatomy."

"You know I love a challenge, Cate."

"It connects the middle and inner ear."

He was about to suggest something which, even by his libidinous standards, was weird, but decided to remain attentive.

"It's normally collapsed."

"What is? Do I call the nurse?"

She laughed and slapped his hand, which had crept further up her leg.

"Swallow, Mark."

"Swallow what?"

"Just swallow. Right, well done. You've just cleared your Eustachian tube by equalising the pressure."

"How long did you say this course lasts?"

She stood up and pulled her panties back up to cover her buttocks. As she sat down again, she told him that if she passed every examination at the first attempt it would be a minimum of three years.

"I suppose there must be a lot of tubes for you to learn about," he said.

"The human body has two hundred and six bones and six hundred and forty muscles and that's just for starters."

Mark went back into the kitchen with the empty coffee cups and returned with two glasses and a bottle of champagne.

"Don't get too excited, Cate. It was on special offer."

He poured them each a glass and kissed her softly on the lips before taking a sip.

"Are we celebrating something?" she asked.

"I don't think 'celebrating' is the word I would use, but Silicon Capital is moving to the West End. We feel a fresh start will help everybody."

"Have you seen Adrian?"

"The only thing left to remind us of him is a cardboard box containing the personal items from his desk. He hasn't replied to any of our communications." He stood up and went to look out of the window. There was a white covering of snow on the streets of London. "It's as though he never existed."

Cate tidied her books into a neat pile and carried them over to the table. She turned and walked slowly back towards her partner.

"Did you enjoy not having sex, Mark?"

"I don't enjoy trick questions, Cate!" he laughed.

"It's a genuine question. How did you feel when we just held each other the other night?"

He turned and faced her.

"I'm probably going to regret saying this, but I liked it."

"You weren't frustrated?"

"There was a different kind of satisfaction."

She stood up and went into their bedroom. She returned a few minutes later wearing her dressing gown.

"Mark, do you remember your crazy outburst? We're all monkeys and sex is about genital areas and you just wanted me to bend over for the rest of our lives together."

"Er… I don't think…"

"We should all watch pornographic films because the

191

producers know that they must show sex from the rear because that's what happens in nature and that's great."

"I'm being misquoted, Cate. What I said was that…"

"What you said was that for you sex is all visual, whether I'm wearing suspenders and my nurse's uniform, or whether I agree to go in the shower in my clothes so you can enjoy your wet T-shirt routine."

"So why do you spend so much of your time on your appearance?"

"Because I'm a woman and I want to look my best for you."

"Exactly. You'd be devastated if I told you I wasn't attracted to your body."

She drank her champagne quickly and opened up her dressing gown.

"You do fancy me, don't you, Mark?"

He stood up and wrapped himself around her. As the CD of film scores reached track six and the theme music from 'Doctor Zhivago' played, he briefly waltzed her around the room.

"In all seriousness, I know that I owe our future to you, Cate."

He sat her down and explained that he had also read *Fifty Shades of Grey* and genuinely understood her concerns about their relationship. He said that men are just horny and the sexual urge was fundamental to the co-habiting of two people, but he'd also wanted them to grow closer emotionally. He then said that her decision to change her career and his determination to see his business through its regulatory problems had seemed to be the catalysts to the next stage in their relationship. He then picked her up and took her into their bedroom where he undressed her, before stripping off himself and snuggling down beside her. He put the phone on answer service.

The following morning Adrian received another text message.

Eight days to go. This webb never meant you to escape but don't see red.

He had not slept following the acrimonious meeting with Annie and their two daughters the previous evening. Honeysuckle had completely flipped when she'd realised the implications of her mother's news. She'd variously suggested that they dial 999, call the doctor, telephone the specialist, sue the hospital – before storming from the room to contact her husband.

Clare had edged up to her mother's side and taken her hand.

"Is this what you and Daddy really want, Mummy?" she had asked, tears in her eyes.

He re-read the text message wearily and contacted Michelle, who told him to come to their offices at around midday.

"You look tired, Adrian," she said as she greeted him. "Let's go and have something to eat. Pollett's following something up. He'll be back later."

When he and Michelle returned from a hearty lunch, they found that Pollett was indeed back and engaged in an animated conversation with Adelene. He looked up as soon as he realised there were others present.

"We need to find De Groot. We know he's gone to ground and it's a safe assumption that he's waiting, for reasons only he knows, for the 14 February in eight days' time. He'll be in a secure flat somewhere. We've tried all the hotels and I even visited some of the more obvious ones. We're speaking to a contact of Michelle's in South Africa who's trying to monitor his credit cards. He's using a different mobile phone every time he sends a text, so he knows that we're unable to trace the source. But, as the boss would say, we must think wider. Just ask yourself. What is De Groot doing?"

Adrian looked at Pollett with a growing respect. It was a fair summary of the situation.

"Waiting," he said.

"There are twenty-four hours in each day. How's he occupying himself?"

"He'll be eating, reading, watching television and, no doubt, pursuing his business interests."

"What about sex? From what I've read in the files, Mr De Groot has some rather extreme tastes."

"Er… I should mention that Sonja cut off his penis. That might make things a bit difficult in that area," said Adrian.

"Not ideal from his point of view, I imagine. I've even heard that the Chinese tried to carry out a penis transplant, but it was rejected by the patient!" Pollett said.

"I guess he'll have to take up another hobby," laughed Adrian.

"Not necessarily," responded Pollett. "He's had the end of his penis removed. Although the gland is sensitive, and plays an important part in the sexual act, he's still got all the other bits of equipment. There's no reason why he shouldn't be able to ejaculate."

"Pollett, with respect, this is getting obscene!" chided Michelle.

"And surely," cried out Adelene, "he wouldn't want anybody to see his damaged manhood."

"Unless," said Pollett, "she was being paid a lot of money. Just think about it. Because he's got so little of his penis left he'd have great difficulty masturbating – but his urges would be normal."

"So he'll need lots of help?" Adelene said.

"He can watch porno films," suggested Michelle.

"He'll need more than that. He'll want a woman. But she'll have to be both discreet and understanding."

"I'm lost," said Adrian.

"The most likely way for him to get some sort of satisfaction is by making a girl parade in front of him and tantalise his senses. The right prostitute would know exactly what was required. He'd probably complete the act out of her sight but she'd work with him almost to climax."

"She'd need to be special and she'd be expensive."

"Probably a woman working on her own."

"No. Wrong," said Pollett. "It would have to involve an agency because De Groot would have to explain his situation and special needs to the Madame. He's been here many times before, so we reasoned he'd be likely to go to a place he'd already used."

"Sounds like the needle in the haystack is getting a little bigger," Michelle said.

"When you get my expenses later this month, sister, you'll find that I've spent over six hundred pounds in bribes."

"That'll get you a serious reprimand, brother," she replied.

"No problem. It's also got me the name of the girl who's visiting Nigel de Groot."

Detective Chief Superintendent Khan looked up from the file.

"The Met would like more information. Mr Dexter has caused enough problems already, Sarah."

"I know that, Gov, but the dilemma we have is that we believe the threat from De Groot is real. There is most certainly a 'threat to life' and we must consider all the possible outcomes carefully. If De Groot does attempt a killing, who else could be hurt? Are the Met issuing an Osman warning?"

"Ah! The 1988 case when we were held responsible for not protecting a pupil who was shot by a teacher."

"If I remember correctly, his father was killed in the attack," continued Sarah. "It led to us issuing warnings and I'm sure the Met will do that because they'll want to tell Mr Dexter what can be done to protect him; safe refuge, a hotel or whatever he feels is required to ensure his personal security. We have the problem that it's not on our patch." She paused. "His girlfriend is, but she's not being threatened as far as we are aware." She thought carefully.

"The 14 February deadline is a week away. I've still got three days' compassionate leave owing to me. I want to wrap up the High Street assault charges, which should be done tomorrow. Do you mind if I take a long weekend off?"

This webb never meant you to escape but don't see red. He smiled. "I can sense that Detective Chief Inspector Rudd is on the case!"

"I better be, Gov, because at this moment in time I haven't any idea what it means."

"I rather think that is exactly what Mr De Groot intends, Sarah."

She returned to her office and re-read the whole file from the first time she met Adrian Dexter, through the events that subsequently took place, her own injuries and recovery, to the recent development involving Nigel de Groot.

She decided to focus on what was likely to happen. On 14 February, the South African would try to shoot Adrian and then make good his escape. He would see it as an act of revenge. He was in London, but it was unlikely the police would find him. He had offered a clue to the shooting and, as things stood, that was the only thing they had to go on.

Nigel de Groot was still surprised at the extortionate cost of the flat on the north side of Holborn. But for him location was everything; he'd only need to travel two miles to kill Adrian Dexter.

Alan Joyce stretched out his right leg and tried to stuff a pencil down inside the plaster to scratch the itching skin.

"God knows what it must be like when you've actually broken your leg," he laughed. "Still, it fooled them all!"

The South African listened carefully. He remained confident, because he knew that his plan was a masterstroke. However, the riddle had been a mistake and he regretted his largesse. "Surely somebody will solve it," he said to himself. But now he just needed to focus on completing the entrapment for 14 February. He was due to speak to the BT engineer early the following morning.

The girl arrived at nine o'clock and reassured her client that nobody, except for the Madame, knew where she was. She went into the bathroom and returned a few minutes later wearing a chiffon robe and a thong. She sprayed the room with perfume and put on some soft orchestral music, before pouring him a large scotch and adding several ice cubes. She dimmed the lights and went to lie on the sofa so that she could look at the man opposite her.

"I've brought some special toys so I can satisfy myself," she said.

She began to gyrate and she saw that he had begun to sweat. As on the previous occasion he remained silent. But suddenly he stood up and went over to her. He turned her over and smacked her across her buttocks. He then took off his belt and brought the leather down from a height, smashing it into her skin.

She bit her lips and tasted her own blood. The Madame had warned her what might happen – which was why she was being paid over twelve hundred pounds.

He put his belt back on and sat down.

"Probeer bliksems harder," he sneered.

"Try fucking harder," he repeated.

Chapter Fifteen

February 2013

Honeysuckle and Clare had drunk most of their bottle of apple juice by the time Victoria joined them on a conference call.

"Right," said Honeysuckle, "we need to act now. Mother is of a sound mind and can change her will without a problem."

The loud-speaker on the telephone trembled as Victoria exploded at her sister's opening salvo.

"She's not dead yet, Honeysuckle, and with our love, care and attention she could have a number of years ahead of her. I don't want to be involved with your selfish plotting."

"Victoria," interrupted Clare, "it's a pity you weren't able to be here when we were with Mummy. She was clear in her thinking. She thinks she's dying and, from what we heard, that's what the specialist believes. She's a proud woman and she can't contemplate being opened up and stitched together again. Even if the operation could prolong her life, it wouldn't cure her. And she doesn't want the debilitating treatment after the operation. She has asked us to help her end her days with dignity. She wants to make the most of what time she has left and she wants to see the grandchildren. She and Daddy seem reconciled to her making this decision."

"That's because he'll inherit all her fucking money and then he can have as many girlfriends as he wants! He'll be shacked up with Helen and her baby before Mummy is even in her grave."

Victoria had always been the closest of the three of them to their father but the tide of emotion seemed to be shifting.

"I don't think so," said Clare. "He phoned me last night, quite late on. He'd been drinking, but I'm pretty sure he was telling the truth. Helen's chucked him out. She wants to go it alone."

"Good for her," said Honeysuckle. "By the way, we've agreed Mummy will be cremated."

"Who's decided that?" shouted Victoria. "She's not even dead yet!"

"It makes sense these days, Vicky."

"But we're not focusing on the key issue," continued Honeysuckle. "Mummy is worth around seven million pounds and she hasn't made a will. It'll all go to Dad."

"So what? Daddy is a generous man and I'm sure he'll share it with the family," said Victoria.

"You always were naïve, Victoria," responded her eldest sister. "Are you aware that he's already lost two million pounds of Mummy's money?"

"You're hysterical, Honeysuckle."

"Mummy gave him one million pounds to start his fund for small businesses. Instead, he used the money to buy the South African stake in MXD Capital which is now worthless. Mummy also provided the ransom money and the police have never recovered any of it. She now thinks that she's paying out around five hundred thousand pounds to buy a flat for Helen and William. Dad hasn't yet told her that Helen has ended the relationship."

Victoria said she was too upset and was ringing off. Thirty minutes later, she rejoined the meeting to find that Honeysuckle and Clare had polarised their position.

"Let me sum up for you," said Clare. "We feel it's our responsibility to talk to Mummy and ask her to make a will. That's something any reasonable person would do. In fact, she did mention it when we were with her. The tricky bit is suggesting that her wealth is divided amongst the family. The obvious solution is four ways: Daddy and the three of us."

"Why would she object?" added Honeysuckle. "He's proved that he can't be trusted with money and I'm certain Mummy will want us to be able to bring up our families better because of our inheritance."

"How do you do that without offending her?" asked Victoria. "I'm with you both that she should be encouraged to make a will – but surely her dignity will be savaged if we tell her effectively that we don't trust Daddy."

"Will it?" asked Clare. "She already knows there is a lot of friction between us."

"They've been married many years and the way Mummy stood by him during the Helen issue showed that, in their own way, they're much closer than you might think."

"And does that way include the South African lover, Victoria?"

"I'm putting the phone down. You two have already decided everything. You're playing with me and with Mummy. Do what you will. Just don't include me in your shabby games."

He knew what it would say.

Six days to go. This webb never meant you to escape but don't see red.

He telephoned DCI Rudd on her mobile and, in some surprise, listened to her response. She told him that she'd meet him at Carluccio's in St. John's Wood and he could buy her a late breakfast. An hour later they were sitting at a window table watching local residents sliding around on the icy pavements. They both ordered scrambled eggs on brown toast and coffee. Sarah Rudd went quiet when Adrian told her about Helen's decision to break off their relationship. She was surprised that he hadn't tried to contact her.

Adrian was relieved when she told him she was taking some leave over the weekend to do some work on the text clue. She returned to the De Groot conundrum and asked if he'd had time to consider it further. She was unimpressed when he replied that he was leaving that to Cyberforce Investigations.

"Can I ask you a question please, Sarah?"

"Go ahead."

"Do you think that De Groot really means for me to solve the clue?"

She finished her coffee and waved her arm in the air to signal that she'd like a refill. The waiter came hurrying over, spurred on by the sight of the police car which his customer had left outside the restaurant.

"I've been giving that some serious thinking time," she replied. "De Groot not only intends to shoot you – he's also hurting very badly. With fraudsters like him, self-esteem plays a massive role. You defeated his hostage escapade and, of

199

course, going back a few months, you also stopped him taking control of MXD Capital. I re-read the whole file and you were very smart in the way you defeated him."

She re-arranged the plates in front of her.

"But let's return to your question, Adrian. We simply don't know, but my instinct is that the clue can be solved, and De Groot has written it in such a way that it's possible to unravel it. What surprises me most is that nobody yet has any ideas. We're going round in circles with spider webs and the rest."

"So what do we do now?" he asked.

"I've managed to stir up the Met and they're trying to find De Groot. There's a standard procedure which they're following, but their workloads are such that the necessary manpower is simply not available. I know all about austerity and government debt but the cuts are hurting us badly."

They left the restaurant shortly afterwards and Adrian watched as the detective drove off. He did not see her turn east and head for the home of Helen Greenwood.

Sarah arrived about an hour later, having stopped on several occasions to take phone calls. Helen responded to her knock on the door and had William in her arms when she answered. She made a pot of tea and Sarah asked to use her bathroom. She noticed that the flat was spotless. She checked in the medicine chest and was relieved to find that there were a few standard prescriptions and nothing else.

She went back to the living room, sat down and asked if she could hold William for a few minutes. Helen placed the baby on her shoulder with a cloth to protect Sarah's jacket.

"He's just been winded so fingers crossed," she said.

They chatted about childbirth and Helen showed a special interest in the police officer's recovery from her facial operations. Sarah then gently raised the issue of Adrian and told her that she knew about the break-up of their relationship.

"I never doubted that," said Helen. "My instinct, though, is that you have not come about my decision to bring William up on my own."

"On your own?" questioned DCI Rudd.

"Well, I did have an unexpected visitor last night. Those are the flowers he brought." She pointed to a vase containing twelve red roses. "But that's not the reason why I made my decision," she said hurriedly.

"You don't need to justify yourself to me, Helen."

"I've hurt him rather badly, haven't I?"

DCI Rudd decided that she was not going to tell her about the threat from Nigel de Groot. She wanted to confirm for herself that Helen was not involved, however unlikely. She needed to ensure that she was safe.

"So this new man?" she asked.

"He's taking me to the pub tonight. The lady two flats down is babysitting. I'll have my mobile with me at all times."

"Tell me, Helen – does the word 'webb' mean anything to you?"

"In what context?"

"Any sense."

"No, sorry, not a thing."

DCI Rudd left shortly afterwards and returned to her office. She was preparing to spend Saturday with her family and then to apply herself seriously to the solving of the De Groot clue. She decided to rule out the possibility that De Groot might try to kidnap the baby in order to lure Adrian to a possible shooting scene: there were too many things that could go wrong, and the South African was smarter than that.

Pollett, Adelene and Michelle were drinking coffee. The office manager was becoming concerned at their daily intake and was quietly substituting decaffeinated drinks. This had not stopped the three partners from raising their voices.

"Pollett! Start again, please."

"Only for you, Michelle. We have to find out where De Groot is. That's the best chance we have of stopping him shooting Adrian. He's almost certainly in hiding and he knows exactly how we'll try to locate him. He's careful with his limited use of mobile phones for texting. He's obviously carrying a wad of cash so he doesn't have to use his bank accounts. He's got a gun or probably more than one but he'll have bought them when he was in Northern Ireland. I did spend an evening in some North London pubs and I managed to speak to one of the main dealers, or rather his associate. They checked things out for me and De Groot is not known to them."

"Go on Pollett, please," asked Michelle.

"As I've already told you, we found the hotel in Park Lane where he was staying. While he was there they do not think he had any female visitors. Then I had a stroke of luck. I paid some money over and I was given a number which I could phone to hire a woman. I posed as a London businessman and, after trying and trying, managed to get the woman to see me. I sensed that she did not trust me. I went to see her and explained that I had some strange tastes and was happy to pay the going rate. She then asked me to leave."

"So that was a waste of time and money?" said Michelle.

"As I was leaving, one of the girls who had been sitting around came up to me. She slipped a card into my hand and whispered that this person could help me. There was a photograph on the card. A really hot girl. I phoned her and she was even more guarded than the woman. However, she did agree to meet me – but then she said she was booked last night because 'I have a rather special client to visit'," he mimicked.

"What's her name?" asked Adelene.

"Monique Arendse. That's what's on the card."

"That's a coincidence. A South African sounding name."

"I'm seeing her tonight at the Hotel Russell."

"How much is this costing?" asked Michelle.

"She quoted six hundred pounds."

"Not a chance," Michelle ruled.

"So how are you going to find De Groot, Michelle?"

"Have you given this any serious thought, Pollett?" asked Adelene. "She's expecting to go to bed with you. That's after you've booked the room which will cost another three hundred pounds. And we don't know whether she's even visiting De Groot. It's totally speculative. What happens when you're with her?"

Pollett smiled. "What did you teach me, Adelene? 'Every person has their breaking point.' I need to find hers."

The doctor on call was a locum. He spent nearly half an hour with Annie and then re-joined Adrian in the kitchen. The Labrador was asleep in her basket. He asked Adrian to take him through the recent events involving his wife's health.

"Your wife is saying that she's decided to refuse the surgery suggested by the specialist, Mr Dexter."

"That's the choice she's making. Our daughters are fully informed of her decision."

"And what do you think about that, Mr Dexter?"

Adrian pondered the question carefully. MXD Capital was finished and his investment was lost; his lover and her son had left him; Sonja was in South Africa; two of his daughters blamed him for Annie's condition and a gunman was preparing to shoot him on 14 February.

"The last six months have been difficult. I could have done more."

"That's not what Mrs Dexter is saying."

"Annie is special. Is she suffering very much, doctor?"

"Modern medicines are pretty efficient. I can't be sure, and I've only seen your wife on this occasion, but what I was struck by most was her calmness. The bleeding that you called me out for is probably coincidental to her overall condition. Call me again tomorrow, but I think I've stopped it."

He paused and looked down at his phone messages.

"I don't know whether this will help," he continued, "and I might be wrong. My guess is that your wife has been fighting the inevitable for quite some time. She mentioned that there had been several periods of respite. That can so easily happen. But inside she knew things were wrong. She's now decided that she is living her last few weeks and is finding some peace of mind in that knowledge. I must warn you, though, that it will be short-lived and, when she does start to deteriorate, it will not be easy for her or for you."

"How long, doctor?"

"I can't say. The specialist knows better than us."

"How long, doctor, please?"

"She'll be lucky to celebrate Easter, Mr Dexter."

He had a knife in his right hand. He was wild and unshaven, speaking a foreign language. He was threatening Helen who was trying to hide William behind her back. She knew that there was only one chance of saving their lives: she had to place herself between the hoodie and his intended victim. She tried to reason with him but the words would not come out of her mouth. He was now within three feet of Helen. She tried to use her phone but it was turned off – who had turned the fucking thing off? She shouted again but still no sound. Somebody was selling *The Big Issue* and asked if she wanted a copy. Still he came forward. Somehow he'd now got a much bigger blade. It had blood on it. The barman came over to tell them that it was last orders. She finally managed to grab the tray from the table. Somebody was singing a song. She knew that she was going to die. But she had to save the lives of Helen and William. She remembered that she'd forgotten to ask how much William now weighed. The thug was laughing. Bastard! She'd teach him manners. Finally he lunged with the knife, now inches away from the mother's stomach. She brought the tin tray up and thrust it in front of Helen. The man pushed it to one side and plunged the weapon deep into her midriff.

Detective Chief Inspector Rudd sat upright in bed and screamed.

"It's alright, Sarah. You were dreaming."

She was drenched in sweat and Nick put his arms around her, saying that she was safe now, it was just a nasty dream. He led her into the bathroom, took off her night shirt and put her under the shower. He went to check on their two children and then returned to towel her down. A few minutes later they were in the kitchen drinking English tea; he had put some sugar in hers. Sarah regained her poise remarkably quickly.

"Sorry, darling. I'm being silly. Let's go back to bed."

"Can you remember what you were dreaming about?" he asked.

"Not really. I was defending a mother. All in a day's work," she laughed, albeit half-heartedly.

"Do you think you were wise not to accept their offer of counselling, Sarah?"

"What would that achieve? I know what this is all about. You've only to talk to other officers who have been in dangerous situations. They nearly always ask themselves the same question – if it happens again, what will I do?"

"We're back to when you saved the life of Helen and her baby."

"I hit a gunman. That's all I did, Nick."

"But you're worried that given that situation again you might not react in the way you're trained to."

She put her hands around his face and kissed him.

"Nick. There's no training for this. It's about Sarah Rudd and her true self."

"What are the odds of you facing a similar situation?"

"No bloody idea. But I'll tell you one thing, Nick. There's one hell of a lot of nasty people out there."

Nigel de Groot was lying on his bed feeling sorry for himself. His penis had reacted badly to their last session, but he dared not phone his doctor and break his cover. He grabbed the glass of whisky and farted. The clock said there were just a few minutes to go until midnight: one less day until it was time to shoot Dexter.

He moved himself around on his buttocks until he felt more comfortable and scratched around his scrotum.

He went over the plans which he had so carefully drawn up. Like all the best strategies, it was so simple. Dexter would be there. He would shoot him. He would then escape and be back in South Africa within three weeks. He would join the hunting party and they'd disappear into the national park. He could already feel the sun on his body. He would enjoy the moment of killing for many months ahead.

'Niemand fok met Nigel de Groot nie,' he thought to himself. 'Nobody crosses Nigel de Groot.'

Chapter Sixteen

Saturday 9 February 2013

The text message which arrived was not the one he was expecting. She usually communicated when she knew he'd be in his study late at night.

Missing you dreadfully. No news here. Love you very much. S x

He was being collected at nine o'clock. He'd been with Annie since the early hours. She seemed better in herself and there had been no further bleeding. She was keen that he should leave the house on time. He'd told her about Michelle's new venture and that she had asked for his help on a new case, and Annie was happy to be left. Clare would be arriving in the late morning and, after taking the dog for a walk, she would prepare her mother's lunch: she was bringing in a special fresh seafood bake. He had reassured her that he was wearing warm clothing and that his walking boots were packed in his bag, together with a change of socks, towel and drinks.

The dark blue Mercedes C-Class saloon drew up outside the house on time. Michelle jumped out and handed Adrian a bunch of flowers. She told him to say to Annie that they were with the love of Cyberforce Investigations. Annie was delighted with the bouquet.

Michelle and Adrian were away within minutes. The radio was offering Classic FM and they drove in silence up through North London and onto the M1. The weather had turned milder and the snow had been washed away by the rain showers.

"We'll stop at the services on the M40," Michelle said. "I think it will take two hours and a bit to get there. We'll pick up the route from Oxford."

Adrian broke the ice as they reached the turning west onto the M25.

"Dark blue. Strange choice for a modern woman," he laughed.

"We reason that most of our clients will be Conservative

voters. Business comes first." She accelerated to overtake a series of lorries which were slowing as they climbed the gradient around the Amersham turning. "You may chuckle, Adrian, but these things matter."

"Conforming is important."

"It's all about trust. I arrive in a car which makes the client feel that I'm part of his community." She laughed and turned off the radio. "If my father had been an Austrian automobile entrepreneur, this car would definitely be called a 'Michelle'."

"Are you referring to the bloke who named the car after his daughter?"

"You're on form today, boss. Mercedes was the offspring of Emil Jellinek, who built up Daimler. She was quite a girl. She married two barons and died at the age of 39."

They had now reached the turning north for the M40 and were travelling quickly up towards the Oxford junction.

"Of course, I'm not the boss anymore. How is Cyberforce getting on?"

She found it hard to contain her enthusiasm. She, Adelene and Pollett were merging into a strong unit. She told him about their first success and explained how there were signs of increased levels of new business in the City. They were hoping to hear shortly that they'd won the contract to investigate a Vietnamese mining company whose directors were applying to join the London market.

Following a stop for breakfast at the services, they rounded Oxford and reached the A40. They were now heading west through the English countryside towards Cheltenham.

"Michelle, where are we going?"

"Eskdale's too far," she laughed.

"What's that to do with it?"

"You, Adrian Dexter, need a dose of Michelle's magic treatment. We're going to a place called Bibury. When we get there we're completing an eight and a half mile walk."

She handed him a guide book. He immersed himself in the wonders of walking in the Cotswold Hills – sixteen hundred miles of public footpaths covering the area from Meon Hill at Mickleton in the north to Bath at the southern end.

Bibury was a few miles north east of Cirencester and, as soon as Michelle parked the car, Adrian knew he was going to enjoy his afternoon. He telephoned Clare who was distraught because she had burnt the potato topping on the seafood bake.

Michelle had prepared a healthy pack of oatmeal bars, cheese and juice. Before setting off, they changed their shoes and put on warm clothing. They left the Saxon Church behind them and began following the river Coln, passing the cottages in Arlington Row. After a little over one mile, they picked up Akeman Street, an old Roman Road.

It was not an arduous trail and soon they were side by side.

"Have you heard from Nigel de Groot?" she asked, as they climbed over a style.

"Nearly every day," replied Adrian, before laughing rather nervously. "He must have overslept this morning because I haven't heard from him yet. Anything your end?"

She told him about Pollett and his meeting that evening with a possible lead. She decided not to give away too many details because she did not want to raise his hopes. She also had serious doubts about the strength of Pollett's enthusiasm for Monique Arendse, even if she turned up. But Adelene had urged her to support him, despite the ever-increasing expenditure.

They were now deep in the Coln Valley and beginning the second half of the route. After stopping for something to eat and drink, they followed the river all the way back to Bibury. The sun was drifting away in the western sky and it was becoming colder. They increased their pace. Adrian told Michelle about DCI Rudd's involvement and her doubts that the London police would make any progress.

"I've given the matter a lot of thought. As you know, I climb mountains and I've found that often, if you have a problem, the physical exercise allows you to clear your mind. Often the solution will appear from nowhere quite late in the day."

"Is that what today is about? I'm really enjoying myself but I can't imagine we're going to solve the question of Nigel de Groot in the Cotswold Hills…"

"Nigel de Groot is a violent and vicious man who is going to shoot you on 14 February. He's probably lying low in London.

He's almost certainly armed with whatever weapon he needs. He'll have planned this meticulously and he's confident that he'll escape. He has given you a clue to solve because he wants you to suffer. As each day passes, he reminds you that the shooting is getting ever nearer. He is defeating the combined detective skills of Cyberforce Investigations and DCI Rudd."

After passing Court Farm they crossed the river and could see the village where the car was parked in the distance.

"But there is one piece of the jigsaw puzzle that really doesn't fit for me, Adrian." She stopped and turned to face him.

"Nigel de Groot does not make many mistakes and my guess is that my summation is pretty much correct. I therefore ask myself one key question."

"Which is what?"

"How does he know where you'll be on 14 February?"

"You haven't eaten your seafood bake, Mummy. Were the prawns cooked properly?"

As she lifted the tray off the bed she looked at her mother and smiled.

"Do you want to have a sleep now?"

Annie was trying to pull some tissues from their cardboard container. Clare was surprised by how little strength she seemed to have in her hands. She sat down on the side of the bed, pulled a few out and gave them to her mother.

"Can you stay for a few moments, Clare? There's something I want to talk to you about. But, first, please tell me what's happened to Helen and William."

She lay back with her head on the pillows as she heard that she would never see William again.

"Oh well, I thought that might happen. Helen loved Adrian for his position. It's ridiculous that she'd want to spend her life with an older man. As soon as MXD folded I wondered if she'd move on. Can you get me her details, please?"

"Is that a good idea, Mummy? Why not let matters rest now?"

"That's not the reason I want them, Clare."

Annie then explained to her daughter that she had contacted a solicitor who would be coming to the house in the next few days with a draft will.

"It's all quite simple really. My financial adviser has provided me with a statement of my affairs. I want him and the solicitor to be my executors."

"But surely there must be a family member as well. That's what Honeysuckle is expecting."

"There will be, dear. I'll be nominating Victoria. She's very level-headed, you know."

She moved around in the bed to ease her aches. "I'm worth around six million pounds. I'm leaving the three of you one and a half million each. There will be a number of smaller amounts for the grandchildren, but those will be put into trust until they're twenty-one. Helen and William will receive two hundred thousand pounds."

Clare gasped and quickly added up the numbers.

"That leaves about half a million pounds, Mummy. Is that for tax purposes?"

"No. The six million is after tax is paid. The balance is five hundred and fifty thousand pounds. That goes to your father. He also gets my share of the house."

"Have you…?"

"I'm of sound mind, Clare. I've checked carefully. There is no way that the contents of the will can be challenged by anybody."

"Does Daddy know about this?"

"He'll find out when the will is read."

"Has Honeysuckle been trying to influence you?"

Annie snorted. "When she hears that she's getting one and a half million pounds, nothing else will matter to her."

"What about Daddy?"

"My belief is that your father will be getting on a plane flying south."

The Bloomsbury area of London contains Russell Square Gardens, which are overlooked by the Hotel Russell. Its Victorian facade reminds local residents of a bygone era, while the three hundred and seventy-three bedrooms accommodate business people and tourists. The grand Tempus Restaurant is said to have been inspired by the dining hall on the Titanic.

They were to meet at seven o'clock in the evening in the expensive and elegant lounge bar. Pollett recognised Monique Arendse the moment she entered, if only because of her dazzling looks and long, black hair. She was carrying a raincoat over her arm. He showed her to an armchair and responded to her request for a large vodka and tonic.

"What do I call you?" she asked.

"Do you need to call me anything?" he asked.

"I prefer a name."

"Pollett."

"Pollett?"

"Pollett."

Their conversation continued awkwardly and, before too long, she asked him if they should go upstairs to his room. She seemed puzzled that he just wanted to talk, but responded to his ready wit and charm. She refused to say much about herself. Any questions about her occupation were ignored – although she did seem prepared to discuss transportation around London and the dangers of travelling on tube trains late at night.

He tried a number of times to raise the subject of her other clients, but she either stayed silent or changed the subject. She refused a second drink and he realised she was growing more uncomfortable. He decided he must act. Pollett stood up and guided her to the lift. They got out on the fifth floor and paused outside one of the doors. He opened it and let her go first into the bedroom, whereupon she said that she needed to use the bathroom. When she re-appeared she had changed into very little and asked for her fee. When Pollett handed her a brown envelope she tore it open and proceeded to count the notes inside.

She went over to the bed and lay down.

"I need to explain something," he said.

She sat up and tensed.

"This is my first time outside my marriage."

212

"Happens to a lot of men," she said.

"No. That's not what I mean. The truth is embarrassing."

"I've heard everything."

"I can't get an erection," he said. "I don't want sex with you. All I ask is that you help me to manage one."

"I can certainly do that," said Monique.

"What do we do?" asked Pollett.

"Get undressed and come and lie by me."

"Ok, but I don't want you to touch me."

As he climbed onto the bed, he knew he must use the technique that he had read up on to its full effect. He would not be looking at a woman. He could only see a teddy bear. He continually counted numbers forwards and backwards in his mind. He had also placed a pin in his scrotum and he found that by moving his position he could inflict quite a lot of pain on himself.

She started to move around provocatively. She played with her breasts and then moved her hands downwards. She stroked the inner flesh of her thighs and then put her fingers inside herself. She then turned over and showed her buttocks. Pollett was surprised to see stripes across the dark flesh. His penis remained limp.

He laughed out loud and suggested that she needed to work on some new techniques. She began to get angry.

"Why aren't you turned on?" she asked.

"Don't blame me. You don't stimulate me."

She began to repeat her routine and pulled up a chair. She sat down, opened her legs and started moaning. The sweat was now running down her body and her face was creased with frustration.

"Let me touch you," she pleaded.

"I've told you that's not what I want," said Pollett. "I want you to help me grow."

"That's what I'm fucking well trying to do!"

Pollett was surprised that she had cracked so early on. He was thinking about Adelene's dictum that every person has a breaking point: Monique had reached hers at a much earlier stage than he had expected.

"I doubt if you could get a horny teenager excited," he chided.

"Fuck off! You're ill. You need help. I'm going!"

"I'll tell them at the agency that you're bloody hopeless. I'll suggest they keep you for Middle Eastern eunuchs."

"This isn't about me, you pervert. Yeah, you probably need little boys."

"I need a woman who's got fucking sex appeal. You're just boring. You'll never excite anybody."

"I'm through with this. You're wasting my time."

"When did you last get a man going, Monique?"

"Since you ask, you prick, I did amazing things just the other day with a client who hadn't even got his full…"

"Full what, Monique? What clever thing did you do because you completely failed tonight." He paused. "Maybe you should give me his name so I can ask for a reference!"

Tears of anger and frustration welled in her eyes.

"I can't and I won't. Anyway, he's leaving Holborn shortly. He doesn't want to see me again."

"Where in Holborn, Monique?"

"Off Red Lion Street, but he'll be gone. Oh God, I shouldn't have said that."

She stormed into the bathroom and re-appeared a few minutes later fully-dressed. She left, slamming the door behind her.

Pollett returned to the offices in Old Broad Street fifty minutes later. Adelene gave him a big hug, and even Michelle said congratulations.

"He's in London, in Holborn, near to Red Lion Street, and he's preparing to leave. That should be enough to interest DCI Rudd and her Met friends."

As they walked away from the office, Michelle hailed a taxi and left her two colleagues walking away together.

"Fancy a drink?" asked Pollett.

"Sure thing," replied Adelene.

A little later, in the pub, she placed her hand on Pollett's leg.

"Do you think we should just make sure that this loss of an erection is only a temporary matter?" she asked.

"That sounds like a very good idea – but would you mind if I removed the pin first? It's bloody painful," said Pollett, as he started to undress Adelene in his mind.

DCI Rudd was not amused to be awakened at one o'clock on a Saturday night, but she allowed Michelle to go through the evening's events and then asked how this new information helped Adrian.

"Surely you can arrest this Monique and make her tell you the address where she saw this man?"

"Arrest her for what?"

"She knows where De Groot is."

"Where are your facts supporting that? You have no hard material evidence here. Yes, it might be that De Groot is somewhere in Holborn and perhaps in the Red Lion Street vicinity, but these brothels have very expensive lawyers acting for them. I'd be in danger of being sued for harassment."

"But she says she knows where he is."

"She'd just been humiliated by your colleague. She was ready to say anything. I'm sorry, Michelle. I know you're trying to help, but let's talk in the morning."

Sarah Rudd hung up the phone, turned over and shut her eyes. She felt her husband's hand around her waist.

"Not now, Nick, please. I have an early start tomorrow."

Chapter Seventeen

Tuesday 12 February 2013

Two days to go. This webb never meant you to escape but don't see red.

'Shrove' is the past tense of the English word 'shrive', which refers to the obtaining of absolution for one's sins. Its more practical application is when it's attached to 'Tuesday' and the eating of pancakes. The taking in of rich food is advised before beginning the forty abstemious days of Lent.

The five people around the table, however, who were each reading a piece of paper placed in front of them, were restricted to coffee, water and plain biscuits.

"This arrived by text message on Adrian's phone at six o'clock this morning," said Michelle.

DCI Sarah Rudd was both angry and nervous. Officially she was off-duty and taking two days of her compassionate leave entitlement as holiday. She had endured a difficult Sunday which included a rare and personal argument with Nick. They both knew what it was about, but neither would give way and come out and discuss the bedroom tensions that were eating them up. She was annoyed with herself that she'd allowed Adrian to talk her into attending this meeting.

She was also concerned that she was becoming too involved in the situation. She knew that other officers should be taking responsibility but, with police budget cuts and reduced resources, and although the Met was taking the potential threat to life seriously, she held out little hope that Nigel de Groot would be stopped in his attempt to kill Adrian.

She had refused to meet at Cyberforce Investigations and was relieved when Adrian arranged to use a conference room in offices located in Lombard Street near to the Bank of England, obtained with the help of a former colleague.

Adelene was going over and over the events which had taken place on Saturday night between Pollett and Monique Arendse. The following day they had trailed around the Red

217

Lion Street area hoping to spot Nigel de Groot. It proved fruitless and frustrating, and eventually they had called it quits and gone home together.

Michelle had greatly enjoyed her visit to the Cotswold Hills with Adrian. On Sunday she had reflected on their discussions and been left with the single question concerning how De Groot would know where Adrian was on Thursday. She knew that he didn't have any appointments and would not be seeing Helen: that was in the past. She had added this conundrum to the list of issues to be raised in this meeting.

Pollett was lost in his thoughts.

'She was so near to telling me the name,' he was thinking to himself, at the same time wondering whether he could have achieved more. Monique's capitulation had come so quickly. She'd then left in a panic and now her mobile phone was always switched off. All his calls to the Madame were refused. He felt deflated despite the words of praise from his colleagues.

Adrian fiddled with the piece of paper in front of him. He was trying really hard not to let Nigel de Groot's threats get to him, but the truth was that he was scared to pieces. The continuing tensions at home and his worries over Annie's deteriorating state of health were adding to his stress. He was not sleeping for more than an hour or two at any one time, and he was missing his communications with Sonja; she had not texted him for the last two days.

Michelle coughed, tapped the table top and thanked DCI Sarah Rudd for joining them. She summed up the situation and suggested that the purpose of getting together was to review their progress and to try and work out what might happen on Thursday.

"We are agreed that De Groot is in London. With the success that Pollett had at the Hotel Russell, we can be fairly sure that he's in the Red Lion Street area and most probably in an apartment."

"You're placing a great reliance on the words of a prostitute," said DCI Rudd. "She sounded very frightened from what Pollett has said. It might be a reasonable assumption, but we must keep our minds open to all possibilities."

"With respect, detective, I was there," snapped Pollett. "She was relating to me. I'm certain that I've got nearer to solving this than anybody else."

"But Pollett," said Michelle, "can we agree that with two days to go it's unlikely we're going to find him?"

Three heads nodded in agreement. Sarah did not offer an opinion.

"We are also fairly certain that any attempt to harm Adrian will take place on Thursday. De Groot started fifteen days ago and in two days' time it's St. Valentine's Day. Shall we, for the sake of this meeting, commit to the attack taking place on Thursday?"

Three people indicated their support for this proposition.

"I'm sorry to be so blunt, Adrian, but we're also fairly sure that De Groot's intention is to try and shoot you."

"So why doesn't Adrian go into hiding for the day?" suggested Adelene.

Her question hung in the air as it was given due consideration by her two partners.

"What would be the point?" said Adrian. "What would happen the day after? We're not absolutely certain it will be Thursday. I can't go on like this. It's like living with a death sentence."

Sarah realised that De Groot had succeeded completely in terrorising Adrian. It was a very clever game.

She had sent *Hierdie webb het nooit bedoel dat jy onstsnap en nie rooi sien nie*, to the police in Johannesburg. They had replied that the Afrikaans was perfect, but they had no idea what it meant.

"We really only have one option. We must try to solve the clue that De Groot has given us. Adelene, please read it out again."

"*Two days to go. This webb never meant you to escape but don't see red.*"

"Why take De Groot seriously when he can't even spell 'web' correctly?" Pollett laughed.

"You've already cracked that one, haven't you, Pollett? If you're so fucking clever how come you haven't solved the riddle and put us out of our fucking misery?"

He looked wounded at the tongue-lashing from his girl-friend.

Michelle quickly moved on.

"We've run each word through the computer and we have spent hours reading through all the results. It's the classic needle in the haystack."

"Got it. I've fucking solved it!" yelled Pollett.

All eyes turned to him.

"It's so shitting obvious."

"Pollett! Stop using your vile expletives. I've told you before."

"You didn't stop her," he said, glaring at Michelle and pointing at Adelene. "It's about a spider's web. What in London looks like a spider's web?"

The four other members of the meeting looked at him in expectation.

"The London Eye! That's the spider's web. It looks like one; it's built to resemble one; it's where De Groot will try to kill Adrian! We must get them to stop it."

Adelene had now googled the tourist attraction and started reading from the Wikipedia page.

"It was inaugurated on 31 December 1999 and started operating on 9 March 2000. It was called the Millennium Wheel but is now known as the EDF Energy London Eye. It's at the western end of Jubilee Gardens on the South Bank of the Thames. It's four hundred and forty-three feet tall and has a diameter of three hundred and ninety-four feet. Pollett, it says here that it resembles a bicycle wheel."

"Yes, but it could be a spider's web!" enthused Pollett. "De Groot's not that stupid to make it too easy for us."

"Does it say how many people can ride on it?" asked DCI Rudd.

"Hang on. There are thirty-two ovoidal capsules which each hold twenty-five passengers. That's er…"

"Eight hundred people," she said.

She looked at Pollett. "How do you shoot an individual who's one of hundreds. How, where and when?"

Pollett stuttered and tried to suggest that a few well-placed police marksmen could look out for the South African killer.

"Pollett," said DCI Rudd, "are you aware of what Red Lion Street is associated with?"

"It's in Holborn. It…"

"In the last year an unknown person called Captain Shame has been writing what he calls 'an illustrated erotic blog'. He suggests that 'impossible things happen in Red Lion Street'." Sarah Rudd paused to take a sip of water.

"He stopped writing it in October 2012, having completed fifty chapters. It is vile pornography with awful illustrations. There are mostly individual sections featuring various women and their adventures."

She paused and looked firstly at Michelle and then at Pollett. Adelene was googling Red Lion Street and holding her hand to her lips.

"When you set up Cyberforce Investigations, if I understand it correctly, you were proposing to offer a corporate finance service. You're completely out of your depth here – and straying far too near to breaking the law. This Monique Arendse, which, incidentally, is not her name because we've investigated her as fully as we can, has made a complete fool of you."

DCI Sarah Rudd stood up and looked at Michelle.

"My advice to you is to stick to your knitting." She left the room and closed the door behind her.

"Mark, can I ask you a question?"

It was getting late in the evening. He'd been reading the draft financial report for Silicon Capital's next board meeting for what felt like a long time. Cate seemed to be ploughing her way through pages of nursing notes. He had not spotted that she'd slipped into the bedroom and changed into a different outfit.

"I know. There are a hundred and ten bones and five hundred and fifty muscles in the human body. Where is…"

She pretended to sulk.

"You don't remember anything I tell you. Wrong on both counts, actually – but that's not what I want to ask you."

"Go on. I'm ready."

"I'm going to lie flat on my back on the sofa. Where on my body is 'Ophelia's flap'?"

"Pardon?"

"'Ophelia's flap'. Where is it? It's a very simple question Mark. You must have heard of it."

"Am I allowed to ask questions?"

"Perhaps one or two."

"It's on your body?"

"It's part of me."

He knelt down beside her, put his hand on her midriff and asked if he should move up or down.

"That's a difficult one to answer. Perhaps you should move it around a bit."

"I'd prefer to move it downwards…"

"I'm sure you would, but that's not where 'Ophelia's flap' is, I'm afraid."

"I'll go up then."

He moved his hand towards her breast only to be told that he'd passed the flap. He realised that she'd changed into a silk blouse. He ran his palm over the soft, smooth material.

"You've just passed it again!" she squealed in delight.

He repeated the process and discovered within the material something quite firm. He felt around. It was a… a what?

"You've found it, you clever man."

He used his fingers to undo the button of a pocket on her blouse.

"You're opening 'Ophelia's flap'!" she cried.

He pressed down and found something metallic.

"Pull it out!" she gasped.

He was now holding an ancient copper key.

Cate stood up and straightened her clothes. She went into the kitchen and returned with two glasses of champagne. She handed one to her lover.

"What day is it on Thursday?" she asked.

"No, no, no, Cate. You can't catch me out. There are flowers already ordered to arrive on the morning and I'm taking you for a St. Valentine's Day dinner in the evening."

"I'm sure you are, Mark, and it'll be wonderful. Only this year you're coming second. Please drink a toast with me and then sit down. I'm going to read you something."

He followed her instructions and watched as she took a piece of paper out of a drawer. She began to read.

"To-morrow is Saint Valentine's Day,
All in the morning betime,
And I a maid at your window,
To be your Valentine.
Then up he rose, and donn'd his clothes,
And dupp'd the chamber-door:
Let in the maid, that out a maid
Never departed more."

"In case you're interested that's Ophelia, in Hamlet."

"So you made it up, this bloody flap."

"You're so gullible!" she laughed. "Now, what are you going to do with the key?"

"I could open something?" he suggested.

He noticed that she was making exaggerated eye movements towards a certain area of the room. He went over and discovered a wooden casket. He inserted the key and lifted open the lid – inside was a red cushion and, on top of the cushion, was… a gold ring.

Cate took the jewellery out of the container. She held the middle finger of his left hand and slipped the ring onto it. It fitted to perfection.

"Mark. I want you, every day of the week, to look at this and know that I am always with you. No woman will ever love a man as much as I love you."

An hour later, when they were in bed together, he removed her hand from between his legs and sat up.

"How did you know my ring size? It fits so perfectly."

Cate chuckled.

"It's amazing what a girl can do in the middle of the night," she said as she returned her hand to its intended position.

Nigel de Groot smiled and put his hand on Monique Arendse's arm.

"Go over to the table and bring me the leather bag."

She brought him the bag, whereupon he opened the zip and took out two fifty pound notes, which he gave to the surprised girl.

He was elated. Together, they had managed to give him fulfilment. She had learned from the previous occasion – she didn't want a repeat of the lashing – and, after an hour's provocative stimulation, he had finally managed to reach a climax. To her surprise he had encouraged her to watch. Under his breath, he was laughing at a certain vengeful South African woman who thought she had put an end to his sexual days.

Monique had slipped on her clothes and coat and was about to leave. She hesitated and then turned and faced her client.

"There was a man."

"Ja. 'n Man. So?"

"I think he was asking about you."

Nigel de Groot's attitude changed immediately. He leaped up, grabbed her by her arms and threw her on the bed. He removed her coat and tore off her dress. He then turned her over, took his belt out of his trousers and lashed down on her buttocks.

She cried out and then again as a second beating was applied with even greater force. He then made her kneel down in front of him and told her that she would be slapped every time she hesitated with her answers.

Within five minutes he knew the whole story. Monique collapsed in a heap on the floor.

"What name did you say?"

"Pollett," she sobbed.

"What sort of name is that?"

"That's his name," pleaded Monique.

"Where's his number?"

"On my mobile."

"Lees dit hardop vir my," he instructed. "Read it out to me."

Nigel de Groot now had all the information he needed.

Clare and Honeysuckle were talking over a coffee in St John's Wood. They were in complete agreement.

"We get one and a half million each and he gets half a million and the house. I would say that's much more than he deserves." The elder sister rubbed her hands together.

"Can we stop the two hundred thousand pounds to Helen?"

"Forget it, Honeysuckle. It seems to matter to Mummy. She's built up quite a rapport with her and the baby."

"I hate the thought that Victoria is the family executor."

"Well, you won't change Mummy's mind on that one, so you better get used to it." Clare paused before continuing with her further news.

"The doctor was called yesterday. The bleeding has started again and he wanted to hospitalise her. Mummy flatly refused and Daddy was just silent."

"She hasn't got too long to live, has she?" said Honeysuckle with a tremble in her voice.

"That seems to be the way she wants it," replied Clare.

"But we can force the issue if we want to. Daddy's totally vacant at the moment. It's up to us to phone the doctor and insist she goes to hospital."

"She'll refuse to go and, anyway, I'm not sure we've got the right to do that."

"Victoria, the bloody executor! How could she do that to us?" mused Honeysuckle before deciding to phone her husband.

Helen picked up her mobile phone and started to text a message.

She shuddered as she recalled the events of the previous evening. She looked over at William who was wearing his tiny Arsenal Football Club top. He was asleep after she had fed him, winded him and put him carefully back into his cot. He looked so peaceful. She almost wished he was awake so she could cuddle him.

The Area Manager had made it quite clear to her. If she wanted to retain his support, and possibly her position as branch manager, she should consider his suggestion that they went back to his flat before he returned her home. Apart from the practicality that her babysitter had asked that she be back before ten o'clock, she had no wish to develop their relationship at this early stage.

She thought that she handled the situation well. She had kissed him gently on his cheek, giving a hint that the future might hold some promise for him. But he'd slammed the door, screeched away and sped down the road. She knew that the damage was done.

She sat and wondered if she had any right to contact Adrian. She knew that she had treated him badly, but he'd changed and she'd felt that he needed space. She had enjoyed meeting Annie and was amazed by her intuition and understanding.

She picked up the mobile again and started to text. She guessed that he'd be in his study listening to music. She deleted her words. She waited for a few minutes and then tried once more. Again she pressed the delete button. She threw the phone away from herself and shut her eyes.

Chapter Eighteen

Wednesday 13 February 2013

Hierdie webb het nooit bedoel dat jy onstsnap en nie rooi sien nie.

Operating within the world's financial centres are human beings, usually, but not exclusively, male and either acting alone or in pairs (with ludicrously expensive tax accountants not far away in the background). Their sole objective in life is to make money. The quantum is immaterial because they are worth so much, by normal standards, that the actual value has long lost any meaning.

It is, however, the actual making of the money that is their elixir of life. They relish the opportunity to outsmart the pack. Corporate raiders, sometimes called asset strippers, have no problem destroying companies, jobs and, on occasions, lives; they have no social conscience and, in many cases, no morality at all. They are nearly always far too smart to be caught out by the police, the fraud investigators and/or the financial regulators. Those that are, like Bernie Madoff in the United States, effectively give themselves up because their game has lost any real adrenalin and they are bored. For them, it has been too easy to outplay the conventional operators.

Money itself buys them a way of life that most people can only imagine or read about in a Jackie Collins novel. But, after a time, even that becomes routine. One waiter bowing is no different to another showing dutiful respect.

Nigel de Groot was of this exact type except that, for him, money was just a conduit. His real joy in life was killing people, and he was very good at it. His only problem with the police had been when he strayed into financial fraud. He was not quite so astute in that sector.

But if asked to kill a person, he was at the head of the queue for success rates. He always worked alone and relied on no other person with any interconnecting information.

He killed for the sake of killing. It gave him an orgasm of huge proportions: it meant that he was superior. He could remember every single person he had extinguished. The one double murder he had attempted persuaded him never to try that again. The seconds lost as he switched the gun from one victim to the other almost cost him his escape route. It was down to seconds in nearly all cases because most of his targets were well-protected.

He had decided to kill Adrian Dexter purely because of his golden rule that nobody ever gets the better of him. He had also decided he must suffer and he'd achieved this by the seventeen days' build-up.

When the authorities later reviewed the events of 14 February, the one feature that infuriated them was the simplicity of the plan. It was De Groot and it was brilliant. He knew that there would be CCTV everywhere and so he'd decided to use the cameras to help him escape.

During the morning of 13 February, four different-sized BT vans were stolen across the south-east of England. In each case the person involved had no knowledge of anybody else. They knew where they had to be and at what time. They parked up and changed the number plates. Then they waited. They made one phone call using a public facility in a pub or elsewhere. They spoke three words and did not wait for a reply. They were paid twenty thousand pounds each, split half in advance and the balance when De Groot had left the country. They each committed not to undertake any criminal activity for two months after the event. De Groot's underworld reputation ensured they would keep to this restriction. The authorities could not understand how British Telecom could lose four vans without knowing, but the truth was that such was their fleet size, and the issues of absenteeism and sick leave, that they were often chasing their tails.

The other key player in the events that were to take place was a council employee who needed some money quickly. He had tried to get through a short-term cash crisis by taking out a 'same day' loan. He was sinking deeper and deeper into trouble and was surprised when he was offered the chance to recoup his losses.

There was no aspect of the killing of Adrian Dexter that Nigel de Groot had not considered. It would hit the headlines and the media pack would slaughter the local police when it became known that there had been a series of warnings. It would be, according to De Groot himself, the murder of the decade.

Annie finished the session with her solicitor and lowered her head back onto the pillow. She accepted that he had a job to undertake but it had taken so long. The setting up of the trusts for the grandchildren was more complex than she had thought and the settling of the provisions, to be included to prevent one of her daughters losing half of her wealth in a divorce, was difficult. The solicitor was uncomfortable with the two hundred thousand pounds for Helen and William and, in the end, Annie was forced to agree that all the money went to Helen.

"I guess I'll have to trust her," she decided.

He collected his papers and prepared to leave.

"Is there anything else we can do for you, Mrs Dexter?"

"I'm very fortunate, thank you. I have a husband and three loving daughters who make sure I have everything I need."

As she heard him leave through the front door and her daughter return to the lounge, she buried her head under her pillows. Annie knew that the solicitor did not necessarily agree with what he had just been told.

Annie decided that all her tasks would be complete once the final copy of the will had been signed. She had spoken to the doctor without Adrian knowing and she was to receive a visit from a pain management consultant. That would take place the following week. She mentioned to the doctor that she thought that Adrian seemed under stress; more so than usual. The doctor suggested that she try to persuade him to come down to the surgery. "We'll check him over," he said. "It will give me the chance to assess his blood pressure and his cholesterol levels."

"I think he'd rather be shot first," Annie had laughed.

Detective Chief Superintendent Khan nodded in approval as DCI Rudd confirmed that she was back on full-time policing duties.

"I spoke to the Met, Sarah. They're treating the threat very seriously. However, they can only allocate a few officers to the case and, in fairness, we all know that the 'lone wolf' is a security nightmare."

He paused as he offered her a plate of biscuits. She refused and continued drinking her cup of coffee.

"Only last month," he continued, "I was reading that, for Obama's inauguration in Washington, there were eight thousand police officers and thirteen thousand five hundred troops protecting the President and he was in 'The Beast'."

"The what, sir?"

"His armoured Cadillac. It can't move that quickly because there's so much armour on it."

He was warming to his subject.

"Do you remember that wonderful Clint Eastwood film, 'In the Line of Fire'?"

"No, not really my scene," she replied.

"Eastwood played the part of a secret service agent, Frank Horrigan, who blamed himself for allowing the assassination of President Kennedy. He redeemed his reputation by saving the life of the current President. John Malkovich played the part of the 'lone wolf'. He had a great name: Mitch Leary. He was brilliant."

"What happened?"

"It was a bit of Hollywood-style heroics. Eastwood threw himself in front of the President and took the assassin's bullet on his vest." He laughed. "An unlikely event, but good fun nevertheless."

"I think I'll give that one a miss, thanks, Sir."

"Your husband might like it. Eastwood's courage wins him the heart of Rene Russo and they sail off into the sunset together."

She smiled at the Chief Superintendent.

"I think I'll keep him to Harry Potter films, Sir. Renee Russo might be too much for his blood pressure!"

Alan Joyce had spent the best part of two days with Nigel de Groot, preparing for this moment. They had gone over the script repeatedly and rehearsed for all eventualities. Finally, at around three o'clock in the afternoon, he made the call. As he did so, he looked through the window of the apartment and saw that the snowfall of earlier in the day was turning to slush as the south-westerly winds brought heavy rain showers. The problem would be the freezing temperatures expected later in the evening. He resented having to walk on the dangerous pavements using crutches to protect his 'plastered' leg.

"Mr Dexter?" Alan Joyce asked, putting on an authoritative government-style voice when his call was answered. Having received the expected confirmation, he continued: "My name is Robin Pemberton-Roche. I work in the Treasury. May I ask for a few moments of your time?" Again he received an affirmative response. "Mr Dexter, I'm calling you on your mobile. Would it be possible to call you on a landline? Ah! You're at home. The number would be helpful."

A few moments later, the two men were speaking to each other, with Adrian sitting in his study in St. John's Wood.

"Mr Dexter. I really do appreciate your courtesy. I won't take up too much of your time. Can I please complete the intro-duction? As I said, I'm Robin Pemberton-Roche and I'm part of the Enterprise Team within the Treasury. We focus on the provision of equity finance for small and medium-sized busi-nesses throughout the United Kingdom. I'm led to believe that this is a subject close to your heart. Before you answer, let me say that we've monitored your excellent work at MXD Capital for some years."

Adrian interrupted to explain the present situation with his former company.

"Yes, yes, we know that, but we don't involve ourselves in those matters. We've heard that you're setting up a fund for investing in smaller companies. We are interested to learn more and to see if we can help."

The next few minutes were taken up with a rather full expla-nation of Adrian's ideas for the use of the one million pounds.

231

He did not mention that the money had already been used for other purposes.

"Of course, the Minister knows of you and your splendid contribution to the work of the company financial sector. He holds regular breakfast meetings to which we invite people of your stature and experience. The next one with a space available is in the third week of April. Would you like me to send you an invitation?"

Adrian found it difficult to temper his enthusiasm. For years, he had felt that his work as a corporate financier working with smaller companies was undervalued by the City.

"That's terrific, Mr Dexter. I'll pop something in the post. Look, this is a little presumptuous of me but I'm sure you'll understand my candidness. It is rather short notice, I know, but we have a breakfast meeting tomorrow morning and, in the last hour, I've had a cancellation. One of the guests can't reach us from Somerset. I've been meaning to contact you for some time anyway. I know that you're a busy man, but it crossed my mind that you might... oh, you can? That's marvellous. You've just saved my career!"

Adrian laughed dutifully.

"It's too late to get the invitation to you by post, but we're at 1 Horse Guards Road. I suggest you drive because we'll want you here at seven-fifteen and we've recently had several guests who were late because they couldn't find an early morning taxi. The Minister dictates that we start bang on seven-thirty – and I have to make sure his bacon is cooked as he likes it!"

Alan Joyce could barely stifle his laughter.

"Just drive under the Arch and turn left into Horse Guards Road." He hesitated as he responded to the next question. They had discussed in great detail the possibility that Dexter could choose to drive down Whitehall. That, however, would take him into Parliament Square and he would have to find Great George Street. It was unlikely that he would select such a route. They intended to place the thought firmly in his mind that he should go under Admiralty Arch.

"Yes, past Spring Gardens and left at the lights. You'll see the security men about two hundred yards down on your left and I'll have a parking space reserved for you. Can you give me your vehicle registration number, please? … GK 12 and the letters… Thanks, Mr Dexter. Please don't speed. There are cameras everywhere in the area. We have to keep the PM safe."

The third break for laughter tested Adrian's stamina but he was elated by this development.

"Well once again, Mr Dexter, thank you so much. I'm person-ally really looking forward to meeting you. Can I just repeat, and do forgive me, the Minister must start at seven-thirty so we'll expect to see you driving under Admiralty Arch at around seven o'clock."

As Alan ended the call, he realised he was shaking. Nigel de Groot enveloped him in a massive bear hug.

"Wel gedaan, my geleerde vriend."

"You have done very well, my aristocratic friend," he repeated.

Adrian immediately smelt a rat. He had given up years ago believing anybody would really take an interest in the smaller company sector. The press and the politicians much preferred investment bankers, hedge fund managers and Russian oli-garchs. He redialled the number on his mobile phone and found himself talking to Robin Pemberton-Roche.

"Yes Mr Dexter. I was just wondering where Jeila, my PA, was so I answered the phone myself." He listened to Adrian Dexter's question. "Yes. Absolutely. I'm sure the Minister will welcome a short presentation from you. What area will you be covering?" He nodded as he evaluated the reply. "Gosh. How exciting. A world initiative. A junior stock market that elimin-ates investor risk." He held the receiver away from his ear. "Right. Not 'eliminates' but lessens. Terrific. Can you say your piece in around four minutes?" He heard the reply. "A hand-out. That is really good of you. I can photocopy it here if that'll help. There are nine other guests." He wiped the sweat off his forehead as Adrian Dexter finally finished their conversation.

Alan Joyce slumped back into his chair and Nigel de Groot remained silent. He could see that his co-conspirator was near-ing nervous exhaustion.

233

Adrian went to the cocktail bar and poured himself a large scotch, much of which he quickly drank.

"Jeila," he repeated to himself. He went to their landline phone. He dialled 118 118 and asked for the phone number of The Treasury in Horse Guards Road. "Khan" he said to himself. "It must be Khan."

He accepted their offer to put him through and within seconds a voice announced "The Treasury." Adrian asked to speak to Jeila Khan. In answer to the next question he replied that she worked for Robin Pemberton-Roche in the Enterprise Team. "I'm sorry Sir. Ms Khan's phone is engaged and Mr Pemberton-Roche has now left for the day." Adrian quietly smiled to himself.

The man in the BT van in Regents Road nodded to the woman and texted to Nigel de Groot that the expected call had been made. He asked if he should divert the Dexter line back to normal. De Groot sent a single word reply: *yes*.

Adrian sat back in his chair and drank more of his whisky. He quickly phoned Victoria, who was thrilled at the official recognition of her father's work. She was free and agreed to stay the night so that she could look after Annie in the morning. Meanwhile, Adrian rushed around the house and found his best business suit. He hurried into St. John's Wood High Street and paid his local dry-cleaner twenty pounds to have the jacket and trousers cleaned and ready for collection by eight o'clock later that evening. He then went back to the house and took his car down to the local car valeting service, where he tipped the three Polish workers to give it the clean of the century. He returned home and spent an hour on the Internet trying to understand the structure of the Treasury, the Enterprise Team and the most recent press releases. He looked in the mirror and sprinted back into the High Street where he managed to persuade the uni-sex hair salon to stay open so that they could wash and trim his hair.

Later that evening he collected his suit and walked slowly back home. Victoria had prepared his supper and he went to bed at nine-thirty. He programmed his alarm clock for five a.m. and also arranged for an early morning call.

Tomorrow morning would belong to Adrian Dexter and he was certain that he'd be able to impress the Minister.

Nigel de Groot could go and fuck himself.

The attack on Pollett was cynical and vicious. As he left a pub near to Liverpool Street Station, he was accosted by two men in hooded tops, and dragged behind the hoardings concealing the building of an office block. Several late evening workers saw what was happening but followed the golden rule in London of averting one's eyes.

One assailant held him against the wooden fencing with his gloved hand across Pollett's face, at the same time stuffing a gag into his mouth. The other hit him in the stomach. As he doubled over he brought his knee up into his face. Pollett collapsed to the ground, whereupon they systematically broke his ribs by using the heels of their boots. The smaller man then kicked him between the legs, causing grave injury to his groin.

They finished him off with one attacker placing his boot at the side of Pollett's face and the other kicking sideways into his chin and breaking the jaw bone. The real damage was done by the second blow which shattered the structure. Pollett would have his face wired up for over four months and during that time was restricted to taking in fluids through a straw.

As they abandoned him on the ground, one of the men pinned a note to his shredded coat.

Nobody messes with me.

As the police had no hope of finding Nigel de Groot and the cameras in the area somehow missed the attack, Pollett became just one more crime statistic, and one more Londoner who would require hours of surgery and committed nursing care.

In the weeks that followed Adelene rarely left his side. Michelle, however, had already decided to abandon Cyberforce Investigations and was ready to return to the City with a finance house at an astronomic salary. Her reputation proved unshaken by her entrepreneurial interlude.

It was the third argument they'd had in a matters of days. It was getting to the point where they weren't even able to hide the warring from their children. She knew that Nick was frustrated but she resented it at the same time. She was still hurting and her mind was on Nigel de Groot: she was more and more certain that he was going to kill Adrian Dexter.

She looked up – the office clock showed just minutes until February 14. She stood up, walked around her room, left and visited the canteen for a coffee. She then went downstairs and out into the street, where she took a deep gulp of freezing air. On returning to her office, she filed her papers and then sat down at her desk with one folder in front of her. She re-read everything, not missing a single sheet.

At five o'clock in the morning she woke up and realised that she had nodded off to sleep. She went to the rest-room and splashed her face with cold water. Back at her desk, she started to cry. Her tears of frustration flowed as she went over the threat from Nigel de Groot again and again in her mind

One day to go. This webb never meant you to escape but don't see red

She was never, ever, able to explain even to herself, why at that moment she should think of two men.

"Think laterally," Nick so often said to her. "Sarah. Think laterally."

"Nick. I am. I am. I'm thinking laterally, sideways, upside-downways…"

And then she stopped in her tracks. "What had Pollett said?"

Why take De Groot seriously when he can't even spell 'webb' correctly?

Nigel de Groot did not make mistakes. 'Webb' was spelt correctly. She googled the word 'webb'. Surely Cyberforce Investigations had done this already? It was all names, one after another. She quickly scrolled down the list of people called Webb, page after page of them, looking for a connection, and there it was, staring her in the face.

Aston Webb designed The Mall in the early twentieth-century for major national ceremonies. She read on: *The surface of The Mall is coloured red to give the effect of a giant red carpet leading up to Buckingham Palace.* She then googled him individually and found

236

that Aston Webb was considered to be the most gifted architect of his generation.

It was so simple. Aston Webb did not mean for Adrian to leave his wonderful design but, for his own good, he should not see the red surface – he should get out.

"The Mall!" she shouted out. "He's going to kill him in The Mall!"

She looked at the clock. It was six-twenty in the morning. She dialled Adrian on his home number and was surprised to hear a female voice. She asked to speak to Adrian urgently.

"My father's left already. Are you from the Treasury?"

"The Treasury? What are you talking about? This is Detective Chief Inspector Sarah Rudd of the Islington Police. I insist on speaking to Adrian Dexter."

"You can't, Inspector."

Victoria explained the events of the previous afternoon and how proud her father was to be invited to the Treasury breakfast to meet the Minister.

"Did they email confirmation?" Sarah asked.

"Funny thing, Inspector. My father was surprised that they hadn't bothered to do that."

"I'll phone him on his mobile. Thank you."

"No point, Inspector. My father was told that there are lots of cameras in the Horse Guards area, so he told me not to call as he wasn't going to risk using his mobile in the car. He has to be in The Mall by seven o'clock. He left early to make sure the weather didn't make him late. Inspector, what's this all about please?"

"If he contacts you, tell him to phone DCI Rudd urgently."

It was now six-thirty-five. DI Blake walked into the office.

By this time, Sarah Rudd was on the phone to Detective Chief Superintendent Khan.

"Sir! They're going to shoot him at seven o'clock in The Mall. Tell the Met. DI Blake and I are leaving now."

She chose not to hear his order that she was to stay where she was.

"The car, DI Blake. I'll explain on the way. Admiralty Arch as fast as you've ever driven."

When they reached his vehicle, he stopped and opened the boot. DCI Rudd shouted at him but he remained firm.

"Gov, we're not leaving until you put on this bullet-proof vest."

She knew that resistance was pointless and so she stopped, took off her jacket and put on the protection. She was a fairly well-built woman and had to loosen the retaining straps. For some irrelevant reason she thought of her husband.

She leapt into the car and told DI Blake how to get to their destination as quickly as possible. She would not allow him to turn the police radio on.

At just before seven o'clock, DI Blake was desperately trying to hold the road surface and clear the windscreen as the snowfall started to gain in intensity. DCI Rudd was on her phone for the whole journey. They reached Trafalgar Square.

On the Whitehall corner he lost control of the car. It slid across the road and hit a parked vehicle. DI Blake swore and recovered the momentum. They prepared to enter The Mall and drive under Admiralty Arch.

In the early hours of the morning Cate woke up with a sudden thirst. She got up and downed a glass of ice-cold water. She then put the kettle on and dropped two tea bags into the white pot.

Mark came staggering into the room and sat down. He indicated that he'd also like a cup of tea.

"We're not sleeping that well, are we?" she said.

"We have too much on our minds, Cate. You're bashing yourself around with your studies and I'm trying to get Silicon Capital into a better situation." He paused. "Did I tell you? Do you remember Michelle Rochford?"

"Who set up her own business? Cyber something?"

"Cyberforce Investigations. Yes. Well, I've heard that it's closing down and she's going to be working for one of our competitors."

"It all seems to have gone a bit wrong for MXD Capital, Mark."

"I'm afraid so, Cate. And from what I'm hearing, Adrian Dexter is a broken man."

Chapter Nineteen

Thursday 14 February 2013

Valentine's Day morning was cold and the air was damp. The overnight snow flurries had left the roads in a treacherous condition, and the gritting lorries were concentrating on the main routes into the capital.

At around six-thirty a.m., and within five minutes of each other, two BT vans approached the Trafalgar Square end of The Mall, passed under Admiralty Arch and stopped on the left-hand side just before the traffic lights and the turning into Horse Guards Road. One of the drivers had come via Red Lion Street. He had slowed to a halt to allow Nigel de Groot to climb in, after putting his weapons in the back of the van. A third driver had reached the location from the south side, after diverting to Lambeth where he had picked up an older man huddled in a rather tatty grey overcoat. The last larger van arrived almost immediately afterwards and the man inside quickly jumped out and began unloading road signs and cones from the back.

Their presence was being monitored by the CCTV security system. Due to budget cuts and staff shortages, only one operator picked up the extra traffic and he had no reason to be suspicious. He went to pick up the phone and check with the police but was reassured by the normality of the activity he was watching. He made a note on his sheet and decided it was time to make himself a cup of tea.

By ten minutes to seven, all those involved in the anticipated killing of Adrian Dexter were in place. A canvas tent had been erected by the traffic lights and the council worker soon managed to disconnect the circuit. The signals stopped working and went blank. Two of the gang positioned a series of notices across the road in both directions, advising drivers that they should proceed carefully as the traffic lights were out of action. A police car on its way to Buckingham Palace passed through the area but the driver failed to detect anything unusual.

Inside the tent, Nigel de Groot was checking his two weapons. Both were FN self-loading rifles. He would use one and have the other in reserve. The guns were originally made in Belgium, but De Groot had known that he would be able to obtain them in Northern Ireland as they had been used by the British Forces. In South Africa, this gun was called the R1. It fired a standard Nato 7.62 x 51mm round, making it more powerful than the Kalashnikov - 47, which De Groot considered inaccurate and only good for terrorists.

He intended to kill Adrian with a single shot. The strategy was simple and, in his opinion, foolproof. The driver in the front van was watching for Dexter to come under Admiralty Arch on his way to breakfast with the Minister at The Treasury. He had the registration number of Dexter's car written in large letters on a piece of cardboard. When he spotted the vehicle he would communicate using a single word on his text messaging system to the gang members in the tent. The council worker would reconnect the traffic-signals but restrict them to a permanent red light. The effect of this would be to cause Dexter to halt his car and wait. Eventually he would get out of the vehicle to ask the workers what was happening. At this point Nigel de Groot would shoot him dead. He would then get into one of the vans and travel rapidly west out of London towards the M4 motorway.

He would abandon the van and get into another car at Chiswick. Their route would take them along the M4, then onto the M40 to Birmingham, west again to link up with the M6, avoiding the Toll Road (which he considered a security risk), onto the M54, then the A5 to North Wales and Holyhead, the ferry across to Northern Ireland and, three weeks later, a flight to Johannesburg.

The CCTV cameras would monitor all the action in The Mall. However, it was anticipated that the operators would have difficulty following all four BT vans which would be driven away in different directions. Each would soon be abandoned and their occupants safely hidden in their homes.

Nigel de Groot was satisfied that his plan would not fail. He was strangely relaxed as he awaited the arrival of his victim.

240

He chuckled to himself as he wondered whether they might have been able to solve his clue, but dismissed the thought at once, such was his contempt for the British police. He looked at his watch and checked his weapons. He raised the gun and pointed it at a vision of his intended victim. He had only a few minutes to wait.

Adrian felt and looked immaculate. The dry-cleaners had come up trumps with his suit and he was wearing his favourite blue tie. Victoria had wished him off with love and Annie had still been asleep. He drove away from St. John's Wood, round Regent's Park, down Portland Road, across Oxford Circus into Regent Street, around Piccadilly Circus, down Haymarket into Trafalgar Square, and on towards The Mall.

He was planning carefully what he would say to the Minister. He was wondering whether the invitation carried any special significance. The Coalition Government seemed keen to encourage enterprise, and smaller companies were becoming more popular – his expertise was clearly being recognised at last.

He had a number of ideas that he would share with the officials. He had been planning the writing of a proposal which would explain how a government-backed enterprise stock market would revolutionise share-trading in London and could become a model for the rest of the world to follow. If his paper was accepted he might find himself on the New Year's Honours List. He had read the criteria for receiving an award:

The submission by a Government department that has identified a candidate doing good work within its sphere of interest.

He felt that an OBE would be appropriate. An order of chivalry established by King George V in 1917: 'An Officer of the Most Excellent Order of the British Empire.'

He would regain his position of respect in the City. He would be offered directorships, and he might even consider sitting on Government committees. The economy was struggling to recover from a long period of austerity and his vision and knowledge could contribute to some forward planning. He looked into his interior mirror and straightened his tie, quickly correcting a veering of his vehicle towards the curb. The flow of traffic was light and the roads seemed safe at low speeds. He checked his watch and saw that he was on schedule to turn into The Mall at seven o'clock. He passed under Admiralty Arch and went past Spring Gardens. He then saw the red light ahead of him. He slowly brought his car to a halt. He banged his fist on the steering wheel in frustration. He checked his watch. He'd been told not to be late.

The two officers in the Royalty Protection Branch Land Rover were continuing the argument that had occupied their attention off and on since the Royal Couple had left Leicestershire at just after four o'clock earlier that morning. They had been due to depart the previous evening but His Highness had explained that the Duchess of Cambridge was still struggling with her pregnancy and had asked that she be allowed to rest for a few hours.

They were being driven in their black BMW and Buckingham Palace was expecting them to arrive before seven-thirty. Despite the inclement weather, they were a little ahead of schedule. The disagreement between the police officers concerned the duty roster for the following day: the younger man had a promising date lined up for that evening and was reluctant to commit to further overtime, although, if ordered, he would have no option.

They never took their eyes off the car in front of them. They were certain that the Duke had gone to sleep but the Duchess seemed restless and at one point in the journey was seen to be wearing a head-set. They guessed what music she might be listening to, with Adele being a popular choice.

They noted that the traffic around Trafalgar Square was flowing freely. They reached the entrance to The Mall and then they became concerned. They immediately registered the red traffic lights ahead of them, the BT vans on the left-hand side of the road and the workmen's tent. They saw that on the opposite side of the road several cars and taxis coming into London were being held up by the red lights. They then saw, to their horror, that the driver of the Duke and Duchess's car had stopped behind a saloon car.

"Drive through, you fucking bastard!" yelled the senior of the two police officers, as he flashed his lights and put on his siren. But the driver was dithering and seemed unsure what action he should take.

The police driver hesitated for a vital few seconds as he wondered if the red light would be changing through amber to green. His partner reached for his weapon and began to open his door. He realised that there was something very wrong with the whole scene in front of him.

Detective Chief Superintendent Khan had succeeded in alerting the Metropolitan Police to the potential shooting in The Mall. Two armed response units were now rushing to the area, one from the south side and the other from Trafalgar Square, where the police had now stopped all traffic just seconds after the Royal Couple had passed through.

The armed police vehicle had its lights flashing and its siren on. It came to a halt as the officers surveyed the picture in front of them. Seven policemen, one from the front and the rest from the back, jumped out and spread out around the parked vehicles. They were bemused by a cry of "Royal Protection Officer!" There then commenced a lot of shouting and waving of hands.

The police officer trying to prevent drivers from entering the area jumped to one side as DI Blake brought his vehicle round from the Whitehall entrance and into The Mall. DCI Rudd immediately saw the chaos ahead of them and, when she spotted the car at the lights, she intuitively knew that it was being driven by Adrian. She told DI Blake to go on the outside, around the armed police, and to pull up alongside the front vehicle. He let out a cry of surprise.

"Gov, it's a Royal Protection vehicle! I'm certain."

The police unit from the south had now arrived and the officers were leaping out and approaching the scene in a semi-circle. The senior leader was calling up his colleague with the loud hailer.

Adrian was becoming confused. His gaze flickered between his watch and the red traffic signals. Now there were sirens and blue flashing lights. He must not be late for the Minister. He wondered whether he should jump the red signal but he looked across the road and, to his amazement, saw a group of armed police approaching him. He was unable to comprehend what was happening.

Nigel de Groot came out of the tent with his FN self-loading rifle in his arms. He was dressed in a grey uniform and was wearing an army cap. He saw immediately that they had pitched it a few yards too far away from the lights and he instinctively realised that he was going to die. It had all gone wrong and he knew from the shouting of the police that the shooting would soon begin. He was determined to take Dexter with him. He advanced forward, ignoring the further warnings that were given.

The Duchess of Cambridge took off her headphones and shook her hair. She did not feel well and needed to get some fresh air. She was sitting on the driver's side and opened the door, being careful to avoid sliding on the ice as she left the car. 'What on earth is going on?' she said to herself as she walked round to take a look. She looked back inside the car to see her husband waking up and shaking his head.

Adrian stayed in his car. He was now turning on his mobile phone so that he could telephone The Treasury to apologise for being late for his breakfast with the Minister. He had recorded the number from the call the previous day into his phone and tried to speak to Robin Pemberton-Roche. He was puzzled: the sound at the end of the line indicated the number was either out of order or unobtainable. He checked his call log and found that he was phoning the correct number. He swore in frustration and called again. He was still unable to connect to the number he wanted.

DCI Rudd saw exactly what was happening. She leaped out of the car. Her legs collapsed beneath her and she went sprawling on the ice and snow, grazing her right knee. She was no more than six metres away from the Duchess, who was now very frightened. She picked herself up and screamed at Kate to get down.

The officer from the Royal Protection Unit was raising his weapon and pointing it at a man with a rifle. He shouted a warning but was drowned out as the armed police also tried to warn the killer.

Nigel de Groot lifted his FN self-loading rifle to his shoulder and looked down the sights. He could not find his intended victim. All those weeks of careful planning – the grooming of Alan Joyce; the recovery from his painful surgery; the tactical plotting; the fun of setting the conundrum; the beating of Pollett, or whatever his name was, and, finally, the murder of Adrian Dexter. He would take somebody with him. Nigel de Groot never failed.

As a hail of bullets struck him there was a flash of recognition as he focused on a beautiful pregnant woman standing by Dexter's car. He fired his gun and then collapsed to the ground, his body riddled with slugs.

The Duke of Cambridge had been fast asleep for the previous twenty minutes. He was disoriented as he awoke and immediately realised that the Duchess was missing. He threw open his car door and leaped out from the black BMW, shouting out her name as he heard a volley of gun noises. He saw her to his left-hand side and immediately moved to protect her. He was too late. A small piece of lead was hurtling towards the chest of the future Queen of England.

The police quickly secured the area. Four officers gathered around the Duke. The drivers of the BT vehicles were thrown to the ground and handcuffed and the older man was found inside the tent with his hands over his head. The area around The Mall became a police incident area. A number of ambulances raced to the scene. Within minutes one was being led by motorcycle out-riders racing towards a casualty unit where the medical team was responding to a high alert warning. Downing Street was quickly advised and the Chief Constable arrived to be fully briefed. The Royal Protection Officers were taken away for interview. Buckingham Palace was kept fully informed as they awaited the arrival of the Duke of Cambridge. The news reporters were already in the vicinity and the shooting in The Mall was to dominate the airwaves for weeks and months to come. The body of Nigel de Groot was left lying on the ground with a canvas cover over it. Adrian Dexter was found by DI Blake standing by his car. He was bemused and befuddled, holding his phone to his ear. The number he was trying to call remained out of service.

The medical officer took her husband to one side and asked that they move into a private side room. He explained that they had done all they could.

"Your wife is battling for all she's worth," he said. "This is one of those occasions when we simply have to stand back and let nature take its course." He paused. "I suggest you sit and talk to her. She'll know you're there."

He let his words sink in. He so wanted to say that it was almost certain that his patient would make a full recovery but, as with all trauma cases, there was an area of concern and doubt. He wanted to break the silence in the room.

"How do I know she's fighting for all she's worth?" he continued.

"Yes, that's what I said." He ran his fingers across his tired eyes. "As a doctor you sense it. It's the nature of her skin, her breathing, the eyelids when they flutter. They are signs that tell me the patient is working with me."

His call monitor vibrated in his pocket.

"Your wife is brave and she's fighting for her life." He stopped again.

"I'll save you asking me the question you are pondering." He paused.

"The next forty-eight hours are critical."

Chapter Twenty

February - May 2013

Since 1954, the Queen's Police Medal for Gallantry has only been awarded posthumously.

For five days, following the shooting in The Mall on Valentine's Day, the family of Detective Chief Inspector Sarah Rudd sat by her bedside and took turns to hold her hand. She passed the forty-eight hour barrier but still she struggled to regain consciousness. Although the protection vest had stopped the bullet in its flight, her chest had been crushed by its impact. She had also torn the muscles in her left leg as she had thrown herself in front of the Duchess of Cambridge. Her body was racked with pain and shock.

She began to improve on the sixth day. She woke up in the early hours and asked for a glass of water. During the next twenty-four hours only the medical staff and her family were allowed into the room. After much deliberation it was decided to permit DI Blake to visit her. A day later, and after the royal couple had left, the Chief Constable arrived and spent over an hour with her family before conveying to her the respect of the British police force.

DCI Sarah Rudd was discharged from hospital two weeks later.

The British media went completely overboard with the story. Day after day, Sarah was front page news. The Queen issued a special message of gratitude; the Duke spoke of his inability to express words that could convey his sense of appreciation that DCI Rudd had saved the life of his wife and their baby; the Prime Minster spoke beautifully in the House of Commons; the Chief Constable described it as perhaps the greatest single act of courage by a serving British police officer; and Nick told the press that he was very, very proud of his wife.

It was worldwide news and there was a special message to Sarah from Nelson Mandela. Meanwhile, Nigel de Groot's body was flown back to Johannesburg where the authorities removed his name from all official records. DI Blake was promoted and had lunch with the Detective Chief Superintendent. The two officers from the Royal Protection Unit were transferred to other duties. The driver of the Duke's car was sacked. The four drivers of the BT vans were charged and sentenced to two years in prison. The council worker was taken ill and remained off work for the next year. He was never accused of a crime by the police. Alan Joyce removed the plaster cast from his leg, fled the country and was now thought to be in South America.

Annie Dexter died peacefully at home on the third Tuesday in March 2013. She simply gave up the fight to live. The loss of Helen and her baby seemed to sap her will to continue. There was a private funeral to which only close family were invited and, afterwards, a tense reception at a local hotel.

Within an hour Adrian was asked into a private room where he discovered that a solicitor was preparing to read the last will and testament of Annie Dexter. He was even more surprised when Victoria walked in holding a five month old baby. Helen was at her side.

As the lawyer read out the provisions of the will Honeysuckle and Clare remained impassive. Helen, who now had her son on her lap, heard the news of her two hundred thousand pound bequest and bowed her head. Victoria was looking from one person to another. She so regretted agreeing to what was to follow. She wondered how near her father was to a complete breakdown.

Once the legalities of the meeting were over Helen made it clear that she was not willing to talk to Adrian and she left the room without saying a word.

When, two hours later, Adrian arrived home, he found that his three daughters were waiting for him in the lounge. Clare and Honeysuckle were sitting on the large sofa and Victoria was close by. An empty chair opposite them awaited him.

Honeysuckle asked her father to sit down. He noticed that Victoria was avoiding his eye.

"Dad, why do you think Mum died?"

He ran the back of his hand across his lips and blinked.

"You know the answer, Honeysuckle. Your mother's nerves had been getting worse, she was eating less and was taking little or no exercise. The doctor said she had run out of determination to fight on."

"Why?" snapped Clare. "Why was that, Dad? Mummy always had courage and resilience. What had happened to her to make her give up?"

"Dad," said Victoria, softly, "please help us to understand."

"You girls should appreciate that I have lost my wife. Your mother and I were very close."

Honeysuckle stood up and laughed out loud.

"You were screwing other women most of the time! How close is that?"

"Not today, Honeysuckle," he pleaded. "Can we do the inquisition bit another time? We've only just cremated your mother. Let's talk about happier memories."

"It's not as simple as that, Dad," said Victoria. "I think you should listen to Honeysuckle."

He realised that he was being handed an envelope. He opened the flap and took out a sheet of paper containing a brief explanation of how his daughters considered him responsible for the death of their mother. It was signed by all three of them. Adrian later remembered how he had noticed Victoria had the neatest writing.

"We have given considerable thought to this situation," said Clare. "To put it in simple terms, we want you out of our lives. Our children do not want you as their grandfather. Not after you've taken away their granny. Please, just disappear. Go away."

Honeysuckle walked up to her father and slapped him across the face. She looked almost as shocked as he at what she had done. She burst into tears and rushed out of the room. Clare followed her, not looking at her father.

Adrian was left rubbing his cheek and looking intensely at Victoria.

She came over and kissed him.

249

"Good luck, Dad. You're going to be a rather lonely man, I think. Phone me on my mobile whenever you want."

She was hurting very badly. Her muscles and tendons were in trauma. She intended to suffer. She wanted to be alone which was why she had waited for Easter to come and go. She chose three mid-week days to find the solitude she so craved. It had taken weeks for the tears to come. Not the crying that was a reaction to all those wires and tubes. The emotion which comes from the inner self. The self-flagellation which was her way of promoting the healing process. She was alone in the sense that no other person sought to blame her. It happened. Life happens. Life goes on.

She had chosen to take the Seathwaite Route via Sowmilk Gill and Windy Gap. The standard timing was around five to six hours but Michelle Rochford was determined to complete the pilgrimage in under four and a half hours. She ignored the views of the Scafells to the south and hardly bothered to look at Wastwater now far below her. She would scale the near three thousand feet to the summit of Great Gables, she would cry her final tears, and then she would descend back to civilisation and to her new job in the City. She would earn vast sums of money and she would find the man who had no history and would love her to death, for evermore.

The closing down of Cyberforce Investigations brought her into the British bureaucratic system at its very worst. Despite the fact there were no debts and she had borrowed heavily to repay her investors, adding to the money required to ensure his hospital care for the next few months, and a pay-off to the office manager, she spent hours filling in forms and going through the process with her accountants. Adelene had refused, point blank, to accept any redundancy payment and had ended their final conversation with the suggestion that she 'fuck off' and leave the two of them together.

She had tried to kiss Pollett but there were so many wires that finally she held and squeezed his hand. He was unable to express his thoughts to her.

250

She had now reached the summit of Great Gables. The sky was clear and empty. She kicked some rocks around and then sank to her knees. At last the tears came from way inside her. She shook as she sobbed. She allowed herself one final memory of Pollett laughing when she had told him of her plans and that he was to be part of them.

She stood up and wiped her eyes. The penitence was complete. It was time to re-join the real world.

Adrian settled down in the business class lounge of Terminal One at Heathrow Airport. He rubbed his shoulder and took two aspirin to try to relieve the tension in his limbs. He read the latest text message from Sonja for the umpteenth time.

In a few hours' time you will experience love-making like you've never imagined. Last time was merely practice. Oodles of love S x

He had spent the last six weeks selling the house, working with Victoria in the clearing up of Annie's estate, seeing some friends in the City (which included a rather liquid lunch with Michelle) and finally, after several calls, meeting with Helen. When she knew that he was going to South Africa she agreed to let him see William.

They found themselves in Finsbury Square. The grass was immaculate and Helen radiated good health in a subdued green dress. William was dressed in a striped nautical outfit and spent most of the time asleep.

"I'm going to carry on renting," she told Adrian. "The money from Annie means we can afford something really decent."

"Why not buy a flat? Move further north where you can get a good property. You'll qualify for a mortgage now."

"I lost my job, Adrian."

She told him about the continuing problems with the Area Manager. Finally, she had just given in and resigned her position. Bearing in mind the ongoing problems with the retail sector as consumer spending remained subdued, she had decided to take a university course.

"Do you ever regret dropping those glasses in my lap?" Adrian suddenly asked.

She looked intensely at him.

251

"You were right for me, Adrian. It just took some time for me to realise there was somebody at the end of your text messages who was more right for you."

She stood up and, slowly taking the pram's brake off, walked William away. She did not look back.

During the flight to South Africa he refused all meals and refreshments apart from a number of large whiskies. He had bought the latest Wilbur Smith novel from the airport shop but struggled to get into the story.

He used a small towel to wipe his forehead. He was tense and excited. The memory of his daughters' letter was fast receding and his focus was on a future life with Sonja. He already knew every inch of her body and he anticipated the passion that lay ahead. He lifted his left arm up off the rest and stretched it out to try and ease the pain. His shirt was wet with perspiration. He was tired. He wanted his new life.

Ten hours after lifting off runway one in London, the Boeing 747 landed at O. R. Tambo International Airport, and the fresh clean air of the Highveld hit him as he stood at the top of the steps. He took in a few deep breaths and felt a little better. It had been a long flight. Forty-five minutes later he had reached the arrivals lounge. He was starting to regret the whiskies.

He looked across the crowded floor and the various notices being held aloft as drivers tried to attract the attention of their passengers.

Sonja saw Adrian from about forty yards away and began to run towards him.

He was standing still because he realised that the lights were going out. His vision was becoming blurred and his legs were shaking. As the crushing feeling around his chest intensified, he began thinking about a baby boy called William. He could see Helen holding him and laughing.

Sonja had now reached him and was hugging his chest. He felt his hand luggage fall from his hands. She screamed and shouted for help as she attempted to hold him up.

The paramedics arrived quickly but they were too late. Adrian was already lying dead on the floor: his heart had given up after the stress of the previous twelve months.

Sonja pushed the medics away, weeping, and cradled his head in her arms. She gently kissed him on the lips.

Adrian Dexter had finally found the love he was looking for. Damn the fatty tissues.

On a Wednesday in May DCI Rudd received The Queen's Gallantry Medal for 'an exemplary act of bravery' in a ceremony at Buckingham Palace. As Her Majesty made the presentation, tears poured down Nick's face. Most of the Royal Family attended the occasion. Prince Charles made some especially warm comments and the Duke of Cambridge held Sarah's hand in sheer gratitude.

Nick watched the official police cars leave the courtyard and the press drift towards the pubs. He and Sarah walked slowly away from Buckingham Palace. Nick's parents had agreed to take the two children home, so he was alone with his wife.

They took a short-cut through to St. James's Park and enjoyed the warmth of the late spring afternoon. The skies were clear of clouds and there were planes flying overhead from the east, on their way to Heathrow Airport.

"So what was that about, Sarah?" asked her husband.

"I told the Assistant Chief Constable that I couldn't face a civic reception. I asked to be allowed to take two more days' holiday and next Monday I will return to community policing in Islington. I also said that I would not accept any further promotion."

She stopped and turned towards her husband. She kissed him gently on the lips.

"I said to the ACC that I'm a police officer and not a celebrity."

"You saved the life of the future Queen of England, Sarah."

They had reached a park bench by the side of the lake. They sat down and took each other's hands.

"Let's have a clear-out, Nick. I'm a wife, a mother and a police officer. End of story."

"You're a national hero and the bravest person I've ever known."

"On Monday I'll be DCI Sarah Rudd dealing with hate and abuse on the streets of North London."

They passed the next few minutes in silence, each lost in their thoughts.

"What is it, Nick?" she asked at last.

"I want to ask you a question, Sarah."

"Ask me."

"You left the file on your desk at home. I now know how you found the South African nurse."

"Good detective work, eh?" she chuckled.

"I just wondered how you felt when you saw Dr Martin Redding?"

In that moment Sarah realised that her husband knew about her affair.

"How did you...?"

"Old fashioned detective work, DCI Rudd!"

"You followed me?"

"Yes, but only after I noticed, when you undressed, that your pants were the wrong way round."

She looked at him in complete horror and her hands flew defensively down to her skirt.

"You never said anything, Nick!"

"I went to see a marriage counsellor."

She looked at him with her mouth open.

"Shouldn't we have gone together?"

Nick laughed. "You were otherwise engaged."

Sarah stood up and walked away from the bench seat. She gazed over the water for several minutes before returning to her husband.

"What did he advise?"

"It was a woman. Normally they see couples together. I only had two appointments because I decided to solve it myself."

"And how did that work, Nick?"

"I went to see your medical lover. We had a chat. He didn't scare easily and it was obvious he was besotted with you."

She sat down and put her hand on his knee.

"Please, Nick, what happened?"

"I told him that I thought we should let you make the decision. I could see no point in forcing the issue. I wanted you to decide whether your future was with me or with him. It was a gamble but I knew I had to take it."

Sarah had always been puzzled about why the passion between her and Martin had suddenly lessened. She had challenged him several times but he had just claimed that stress at the surgery was affecting his libido. Finally, she had decided to go home to her husband and throw herself into rebuilding their marriage.

"He wrote to me in the middle of January," she said.

"So that was the 'Private and Confidential' letter," Nick said. "What did he say?"

"It was a rambling epistle on what a fantastic police officer I am and how proud he was that he'd played a part in saving Helen's baby which, in fairness, is exactly what he did."

"Is that all he wrote?"

"He hinted rather crudely that he'd like to go to bed with me again."

"Did you reply to him?"

"I tore up the pages and threw them away."

"So you don't want to go to bed with him again?"

"I want to go to bed with you, Nick, not Martin Redding."

They stood up and looked up The Mall towards Trafalgar Square. They would never again refer to that episode in their lives. They joined hands and walked slowly ahead.

"So, Sarah," asked Nick, "the sleepless nights, the nightmares when you did drop off, the worries about whether you'd lose your nerve – any chance we might get back to a normal family life?"

"I'm a police officer, Nick. It goes with the territory."

She was suddenly concentrating very hard. She let his hand go. She was not seeing the trees and the water. She could not hear the noise from the cars and the taxis. She knew that her husband was trying to move the goalposts.

There was a change taking place. She felt a surge of adrenalin through her body.

What had Dr Stelling told her?

"Your body reached a point where it had no more to offer"
She had trusted Dr Stelling and she had believed him.

"Go home, Sarah, and wait," he had said. *"You'll get better. Let your body decide when."*

She strode ahead of the father of her two children.

"Let your body decide when."

"You lucky man" she said to herself, looking back at Nick.

She waited for him to catch up with her.

She put her arms around his neck and kissed him. She held him to her for a few more moments.

"Nick" she whispered. "There's one more thing I have to tell you."

He pushed her away as a frown creased his forehead.

"They've given me a new pair of handcuffs."

The End

About the author

Tony Drury is a corporate financier based in the City of London. He is a Fellow of the Institute of Bankers and a Member of the Securities Institute.

Tony has written extensively over the years and is particularly well known for his financial and political books. He blogs weekly for www.enterprisebritain.com – both in his own name and as his alter ego Mr Angry. He is chairman of Axiom Capital Limited, a London-based corporate finance house, and chairman of Ford Eagle Group, a business advisory company, which is based in Hong Kong.

Tony is a member of The Romantic Novelists' Association. His first novel *Megan's Game*, which was published in the spring of 2012, is set to hit the silver screen in 2014. Accredited producer, Paul Tucker believes it will make a great feature film with international appeal! The screenplay is now written and principal photography is planned to commence later in the year.

Tony is also passionate about business and entrepreneurism; he recently chaired a committee of city-based financial market practitioners focussed on how revitalising the Small Cap community can stimulate growth within the UK economy. The paper was delivered in March 2013 to Greg Clarke MP at HM Treasury.

Cholesterol is his third novel.

Follow Tony on Twitter @MrTonyDrury.

Coming next...

A Flash of Lightning

Two people are looking for sex. Jessica, a bank loans officer, wants a baby and Matthew, a City financier, wants women. They live and work in London. They meet and their explosive relationship erupts when a baby is tragically beaten. To add to his problems Matthew's business is the innocent party in a film finance fraud.

Meanwhile, somewhere else in London, terrorists are plotting to blow up a railway tunnel to exact massive loss of life. The Metropolitan Police have been closely monitoring the air frequencies and know something is being planned but do not know where or by whom.

DCI Sarah Rudd, based in Islington, becomes unwittingly involved as she finds all is not what it seems in the leafy lanes of a Bedfordshire village where, in 1963, the Great Train Robbery had taken place.

What happens when Jessica, Matthew and DCI Rudd's paths cross and the plot is unravelled is like a bolt from the blue... a flash of lightning.

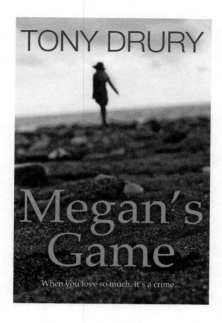

TONY DRURY

Megan's Game

When you love so much, it's a crime...

"City veteran has scheming broker's story to tell."
Daily Telegraph

"Tony enjoys success story." *Leighton Buzzard Observer*

"I have just finished reading *Fifty Shades of Grey* and it isn't a patch on *Megan's Game'*... I look forward to your next book."
Lizzie Lee

"As good as John Grisham!" *Judy Constantine*

"It's a very, very good book." *Austra Laukyte*

"A thoroughly enjoyable read and very moving."
Roger Chapman